"McGregor, is there something wrong?"

He shook his head. "Why don't you call me by my first name?"

She shrugged. "Everyone calls you McGregor."

"But you call others by their first names on the team. Even the boss. You call him Del."

She sighed. "I guess it was one way to keep my distance."

"So, if you finally call me Graeme, I know you don't want to keep your distance?"

She sucked in a breath, then her lower lip quivered. If he hadn't been concentrating on her so closely, he would have missed it.

"No, I just—"

"Say my name, Eleanora." He liked the way her formal name sounded on his tongue.

Her eyes softened. "Okay, Graeme—"

He bent his head then and kissed her. Just a brush of his mouth against hers. The simple touch sent a wave of fire through his body. He never took his hands out of his pockets. When he pulled back, she said nothing for a moment.

She looked as shocked as he did.

"What was that for?" she asked.

He shrugged. "I'm not really sure."

Melissa Schroeder

Hostile Desires

Melissa Schroeder

Edited by Noel Varner and Fedora Chen
Cover by Scott Carpenter

DEDICATION

To Meg Graham Weglarz who not only
shares my love of Wegmans, but she is the
person who suggested that Graeme must
wear a kilt at least once in the book. You can
thank her for the scene.

DEAR READER,

I knew before I wrote this book that I would have to deal with Elle's past and what happened to Jin in the first book. It definitely wasn't easy. Dealing with the aftermath of rape is very personal and is different for every person. I have done everything in my power to show respect for the victims.

If you or someone you love has been a victim of rape, and you feel that you need help dealing with it, please contact Rainn: https://rainn.org/get-help.

Mel

MEET THE TEAM

CAPTAIN
Martin "Del" Delano

Second in Command
Lt. Adam Lee

Regular Team Members
Graeme McGregor
Marcus Floyd
Cat Kalakaua

Medical Team
Dr. Elle Middleton
Drew Franklin

Forensics
Charity Edwards

Contractors
Emma Taylor

Hawaiian Terms

Aloha - Hello, goodbye, love

Bra-Bro

Bruddah- brother, term of endearment

Haole-Newcomer to the islands

Howzit - How is it going?

Kama'āina-Local to the islands

Mahalo-Thank you

Malasadas- A Portuguese donut without a hole which started out as a tradition for Shrove (Fat) Tuesday. They are deep fried, dipped in sugar or cinnamon and sugar. In other words, it is a decadent treat every person must try when they go to Hawaii. If you do not try it, you fail. Do yourself a favor. Go to Leonard's and buy one. You are welcome.

Pupule- Crazy

Sistah- Sister, term of endearment

Slippahs - slippers, AKA sandals

CHAPTER ONE

Elle Middleton jackknifed in her bed, her heart beating against her chest, as she gulped in huge breaths of air. She could smell the dank basement where she had been trapped, the body odor of the bastard who had kept her there. Sweat dribbled between her breasts. She looked around her bedroom, and realized she was in her house in Hawaii. Safe.

It was dark in the room, so she knew it was well before she needed to be up. Going back to sleep was out of the question though. She had learned a long time ago, there would be nothing but nightmares for the rest of the night.

Scrubbing her face, Elle wished she could do the same thing with her memories. Even now, her pulse was elevated, her breathing erratic. The metallic taste in her mouth was from memory. She drew in a deep breath and released it slowly. There was no use lying in bed, so she slipped from under the covers. Raising her hands over her head, she stretched, trying to work out the kinks in her back.

She didn't seem to be getting any better. She had been having these dreams for the last few months. Since they had found Jin.

Elle had known it would be a problem. When she had insisted on going, no matter if they had found Jin alive or not, the situation was bound to bring back the memories. The attack had happened almost a decade earlier, halfway around the world, but it didn't matter. The last six months had been hard on her. Still, she didn't regret it, and she would do it again given the chance. She wished she'd had a previous survivor present when she'd been found.

After a quick trip to the bathroom, she grabbed her mobile and headed to the kitchen. She had help if she needed it. People she could call, and meds that she knew would dull the memories…at least for today. But she had a job to do, and if she kept putting one foot in front of the other, she would be able to make it through the day. Maybe.

Yawning, she made her way through her tiny kitchen to the coffee machine. Before moving to Hawaii, she had always preferred a cup of tea in the morning. Less than two years, and she was an addict of the smooth Kona coffee that was served everywhere—even at McDonald's. With a flip of the switch, she started brewing her drug of choice. She yawned again just as her mobile went off. Without looking, she knew from the ringtone it was work.

"Dr. Middleton."

"Hey, Elle, it's Dennis," he said, his voice quivering a little.

Dennis Chin was a no-nonsense ME for the HPD Medical Examiner's office, with nerves as strong as steel. This was completely out of character for the senior supervisor. Her worries about the nightmares immediately dissolved, and her mind focused on the job at hand.

"Morning, Dennis. Is there something wrong?"

"Well, not really, but I was wondering if you could handle a case for me? I'm at the hospital with my wife, and she's in labor. Mike is down with the flu."

She smiled. "No worries, Dennis."

He sighed, the worry and fatigue easy to hear in his voice. "I'm sorry if I woke you up."

"First of all, it is part of the job, and it doesn't really matter. I was up. Please don't be sorry. I got your back, as you like to say."

"Great. At least it is up in your neck of the woods. The Wiki Mart right by Schofield. There was a burglary."

"Oh, damn, and I stop in there all the time." She sighed. One thing about living and working on Oahu, there was a high chance she would come in contact with people in real life who ended up on her table. When she had worked in London, there was an anonymity to it that shielded her. There was always a slim chance an acquaintance would be part of an investigation, but the odds of that happening on the small island of Oahu were much higher.

She pushed those thoughts aside and focused on the current job—calming the expectant father. "Don't worry about it. I have this, Dennis. Good luck, Daddy."

There was a moment of silence, then he laughed. "Thanks."

She clicked off the mobile just as her coffee finished brewing. She had wanted to watch the sun rise over the Pacific. It was something that soothed her after a night like she'd had. It was one of the reasons she had bought the seriously tiny house just a block away from the beach. When the nightmares had started again, Elle had developed the habit of watching the sun rise every day. It soothed the terrors that had crept back into her conscious the last few months.

But that was not happening today. She had a dead body to process. Fate had always been a bitch to her.

With cup in hand, she headed to her bedroom. She could make it there in under thirty minutes this time of day, and still be able to get into the office just in time to miss rush hour.

It took her less than twenty-five minutes to get to the Wiki Mart. It was still early—even by military standards—so she hadn't hit any traffic on her way to the scene. Two HPD cars were still sitting out in front of the store. Thanks to the time of day, there wasn't a crowd. She would really hate for the neighborhood to see this. If she worked fast, they could get him out of there before many of them did.

After grabbing her bag, she slipped out of her car. She set the bag on her car, retrieved a pair of gloves, then grabbed it up again and headed to the door of the store.

When she stepped in, her mind went back to the first day she had walked in, and the smile that Joe Alana had offered—always offered, in fact. With a sigh, she pushed those thoughts away and concentrated on the job in front of her.

"Hey, Elle," Rome Carino said. Tall, lanky, but still solid, the HPD detective worked hand in hand with Task Force Hawaii as their liaison with the department. Even at this time in the morning, he was dressed in a suit, although he'd finally stopped wearing ties all the time.

"Howzit, Rome?"

"Could be better. Hate when stuff like this happens."

She nodded. "I called and was told they sent a bus to pick up the body."

"Good deal."

Drawing in a deep breath, she pushed everything out of her mind, and set about her task. Joe was lying behind the counter. She squatted beside the body. It was easy to see what killed him, one gunshot wound to the chest.

She retrieved her tools and got to work. After checking the liver temperature, she figured that he had been dead for at least six hours.

"So, I take it was the gunshot wound?" Rome asked

from behind her.

She nodded. "Although, official COD will not be determined until I do the autopsy. Has anyone found a bullet?"

"No one was allowed to touch the victim until you showed."

She smiled. "You are a good guy, Rome. Want to help me roll him?"

Rome stepped over the body, then they rolled him.

"No bullet."

"I'll find it during the autopsy, and have Charity test it. Maybe we'll get lucky."

Rome nodded, as they laid the body back down. "Thanks. I take it the victim is going back to your lab?"

She looked up at him. "Yes, if you are okay with that?"

"No problem, sistah."

She smiled and stood to face him. "I'm going to go in and prep for the postmortem."

"And I have video to look at. I know that Joe had a good system for such a small place."

"Good, because this guy needs to be caught. No one, and I mean not even the Yakuza, messed with Joe. This was a safety zone no matter what. Whoever did this, did it without thought."

"Yeah, we're thinking it was a robbery gone bad, maybe a junkie. I'm sure we'll find prints too, but the video proof will be more helpful."

She nodded and started out of the shop when she ran into Mike Charles, Dennis's morgue assistant.

"Howzit, Mike?" She asked, looking up at him. She was a tall woman, but Mike was a massive man, with a little Polynesian in his blood. His usual smile had been replaced by a grim expression.

"Early morning."

"Any word on the baby?"

He shook his head, as a small smile curled his lips. "Not yet. Doc is kind of a mess."

She nodded. "Make sure you get it to my lab."

"Doc told me. See you in a few."

She watched him go to the back of his vehicle, then shook herself back awake. More coffee was definitely in order if she was going to make it through the day.

She'd skipped breakfast, and the morning was slipping away from her fast. Again. It wasn't done on purpose. She just got so busy. First, the autopsy on Mr. Alana. Then, a sixteen-year-old on vacation from the mainland drowned in high surf. With half the HPD ME staff out thanks to the flu, she hadn't had time to think about eating.

She slid the drawer that held the teenager into the wall and sighed. Her back ached, her head pounded, and worse, she felt as if she could eat three plates of shrimp from Giovanni's Shrimp Truck. She was definitely going to treat herself this week.

"So, all we have is this bullet," Drew Franklin said. She glanced at her assistant with a frown.

"That's more than we sometimes have," she said, taking the evidence bag from him. "They are analyzing the security footage. I bet we will only need the bullet to tie the shooter to the weapon."

Drew nodded. A local boy, he was one of the many people who had known Mr. Alana. Over a quarter million people lived on Oahu at any one time, but people who had lived there all their lives all seemed to know each other, or knew of each other in some way. Drew always said there was only three to four degrees of separation between each local on the island.

"I'll get this down to Charity," he said. Charity Edwards was their forensics tech, and if anyone could find a lead on the bullet, she could. The former Georgia resident had a reputation as one of the top ten techs in the country.

"Don't forget to take the other swabs and fingerprints as well. There might have been more than just one person."

"You got it. You know Charity will find something."

Elle nodded absentmindedly, her mind already drifting. Her lack of sleep was starting to take its toll on her.

"Elle?"

She blinked and realized Drew was still there.

"Sorry. Need anything else from me?" She yawned. "Oh, pardon me. I don't think I have ever been this tired, even during my residency."

Drew nodded. "You should take the rest of the day off."

"I have to talk to Carino about my findings, then I might just do that."

"You work too hard."

She offered him a smile. "You should talk. You work as many hours as I do, and you help your folks out at the restaurant every now and then."

Drew wasn't just a local boy; he was part of a legendary family who ran a well-known restaurant on the island. While he had always wanted to play with dead bodies—his words, not hers—his family had insisted he at least learn the ropes of the business. She would often find him working behind the counter or cooking in the kitchen on his day off.

As she watched him head off to Charity's lab, she walked over to wash her hands. She would call Rome instead of going over. It was the best way to do it. If she went over to HPD, she would get pulled into some meeting or other. She just didn't have the patience. It was one of the reasons that when she had her choice to go with HPD or Task Force Hawaii, she had jumped at the chance to work with TFH.

Elle was drying her hands when her door opened. Of course, Rome would come to find her.

"Well?"

"As you thought. Shot to the chest. He wouldn't have made it to Tripler or Queen's."

"From what I hear, there was no reason. Joe gave all of his money to the man."

Senseless. "Charity has the bullet. She'll run it through the system, and maybe we can give you a name with the face you most likely have now."

"Thanks a lot. Just between you and me, I wish you worked over at HPD."

She smiled as she pulled off her overlay scrub and tossed it into the hamper.

"No, thanks. Too much drama over there. We have it easy over here."

"Yeah, like catching a psychopathic serial killer."

Six months earlier, TFH had been on the search for a serial killer, but what they found out in the end was that a couple of sadistic bastards were working together to abduct, torture, rape, then kill their victims. In the process, TFH had almost lost one of their own.

"Killers."

He nodded. "So, your thoughts are sure it wasn't premeditated?"

Elle shrugged. "More than likely not premeditated, but that's your job to figure out, right?"

His mouth twitched. "Always a hard case, Doc."

"I know your wife. She wouldn't let you get away with that either. But they did send some fingerprints over, and I have some from Joe's shirt. If the subject touched him, we might get something. Plus, I swabbed some matter off the shirt; could be nothing, but it looked like ICE."

"Great. I was pretty sure it was a junkie. Did you have anything else for me?"

She shook her head. "Charity has orders to ping us both when she has any results."

"Thanks. Thought I would stop by to see Del on my way out."

She chuckled. "Have fun with that. Avoid his bride-to-be. Emma is a little...overwhelmed at the moment."

He nodded. "Thanks, Elle."

"Just get the bastard. I really liked Joe. He always had a smile for anyone who stopped by, and he contributed a lot to that neighborhood. He is definitely going to be missed."

"Will do."

"Give my best to your wife and that pretty little girl of yours."

He waved as he walked out the door. She looked down at her clothes and realized she needed to change out of her scrubs. Since the early call had ruined her chances at a shower, she felt grimy. Threading her fingers through her hair, she decided that she would grab a fast shower. It was the first time that morning she wasn't busy doing something. Her stomach growled, and she made a face. She hadn't brought her lunch because of the call this morning, which meant she had to go somewhere to pick something up. But she didn't want to go far. There could be another call, so the coffee stand out front would work.

Graeme McGregor was parking his truck when he saw Elle Middleton sitting on a bench out in front of the TFH headquarters. He turned off his vehicle and watched her for a moment. The woman should have looked out of place, the English rose sitting amongst the tropical flowers. But somehow, she fit.

If anything, she added to the surroundings. Her pristine appearance enhanced the wild fauna that surrounded her. Of course, lately, she had started to take on a certain look.

More local than *haole*. She'd let her short hair grow out just a little, and the humidity had added some curl to her flaxen hair. More and more she had been wearing colorful tropical shirts like the one she had on today. The deep coral color brought out a glow to her skin.

He wanted to avoid her. They didn't get along at all, but while he told himself to walk on, he found himself wandering over to her.

"Out early this morning."

She blinked, then her eyes seemed to focus. "Oh, McGregor. Sorry. I didn't get much sleep last night. Sort of zoned out there for a bit."

He nodded as he studied her. She held a cup of coffee in her hands, and an unwrapped sandwich sat on her lap. She definitely looked like she had been staying up late. In fact, she looked bloody awful. The dark bruising beneath her eyes was getting to be a regular sight on her. It had been that way since they'd found Jin months earlier.

"Did we catch a call?" he asked.

She shook her head. "I'm helping fill in with HPD. Flu is wiping out their folks, and then Dennis's wife went into labor yesterday."

He nodded and, before he could tell himself not do it, he sat next to her. She didn't physically move away, but he felt her pull away just the same. She had been like that since the first time they'd met, and he didn't know why. He had thought with him being from Scotland, and she being a UK transplant, they would have had a lot in common. Apparently, the doctor thought otherwise.

"Was it a tough one?"

"Yes. You know the Wiki Market there right off of Schofield Barracks?"

He nodded.

"Joe Alana was shot in the chest, bled out at the scene."

"Well, damn. Joe was a bloody good guy."

She glanced at him, as she sipped at her coffee. "You

knew him?"

"Yeah. I live up near the North Shore."

She frowned. "I didn't know that. I live in Haleiwa."

He knew where she lived. Not exactly, but the area. He wasn't a stalker. But he knew they lived closer to each other than any of the other people on the team.

"I live in Laie."

She nodded and looked out over the lawn. "It was completely senseless. If you know Joe, you know they have the video of the kid."

He opened his mouth, but her phone rang with a "Georgia on My Mind" ringtone. He smiled.

"I am assuming that's Charity?"

She nodded and turned on her mobile. "Been waiting on the ballistics. Hey, Charity, what do you have for me?"

He watched her expressive face. Graeme had an idea that Elle thought she was cool as an English cucumber, but he knew better. When things really got to her, it was easy to see how it affected her by her facial expressions. He watched as whatever Charity was saying hit home for Elle.

"Are you sure?" she asked.

More silence.

"I'm sorry. It wasn't that I don't believe in your abilities."

More silence.

"Bloody hell, I promise never to ask again. I'll be right in. I was just grabbing a bite to eat outside."

Graeme noticed that Elle hadn't eaten the sandwich, but he knew better than to say anything about it.

She clicked off her mobile.

"Got a lead on the bullet?" he asked.

Elle nodded, her eyes sparkling with excitement. Damn, she was beautiful when she smiled—something he shouldn't be thinking about. He forced himself not to be drawn in by the twinkle in those green eyes, or the way her dimples showed when she smiled.

"Of course she got a hit, and it is linked to a crime from almost thirty years ago."

CHAPTER TWO

Sam Katsu swallowed the bile in his throat as he watched the news. A shiver of need rushed through his body, chilling his blood and making him sweat. He needed a hit. Another one. A big one. But they had him dead to rights, and had been showing the fucking video over and over. He couldn't leave his house. He couldn't call his supplier.

It had been nonstop coverage since they'd found the old man. What was he going to do? It wasn't like he could hop in his car and go anywhere. *Fuck*. He didn't even have a car. He'd sold it several weeks earlier. He'd needed the cash for another hit.

He paced the small living room area, as the reporter droned on.

"People have been arriving at the small Wiki Mart since early this morning, leaving flowers by the police tape. Joe Alana was not only a member of this community, he was the heart of it."

Sam shoved his hands through his hair, as sweat

gathered at the base of his neck. He looked at his hands and saw the blood. He still had the old man's blood on his hands, beneath his fingernails. He shivered as a bead of sweat slid down his spine. Chills raced over his flesh. His stomach roiled, and his throat filled with acid. Running to the bathroom, he collapsed on the floor in front of the toilet. He had nothing to throw up, nothing in his stomach at all, so all he did was heave a few times, then fall down onto the stained, cracked linoleum.

He rolled over onto his back and looked up at the ceiling. It wavered, and he realized he was crying. It had all started with the fucking gun. That was why he was where he was. If he had never found it, he would have never ended up where he was.

What the fuck was he going to do?

Elle was out of sorts by the time they made it back into the TFH conference room. Part of it was her lack of sleep. She'd been fighting insomnia for months now, but that wasn't particularly new. She usually handled it better, but with Graeme McGregor by her side, she couldn't seem to settle her nerves.

He walked beside her; his big hulking frame both irritated and calmed her at the same time. She didn't know what it was, but for some reason, she'd had this reaction from the moment she met him. She knew why he agitated her, but why she seemed to want to see him from time to time was just insane.

At first, she had blamed it on his long golden hair, which had earned him the name of Goldilocks. But he had cut it off a couple of months ago and grown a goatee. She had never been a woman for facial hair, but damned if it didn't make him even more attractive to her. It suited his face and his character. More than once she had wondered what it would feel like against her skin.

There were more things that intrigued her about him, but mostly she wanted to see the tattoo that everyone had talked about. It covered his back, or so they said. She pushed those thoughts aside and concentrated on what was going on in the room beyond the glass doors. Charity was standing next to the conference table talking to Del. She smiled when she saw Charity's hands flapping around and her mouth moving. She was definitely enthusiastic about her find.

"Lass seems to know something exciting," Graeme said with a chuckle.

His rich brogue danced over her nerve endings. He had one of those deep baritone voices that only Highlanders seemed to possess. But not in real life. They lived in fantasies, in movies, and books. They definitely should not be spending time striding around Hawaii like a displaced Laird searching for his clan.

Bloody hell, she needed some sleep. After she was done today, she would take one of those little sleeping pills her doctor had prescribed. They had been sitting untouched for a month, but when she started having romantic thoughts about McGregor, it was time for drastic measures.

He reached for the door at the same time as Elle did, and their hands brushed against each other. She sucked in a breath and dropped her arm to let him open the door. When she looked at him, she found him looking at her as if he had been struck. His clear gray eyes narrowed as he studied her. He hesitated as if he had felt it too, then he pulled the door open.

She stepped over the threshold and into the whirlwind of excitement that always seemed to surround Charity Edwards.

"What are the chances? I mean, I am not that good at math, but maybe you can ask Emma. I bet she would know about the odds of this happening."

When Del spotted them, relief was easy to hear in his

voice when he spoke. "Great, you're here."

Del's gaze landed on Graeme, and his eyes widened slightly, but he said nothing. Of course, the entire office knew they didn't like each other. Seeing them walk in together was enough to raise a few eyebrows. Still, Elle wasn't thrilled with his reaction. It was moments like this that lead to silly wagers.

"Charity said the bullet is linked to a case from 1986?"

Charity twirled around. She had her lab coat on, but now Elle got a look at Charity's outfit. A bright yellow shirt tucked into black Capri pants. And, as usual, she was prancing around on heels. How the woman did that all day was beyond Elle.

Her eyes sparkled as she nodded. "Yes, unsolved and never used again."

She handed Elle a piece of paper. She looked over the information, then glanced up. "A first generation Glock? I don't know many people who use those anymore."

"A good gun is a good gun," Charity said. "When I saw it, I recognized it. You can take the girl out of Georgia..."

"That sounds like an odd choice of weapon for our young perpetrator," Graeme remarked.

She was nodding when Del stepped in. "I don't think so. Remember, the first description is a young man. Now the video confirms it. If he was in there to do a smash and grab, there is a good chance he just grabbed the gun from somewhere. Desperate for cash, if he was an ICE head."

McGregor nodded. "That is a good point. But how did he get hold of a gun that was in another case?"

Charity practically bounced, as she exploded with the information. "It's from a cold case. And, Oh! My! Gawd! It was huge news here in Honolulu."

"Not big enough to solve it," Del remarked.

"Either way, it made the news," Charity said, her tone dismissive.

"All murders make news here—especially if it is someone local. They didn't solve it?" Graeme asked.

"No. Lots of leads, nothing came of it," Charity said, handing her another page. There was a picture of a young girl.

"A girl?"

Before she could ask for more details, Cat and Adam came walking into the room.

"Is this about the Wiki Mart shooting?" Adam asked.

She nodded and handed him the paper. Adam Lee was second in command and had worked for the HPD for a few years before moving over to TFH. Local and Hawaiian, he was big, strong, and happily bald. He always had a ready smile and something nice to say about everyone.

"Oh, the Jenny Kalani killing. I vaguely remember that. Definitely big news here."

Cat nodded. "Happened before my time."

Adam shot her a look out of the corner of his eye. Elle had to fight the smile. She and Adam were the oldest of the group, but none of them seemed to mention it. They did like to say it to Adam though.

"Are you calling me old?"

Young and small, but one of the strongest women Elle knew, Cat was considered the best shot of the whole group. She beat all the men on the team...and she was the exact opposite of Elle's lab assistant, Drew, who was infatuated with her.

"Not calling anyone old, bruddah."

Adam shook his head. "I don't remember it happening, but I remember when I first started thinking about becoming a cop. I read up on that case and the Honolulu Strangler case."

"I was just saying that you are of a *certain* age. But I remember several of my aunties talking about this. It was when the Strangler case was going on."

"Yeah, a young girl couldn't fight the publicity of a serial killer," Adam said.

"Especially the first ever recorded serial killer in

Honolulu," Del said.

"Wait, go back," Graeme said. "Talk about the serial killer."

"Why is that important?" Cat asked.

"Context. It's always best to know what was going on at the time."

Del nodded. "She definitely didn't fit the profile. She was young, too young. The other women were older, all of them of legal age. She was out of the parameters. Plus, she was shot, not strangled, and there was no sexual assault. So, the press moved on. The Honolulu Strangler was gaining some national press."

"In a place that lives off of tourism, and had fought so hard to clean up Honolulu's image from the early eighties, he was a worry for state officials," Adam said.

"The victims of the Honolulu Strangler were strangled, of course," Del said. "And they had been raped."

"So young," Elle said. "Only thirteen. Shot up close and personal, from what the report said, and left on the side of the road like rubbish."

Charity nodded. "It's not that easy to do, but the truth is, I'm kind of a cold case nut—especially when forensics is involved. I remembered Jenny's case because it was a first generation Glock. That stuck with me. So, I went back and found the pictures of the bullet. The striations match."

Striations were the markings inside the barrel of the gun. Each manufacturer used them and they were unique to each firearm.

"Don't those wear down in time?" Elle asked.

"Usually, and it makes it hard to ID a bullet from the same gun if a lot of bullets have been fired from it. That tells me there weren't a lot fired, or any at all. Plus, we have added DNA."

"DNA?" McGregor asked.

"Yes. I have all the bullets from the scene. Some did not even hit the victim. What I think is the first bullet fired had some DNA that did not match either of them. When I put it in the system, it came back to Jenny. Her murder was up close and personal, so that makes sense there would be blood or possibly some skin cells at least on the barrel. I tested a few other bullets that they found at the Wiki Mart. There are two others with DNA, but each one had a little bit less on it."

"Meaning?" Cat asked.

"It means that I can give the detectives an outline on which bullet was shot first," she said. "I have a feeling this was not premeditated."

"What addict premeditates anything but their next hit?" Cat asked. "It's still murder."

"But all these years later, the gun was used in a robbery. No other hit off of it since," Graeme said.

She could tell from the tone of his voice that he was already thinking about the implications.

"Right."

"Wait," Adam said. "Are you saying that this is connected to the Wiki Mart killing?"

"Yes," Charity said. "Tested the bullet myself. First description is a young male, probably in his twenties, so if that holds, this kid has nothing to do with a murder from almost thirty years ago. The grainy video wasn't that great, but he still looked young."

"So, somehow this kid gets hold of that gun and uses it to rob then kill Joe Alana," Graeme murmured.

"But if the person who killed Jenny all those years ago decided to hold onto it, or hide it, how did this loser come across it?" Cat asked.

"Especially if he's been tweaking out for a few days," Adam said. "I don't see a junkie holding onto a weapon and not selling it off for cash."

Elle nodded and looked up from the report. There was really only one explanation. Her gaze locked with Graeme's. Cold seeped into her, as everything seemed to fall into place.

"So, if he didn't hold onto it, he found it," Del said.

"Or," McGregor said, his voice filled with grim determination, "our current perp might just know who the killer of Jenny was all those years ago."

"And if he does, we need to find this guy...alive," Del added.

"We have another issue here," McGregor said. "We need to keep a lid on the fact that this gun is linked to another murder."

"Wouldn't it be better to put it out there? We might be able to stir up some memories, get someone to come forward," Cat said."

"No. If we stir up memories, we might put this bastard's life in jeopardy. I hate to admit it—other than the bullet that was left in Jenny, he is our only link to the killer," Del said. "And we need to make sure we get the bastard here, in custody, before the owner of the gun realizes we have a connection to it through our perp."

"Because if he is going to kill a little girl years ago, he won't think twice about killing a tweaked out junkie who killed a beloved store owner," Elle said. "You're right. We can't tell anyone."

Del met her gaze and nodded. He knew she didn't like being pitted against the police, not after what had happened in England. The apology that she read in his expression was enough to tell her it couldn't be helped.

"I do have a connection to the old ME, who should have been working here around that time. I might be able to get info about the case under the table, so to speak," she said. "He won't talk."

"Good," Del said. "Let's start digging into the files, but we have to do it quietly at the moment. Don't go through official channels just yet."

She frowned. "I can't start building a forensic profile of the killer without the official documents. But I can say I am working on an article on unsolved cases."

"That will fly with him?" McGregor asked.

She didn't bristle like she had when they'd first met. She had learned that his questions had more to do with curiosity than doubting her abilities.

"Yes. I'm pretty well known for writing about serial killers and what not. I can say I want to rule it out as a possible kill of the Honolulu Strangler."

"She was shot. They will question you right away, and then people might start talking," Adam said. "You know how people are."

She nodded. "But I have a reputation for being extremely thorough. Plus, remember, why would they even notice if I ask for all deaths during the time period of women from the ages of thirteen to thirty? It will just be included."

Del nodded. "Get that going. I'm going to have to tell the mayor and the governor about it though."

"You get to have all the fun," Elle said with a smile.

HOSTILE DESIRES

CHAPTER THREE

Graeme was looking over a report on his last assignment when there was a knock at the door to his office, and seeing his boss wearing a grim face, Graeme knew it was going to be bad news.

"So, I was talking to the mayor and the governor."

Graeme let one eyebrow rise. "At the same time?"

Del rolled his eyes, and walked into Graeme's office. When he shut the door behind him, Graeme's worries increased. If he wanted privacy, it couldn't be something particularly good.

Del grimaced as he sat in the chair in front of Graeme's desk. "No, although that would have been preferable. Sort of like ripping off the bandage. Get it all over with in one hard tug."

"What's up their asses?"

"The case."

"You might want to be more specific, since it seems we're handling about five at once."

"The cold case. Jenny Kalani."

Graeme nodded and leaned back in his chair. "They want us to take it up?"

"As of right now, the HPD does not know of the link. The governor and the mayor agreed with me on keeping it quiet, and the only way to do that is officially investigate it under TFH."

That made him pause. It usually took a lot to get either man to assign TFH a case. It was when they felt it was better to put up with the hassle from HPD or the feds. An assigned case usually meant a bloody mess in the media.

"They think HPD might interfere with the case?"

Del shook his head. "No, but you know that they are much more integrated into the community than TFH. Someone will let it slip. Then it will end up on the news. We want to make sure that we keep this out of the news as long as possible."

"For the sake of their reputations?" Graeme asked, not even trying to hide his irritation with the situation.

"Partly. The HPD got a lot of crap at the time for it. But it wasn't totally their fault. They were knee-deep in the Honolulu Strangler case," Del explained.

"Their first serial case?"

"Yes, and they were very overwhelmed by that. Remember, this was the eighties, long before DNA was being used in cases. Computers were barely used, and there was no national database of anything. No Internet. They were in over their heads, and the FBI was no use to them either. If the FBI couldn't find a serial killer on an island, there was a sure bet the local PD wouldn't, not then," Del continued.

"But, you're saying that the public got irritated over this Jenny Kalani case. Apparently, they didn't seem to complain enough. I've lived on this island a year. The public noticed and were horrified by her death. From what I can find on the case, Jenny came from a good hardworking family. She was just on her way back from the store with a gallon of milk when she was shot. But, with the fear and outrage rising about the serial killings, Jenny's murder faded into the background."

"And she wasn't tied to the Honolulu Strangler case?"

"No. She was shot and not near any area where the women had been abducted. Those victims were strangled. Jenny was much younger than the other victims, and there was no sexual assault, as you said. I have Elle hunting down the ME's report so she can start going over it."

"Hunting it down?"

"Remember, this was before computers. Everything I have found was what I could find in the news."

"And what is the other reason?" Graeme asked.

"If the bastard who killed Jenny Kalani is still roaming the island, they don't want him knowing that gun has been used in a killing. He might freak out. If he doesn't know it is missing right now, we have an advantage." He sighed. "And there is the family to consider."

"Don't you think they want to know if there is a lead in the case?"

"Yes. But we also don't want to get their hopes up. This might not lead anywhere. He might have snatched it from a home, or found it in one of the many drug hangouts. Finding him and the gun is of the utmost importance. If we don't, and we can't figure out how it ended up in his hands, or where it came from before then, we just won't be able to do much."

It sounded like a bitch of a case, and it also sounded as if this was all leading up to something very bad for him. "And you are telling me this because..."

"You're lead."

It took a second to seep into his brain. "I'm lead?"

Del nodded.

"*Bloody hell.* Doesn't Adam usually take these cases? He knows more people on the island than any of us. He'd have an easier time of working it than I would."

"Yes, but he's got a bead on a human trafficking case. Cat and Marcus are working with the FBI and Secret

Service on some kind of threat assessment for an upcoming conference."

"Bollocks. Marcus is working that one because that Tamilya is working the case for Dillon Securities for a few of the corporate bigwigs. Cat could handle it by herself easily."

The former DC cop had a thing for one of the security analysts, who worked at a private firm on the island. Marcus had been more than a little distracted by her.

"Maybe, but he's our best trained terrorist expert after working in DC for so many years. So that leaves you. Any of the team, including me, can help you, but I need someone to lead this up."

Bloody hell, he didn't like this. He hated working kid cases, even if the kid had been killed before he had been born. He could take a straight adult homicide any day, but throw in a kid...Graeme hated them. It was mainly because he never knew how to handle the parents' grief. He knew, even after all these years, the parents would be thrown back into their pain...reminded of their loss.

But he didn't really have a choice, so he nodded.

"Another thing. You'll need help from the doc on this. I know you two don't get along well, but her insight will help you with the case."

"I can work with her, if she can keep herself from being a pain in the arse."

Del shook his head. "Cut her some slack. She's not always that comfortable with policemen."

"She has no problem with you."

Del hesitated, as if weighing something mentally. Then he asked, "I guess you know she was married?"

Graeme nodded.

"He was a cop. Their breakup wasn't pretty."

"Is there a breakup that is?"

"True, but this one played out in the press. They worked together, and she pretty much got shut out after that. It almost ruined her career. She has a chip on her shoulder, and maybe you hit too close to home."

He wasn't really sure what that meant, and he didn't want to. He just wanted to stay away from the prickly Englishwoman. If she stayed mad at him, it would be easier to resist the temptation she presented.

"Okay. You know me, boss. I'm going to go where you send me."

Del nodded. "Thanks. They wanted me to take lead, but with my mom and sisters coming in next week, Emma has been kind of...well, hyper."

Graeme chuckled as he thought of Del's bride-to-be. "Emma and hyper sort of go hand in hand."

"Double it. No, triple it. She is so freaked out about the wedding that she's made herself sick. I have to deal with her and Sean, who blames me."

Del's fiancée, Emma Taylor, had a very protective half brother, so Graeme could just imagine.

Graeme knew the smile he gave Del wasn't pleasant. "Better you than me. I am happily single."

"I was too. Happy in my bachelor ways. So don't get cocky, Graeme, because life has a way of proving you wrong."

After he watched his boss leave the office, Graeme rose from his chair and looked out his window. He liked that he had a view of the outside when a lot of the other offices did not. It was smaller, which didn't bother him. He'd grown up in a three-bedroom house with six people, so he knew how to live in small places. He'd happily traded that space for the view.

He couldn't see the ocean, but he did get a gorgeous view of the gardens and the Palace. He liked to watch all the people mingle about, enjoying the beauty of Hawaii. He didn't think anything could replace his love of Scotland, but Hawaii was a close second. And here he felt he was doing something. After leaving the Royal Marines, he had been at a bit of a loss, but it all clicked when he had interviewed here for the job.

And now he had his first official case to lead…with a woman who hated him. He remembered the first time he had seen her. She'd just finished an autopsy, her scrubs were covered in blood, and she had smiled at him. Just that, a smile, and her eyes had sparkled. He swore at that moment; his heart had actually stopped beating. Even now, he got sweats remembering the way his body had reacted. Hell, he'd wanted to seduce her right there and then, even covered in the muck of an autopsy. Just because she had smiled at him.

Then, he had introduced himself. The moment she heard his accent, all happiness drained from her expression and the prickly attitude had emerged. Even so, he still lusted after her. He couldn't seem to help himself. Which made him an idiot. He'd found a woman who made him itch beneath the skin, and she wanted nothing to do with him. Worse, she loathed him.

Life definitely liked to bite him in the arse, and this time, the bitch had taken a big chunk of it.

Elle waited on the phone, waiting to hear about the ME's report, when the door to the morgue opened. She should have seen this coming. Del had warned her she would be working with McGregor.

"Dr. Middleton?" a voice over the receiver said.

"Yes."

"We have no report for that case."

She frowned. "I saw that in the computer, but that makes no sense. This is an open case. A homicide."

"I understand, doctor, and you are more than welcome to come over here and look, but even the physical ME report is missing."

She sighed. "Thank you. If you should find it, make sure to contact me at TFH. And, could you send over the files about the other cases during the time period I asked for?"

"I will."

She clicked off her mobile and looked at Graeme, who was frowning at her. It was nothing new, nothing that she shouldn't have grown accustomed to over the last few months. It was her fault. She'd been the one who had bristled the first time they'd met. He was only reacting to her behavior, so it was her fault, not his. There was a very good chance that he had no idea why she acted the way she did.

"We have a problem," she said.

"What?" he asked.

"The ME report is missing."

"From the original case? Bloody hell, this gets worse and worse." Then he thought about Charity's findings. "How did Charity match the DNA."

"I talked to her about that earlier. She said that has to do with the Kalanis. They insisted on having a sample of Jenny's blood stored at a separate secure location. When DNA started to get used, they paid the hefty fee to have hers tested and recorded. Most cold case nutters like Charity know of the companies. But there are more disturbing things than just the ME report going missing."

"That isn't the most disturbing thing?"

She shook her head. "It was not logged into the computer system when the others were. So I am not even sure if it disappeared directly after the murder, or if it disappeared later. There's no way of knowing for sure."

"Damn. I really hate to have to talk to the parents if this leads nowhere."

"We might not have a choice, but I have a friend who might be able to help."

"This ME you talked about?"

She nodded, thinking of him. "Yes. If anyone knows anything about the case, it would be Dr. Keahi."

"Will he keep his mouth shut?"

She chuckled, thinking of the man she'd thought of as a second father for most of her life. "Yes. If he knows about it, he will be happy to help, and happy to keep quiet."

Before she could continue, Drew came bursting into the office. Tall, handsome in a geeky kind of way, Drew Franklin was the perfect assistant. He had more energy than she ever remembered having, and he didn't hesitate to lend a hand.

"It looks like they found the killer. It's all over the news."

"They have him in custody?"

He shook his head. "They've surrounded a house he's in. There's a standoff."

"Damn," McGregor said. "Is it a Monday? It feels like a bloody awful way to start the week."

"It is and I agree. Let's go watch upstairs. They have better screens," Elle said.

By the time they reached the conference area, everyone had gathered to watch the breaking news. Elle noticed that there were just three seats, all close together. Graeme waited for Elle to take her seat, then he sat in the one next to her. Drew took the last one left.

"What the hell does he think he's going to do?" Charity asked. "He's surrounded by men with big guns."

"Let's hope he survives. We need him to be alive," Elle said, without tearing her gaze away from the screen. He heard it there in her voice, the need to believe this man was going to help them with the murder from thirty years earlier.

"Oh, there's Carino," Drew said.

Graeme tore his attention away from Elle to look at the screen. Sure enough, the hardened detective had a megafone and was trying to coax the criminal from the house.

"Does he have hostages?" Graeme asked.

"They aren't sure; that's why they're being careful with him right now," Del said.

"They're using a heat sensor to see the heat signatures in the house," Marcus said. "We used it in some hostage negotiations in DC. I'm sure you and Del have used it."

Both men had served in the military, so of course they had used it. She knew for a fact, they had both been active in Iraq.

There was activity behind Carino, and Elle realized they were getting ready to do something. Canisters flew through the air, crashing through the windows. In the next instant, smoke billowed out from the openings.

Within seconds, the door flew open and the suspect came running out, tumbling over the dilapidated front lanai, and then onto the barren yard. He was screaming in pain and coughing. The HPD rushed in and handcuffed him before pulling him up and dragging him over to the car.

"Well, at least now we can see if he still has the weapon," Elle said glancing at Graeme. "Do you think Rome will have a problem letting you observe the interrogation?"

He shook his head. "I'll head over."

"And I can call Dr. Keahi and set up a meeting with him."

Both of them stood, but Del stopped them.

"Remember, no matter how much you trust the HPD, we need to keep a lid on this case. Don't tell anyone you are working this case specifically."

They both nodded and headed off in different directions. Elle just had to figure out how to keep the truth from the man who had known her almost her entire life.

McGregor was right. This was definitely a sucky Monday.

HOSTILE DESIRES

Melissa Schroeder

CHAPTER FOUR

In the past year, Graeme had learned that once arrested, there were two types of junkies. There were the ones who would blather on, refusing to shut up. Unfortunately, Sam Katsu fell into the latter category. He'd been around the block, as the Americans liked to say. The first thing he had done, after trying to run away, was ask for a lawyer, then piss himself while in the squad car.

Since that moment, he had been silent. Part of it was self-preservation. The other part of it was the little bastard was crashing hard. Graeme could see it in his eyes. When he did talk, it made no sense whatsoever. Graeme studied him through the two-way mirror. He didn't look as if he could withstand a strong trade wind. His leg hadn't stopped moving since the moment Graeme laid eyes on him, and the wild look in his eyes, along with the dirty clothes and tangled hair, told him the kid had definitely been living on the streets—or close to it.

Rome stepped into the room and nodded at the officer who had brought Graeme in.

"Hey, Graeme. Is there a reason you're here?"

"Just wanted to see him. This is the bloke who killed Joe?" Graeme asked, not moving his gaze from the suspect.

Rome sighed. "Yeah. And more than likely, high as a kite at the time. Or, he was hurting for a fix so bad he would have killed his own grandmother to get enough money to buy."

"What is he? Sixteen?"

"Twenty-five."

He looked at Rome to see if the detective was joking. His grim expression told Graeme that he wasn't.

"You're telling me he's almost a decade older than he looks?"

Rome nodded. "With a long rap sheet. I'm pretty sure he used his size to fool people too. Petty theft, muggings, and felony drug possession. You name it, he did it to get his next fix. He's definitely an ICE head. He didn't care who he hurt as long as he got a fix."

ICE was what locals called meth. It was just as bad on the islands as it was on the mainland.

"People liked Joe," Graeme murmured.

Carino's gaze sharpened. "You knew him?"

Graeme nodded. "Yeah. I live in Laie. I stopped by every now and then. Joe was one of the first locals to welcome me to the islands. Always smiling."

"Yeah. He's going to be missed."

Graeme glanced back at the young man. "He looks *feart* of something."

"I am going to assume that means afraid, and he should. We have to protect him."

"Who from?"

"You name it. If he is in the general pop at Halawa, he's going to have just about everyone in there after him. All the gangs, no matter their affiliation, are going to go after him."

"Yeah, that's true. The Wiki Mart was one place on the island anyone could shop at and be safe. And they had been until today."

"It is odd that he escalated the violence. Before today, he would normally grab the occasional tourist's purse, or do a smash and grab at a store. He'd never used a weapon of any kind."

"Might have dried up a money source."

Carino nodded. "But we won't find out until his lawyer gets here."

"Does he have a lawyer?"

"Public defender."

Graeme watched as the young man slowed his movements. His leg was no longer banging against the table Suddenly, his eyes rolled back and he slid to the floor.

"Fuck," Carino said, as he started running toward the door.

McGregor followed him, but stayed out of the way, waiting to see if they needed his help. Foam was bubbling up from the man's mouth as he started to convulse.

Carino took hold of his head and tried to keep it still as Katsu shuddered against the floor. Nothing came out of his mouth but gurgling noises, and his eyes were still rolled back in his head.

"Stay with me, Sam. Come on," Carino yelled.

No response. The choking sounds grew louder just as the EMTs came rushing in. As they started to work on Katsu, Carino backed off and walked over to Graeme.

"There are going to be a lot of people very happy this happened," Carino said. "If he doesn't survive, it's going to save the DA a lot of headaches."

"True," Graeme said, as he watched what he thought would be fruitless efforts. And it would be better for almost everyone, except Katsu and Graeme. If he died, it was going to be damned hard to find that fucking gun.

This was turning into one bloody hell of a case.

Elle had the top down on her convertible as she sang along with Jake Johnson on the radio. This car had been the one thing she had splurged on when she moved to Hawaii. She had always had sensible sedans before, and after the meltdown of her career and marriage, she had been very cautious. She'd watched what she spent, and she was careful who she confided in. But when she had seen the two-year-old BMW convertible, she couldn't resist. And why live in Hawaii if she couldn't have a convertible?

As the sweet breeze blew through her hair, Elle turned onto Portlock Road. The neighborhood was quiet, even for the afternoon, but then it wasn't a touristy area. Kids should have been out of school for the day, but she understood. She could walk to the beach, and she took advantage of that every time she got the chance.

Her mobile rang. Turning down the music, she glanced at the screen and felt her pulse speed up when she saw McGregor's name. She drew in a breath and clicked on the speaker.

"Hey, how did the interrogation go?" Elle asked.

"Not well at all. He refused to answer anything until he talked to a lawyer which he means he knows his way around the system."

"That's definitely not good."

"It gets worse," Graeme said. "Katsu passed out and had to be taken to the hospital."

"Good lord. Is he okay?"

"He crashed once, but they brought him back, and have him at Tripler. The police thought he would have more of a chance of being safe there, and they have a guard on the door."

Rome would definitely do everything he could to keep him safe. But getting the info from him now was going to be even more difficult. "I'll call as soon as I get a chance and talk to the doctor," she said.

"Sounds good. I just pulled back into the parking lot. Do you want to meet up and discuss strategy?"

"Sorry. I'm not there."

"Then where the bloody hell are you?"

She tightened her fingers on the steering wheel of her car, as she pulled into the driveway. While she knew her behavior toward him when they'd first met wasn't cordial, the man had the manners of a goat.

"I know the original ME who did the autopsy on Jenny Kalani. Remember, I said I would call him? I'm meeting with him to see if he remembers the case, and to explain what might have happened to the report."

"Oh. Okay." He was quiet for a few moments, and she thought he might have hung up. "So, you want to meet later?"

"It might take me a couple hours here. Doc Keahi likes to ramble."

"Okay. Let's meet at McPherson's."

She blinked. She knew the place was a favorite with UK expats. She went often, but had never seen McGregor there. It made sense, and more people would place him in the rowdy pub before they would think she would spend time there.

"I can get there by six."

He made a sound that was close to a grunt. "You got it."

Then he hung up. With a shake of her head, she clicked off her mobile and slipped out of the car. The man really did have the most deplorable manners, but then, a person always knew where she stood with McGregor. She could handle that better than someone who hid his motives beneath slick smiles and pretty words. She'd had enough of that kind of man to last a lifetime.

She pushed away those thoughts, as she made her way to the door. Portlock Road was one of those areas of Hawaii people dream of living. Set in Hawaii Kai, it housed locals and celebrities alike, but for a price. The homes reached in the millions, and some had seemed to double overnight thanks to the insane Oahu real estate market in the last year.

Doc Keahi started off as a pineapple picker's kid, but a stint in the service along with a sharp mind got him through medical school. After leaving HPD, he had become a legend in the forensics field. His testimony had put more than one killer away in high profile cases, and several of his books had been optioned for movies. Her time with the Doc had started before she had even attended school.

She stopped to admire the gardens and the pretty little koi pond. The fish flitted back and forth, enjoying the warm water. She needed to think about getting a fish. She loved pets, but her hours made it difficult. She didn't want to adopt a dog or cat and then never be there. It would not be fair to the animal.

The front door flew open, pulling her attention away from the fish. On the stoop stood Doc Keahi.

"Dr. Elle Middleton," he said, a wide smile creasing his face. "What a pleasure."

He looked as he always did. His skin was golden brown from his heritage and his time in the sun. Bright brown eyes, rimmed with gold, sparkled from behind horn-rimmed glasses. He might be in his seventies, but there was no mistaking whether he was sharp as ever. His gaze rarely missed anything.

Now that he was semi-retired, he seemed to spend at least three days a week at the beach. Of course, there was always the stunning pool, and she knew he swam almost every day. He regularly prescribed her the same activity. He was wearing a pair of board shorts that had seen better days, and a red clay shirt that said older than dirt.

"Hullo, Doc. How are you doing?" she asked, as she walked toward him.

"Well, although they say I need to use my cane more often. My ortho doc told me I shouldn't be surfing."

"Oh, God, you went surfing again? Mum will have my head if you get hurt."

He gave her one of his trademarked hugs and let her go. His smile faded. "You are not getting enough sleep, Elle."

She shook her head. "I've been pulling double duty. They're a little low on manpower at the moment at HPD."

"I heard. Come in. I've made us some proper tea, as your mother taught me to make it, and we can have us a good chat."

The moment she stepped into the foyer, memories washed over her. When she had arrived over four years earlier, she had stayed with Doc. He had welcomed her, just having lost his partner of over thirty years. They had helped each other through a lot of the pain they had been going through, and he had given her a new life. He had shown her his Hawaii, the one only *Kamaaina* see. She had fallen in love with the island, the people, and the culture. Now she could not even fathom living anywhere else.

"So, you want to talk to me about Jenny Kalani?"

"Yes. I'm working on an article about the Honolulu Strangler case. After working on the Goddess Killer case late last year, I started researching serial killers here in Hawaii, and found this one was the first one."

He was carrying the tea into the living room, and he stopped and looked at her. "Eleanora Middleton, you're not a very good liar."

She fought the smile, but lost the battle. "Actually I am. Ask Mum. But you could always tell when I was lying, so I'm happy you were not around during my secondary school years."

He shook his head. "I don't even want to think about what lies you got away with."

"I wasn't that bad, but there were a few nights Mum thought I was studying." She smiled. "Let's just pretend you believe me today."

He studied her for a moment, then he nodded. "Okay, but I expect a full accounting when this is all over."

"You got it."

"Let's go out to the lanai, and we can talk all about poor Jenny and her murder."

Graeme took a healthy swig of his Guinness, letting the yeasty brew calm his irritation. He was pretty sure high and mighty Doc wouldn't know how to find the place. It was one of the better known places for expats to hang out, but he was also sure it wasn't her kind of place. He glanced at the door for the third time in less than five minutes. Damn, the woman was never late for any meeting. In fact, there were times she beat everyone to the table, including Adam, who was the Boy Scout of the office.

"Bad day?" Will McPherson asked as he dried a glass.

The retired HPD cop hailed from Ireland, and you could still hear it in his voice. Like so many people before him, Will had come to Hawaii for a week and decided to stay forever. His shock of bright red hair was now threaded with grey, and his fair skin was definitely not ideal for the Hawaiian sun, but that did not seem to matter. After retirement, he'd opened his bar and grill, which was just off of the regular touristy area in Waikiki, in an area that didn't call out to the tourists, or even many locals. Instead, it had become primarily a UK transplants and cops' hangout.

"Just a long one."

"And you look like you're waiting for someone."

"He is," Elle said from behind him. He turned to face her. She looked...better. He didn't know what it was about today, but she looked refreshed. And she was smiling. She hardly ever smiled when he was around.

"You had no problem finding the place?"

She raised her eyebrows. "I do know my way around Honolulu, as I have lived here longer than you have. Plus, they have this thing called GPS. Have you heard of it?"

He said nothing, because she was more relaxed than he had seen her in awhile. He knew that filling in with HPD was important to her, but it did seem to take its toll. Covering for them while still holding down regular shifts at TFH was starting to show.

"But the lass knows her way here, don't you, Elle?" Will asked, sliding a glass of white wine on the bar toward the doctor. "I poured it the minute I saw you come through the door."

Her smile turned into a grin. "You're the best."

"You look like you need something to eat."

She nodded. "I just had the best biscuits this side of the Pacific and Atlantic by a Hawaiian who knows how to brew some proper tea, but would love my usual. I seemed to have skipped lunch again."

Graeme looked back and forth between the two of them. "I take it that you are a regular."

"Yep. For months now. We must have just missed each other."

"Doc, your booth is open," Will said.

She nodded and grabbed her wine glass and motioned with her head. As they walked further back into the pub, he realized that many of the people who knew him, also knew Elle. She smiled at a few, waved at more than one, and stopped to chat with one of the cops he knew worked Vice.

She slid into the booth just as he got there. It was one of the cozy ones in the back with the round back where you could sit right next to each other.

Elle slid in and stopped. Of course. He sat down opposite her, wondering why his palms were suddenly damp. The urge to slide around the table and sit right next to her almost overwhelmed him. Instead, he took another quick drink of Guinness.

"So, did the ME have any info for us?" he asked.

She smiled at him, one of those amazing smiles she rarely bestowed on anyone, and definitely not him. It lit up her eyes and displayed the cute little dimples at the sides of her mouth.

"Yes. Thanks to my relationship with him—"

"Your relationship?" he asked, a little more sharply than he meant to.

She said nothing, but stared at him.

He cleared his throat, as his face started to heat. "I just thought the man to be older than Methuselah."

She chuckled. "He would challenge you to an arm wrestling match if he heard you say that. But my relationship goes back to my childhood. He lectured at Oxford with my father. He's actually the reason I go by Elle."

Greedy for any information about her background, he was temporarily sidetracked from the issue at hand. "He is?"

She hesitated, then her shoulders relaxed as she sipped at her wine. "My real name is Eleanora."

Graeme blinked. "Eleanora?"

"I know. It doesn't fit me, does it? When Mum introduced me to him, Doc said it was too big a name for such a little girl. He called me Elle, and it stuck."

He could just imagine a tiny version of Elle, and couldn't fight the smile. "Ah."

"He's one of the reasons I went into this work, so when I came here a few years ago, I stayed with him. Of course, not a bad choice seeing that he lives over on Portlock Road."

"Nice location," he said, knowing it was an understatement.

"Indeed. So, I went out to his house, and he not only remembered the case, he had a copy of the case files." She pulled out a dilapidated file folder filled with paper, and secured with several thick rubber bands. "And he gave them to me."

HOSTILE DESIRES

CHAPTER FIVE

Elle sipped her wine, enjoying the sweetness of mango. She had been married to a wine snob, and many of her old friends were as well. Still, when Elle had discovered some of the fruit wines of Hawaii, she stopped caring what other people thought and just enjoyed.

She turned the page and found the report from Doc. He had a very detailed report—as much as he could back then—and he included many notes. It wasn't odd that he would do that, but it seemed some of them were more recent, and there were a lot of sticky notes in the report. Still, when Elle had talked to him, he had seemed frustrated by the lack of closure. It seemed to be the one case that bothered him.

"Why did he take the files?" McGregor asked, pulling

her out of the report.

Elle looked up from the files. "He made a copy of them, so he didn't technically take them."

McGregor rolled his eyes, and she had to bite back an apology. Gerald had always said she was too particular about the wording. He never understood what it was like to grow up as a single child of two brilliant professors. Even after her mother stopped teaching, she wrote articles and books, one on linguistics.

"Why did he make copies?"

She thought about the way Doc acted during the discussion. "I'm not sure why, but Doc seemed to think someone was dragging their feet in the investigation. More than once he mentioned to me, and here in the report, that it was taking them forever to get information about the evidence from HPD. He also alluded to the fact that there were some in the police department too interested in the Honolulu Strangler to worry about some poor little *keiki* from the islands."

"But I read those files. They were all locals, right? For the Strangler case?"

She nodded. "But this little girl wasn't going to get any notice on the news. Not national at least. And, they had next to nothing to go on. Remember, this was right after Bundy had been executed in Florida. The first ever serial killer arrives in Hawaii, so you know the press was going to be all over that."

"And that hasn't changed."

The whole task force knew exactly how the press reacted to serial killers.

"Unfortunately, all I have is Dr. Keahi's report to go by, and the fact that the bullet had been entered into the system; there was no way to make that disappear. If that hadn't happened, we would have never connected the two."

Before he could ask another question, Will showed up at the table with a plate of hot wings for her, along with the extra carrots.

"There you go, lass. You want anything, McGregor?"

"Burger, rare, with cheese and some chili fries."

"Of course, you McGregors always like things bloody." Will turned and winked at her. "Why is a good Campbell girl like you hanging around a scoundrel like this?"

She smiled. "We're going to catch us a killer. Then, I'll stop talking to him to make you happy."

"Good."

He walked away, and she looked at McGregor. He was staring at her as if she had grown another head.

"What?" she asked.

"You're Scottish." He spat out the words as if he were accusing her of eating babies.

She nodded. "Well, half. My mother's side. I'm actually named for my Granny Eleanora, from Inverness. And I grew up at Oxford, because that was where my father taught. He actually got his doctorate at Edinburgh."

"You never corrected me when I called you a Sassenach."

She shrugged. "Because I am. My father is English, although from York."

His eyes narrowed as he watched her eat. She had seen him do this in interrogation. McGregor seemed like a happy fellow, until you put him in the box with a suspect. While he had come to the job later than everyone else, he seemed to be particularly skilled at making a suspect pour out any secrets. There was a tickle at the back of her throat that was making it difficult for her to swallow her food. Finally, she'd had enough. She dropped her chicken wing and glared at him.

"What?" she asked.

"Why?"

"Why what?"

"Why did you allow me to be antagonistic to you? And why were you such a..."

"Bitch?"

His lips thinned. "Not my choice of words, but okay."

Elle sighed, not wanting to address the issue. Guilt had gotten the best of her more than once in the last few months. It hadn't been McGregor's fault. She had been the one with the chip on her shoulder, not him. He had been reacting to her behavior toward him, and then she had tried to punish him for it.

"When I found out you were from the UK—"

"I'm Scottish."

She rolled her eyes. "Still. You know when big news hits, especially scandal, Scotland hears it too. It didn't make the reports here in the US, but it was all over the UK. I had not realized you had been deployed with the Marines during my tenure with the Met."

"And?"

Of course, he wasn't going to let her off so easily. He wasn't a man who was easy to handle, and that was one of the reasons she had avoided him. He would pick and prod into her business, or worse, ask around about her. If that started, it could end badly.

"There was a case, a big one, that I worked on with my husband."

"The police officer."

So, he knew about that. Now she wondered how much he did know. She nodded.

"It made the news, then it made the rags. In the end, our marriage fell apart and I left. I just...I have sort of a chip on my shoulder. It almost ruined my career. And, many of the police blamed me. They sided with my husband, of course. It was just horrible."

"And you thought I would too."

She shrugged. The memory of those days came rushing back to her, and she suddenly didn't feel so hungry.

"People I thought of as close personal friends refused to acknowledge my presence. Not only was I being vilified in the press, but my support system had dissolved almost overnight. When I found out where you were from, I had a knee jerk reaction. I didn't understand it at first, but now I do. I am very sorry for it."

He studied her again for a long moment, as if weighing her words for their truthfulness. "And you don't want to talk about the case?"

She would rather walk naked into her mother's funeral. "I would rather not."

He nodded. "Okay. So, on to the other case."

She blinked. "Just like that?"

His lips curved, sending a flash of heat through her blood. "I'm easy, lass."

"So I've heard, McGregor," Will said, as he returned with the burger. He looked down at her plate. "Eat, Campbell."

"I will, don't worry. It's been over a month since I've had these."

"Just make sure you do, or I'll be talking to the Doc Keahi."

"I was just there today, and he filled me up with tea and biscuits, so everything is fine."

"That's good." He looked at McGregor. "Don't let her forget about her food." Then he left them alone.

"So, what did the good doctor tell you?"

"Not much. I got the autopsy and the description of the scene, which might help us more these days with profiling."

She sifted through the papers, then handed one to him. He set his burger down, wiped his mouth, and took the paper.

"He covered her face," he said. His piercing gaze rose to hers. "The killer probably knew her."

"Could be a she. And there is an indication of that. Or just felt badly about it. It tells me there's a good chance this wasn't premeditated."

She noticed something on the TV, and then Rome's face. He was talking about Sam Katsu when the reporter opened up with a question about a linked case. Her heart started to sink. This was just what Del had wanted to avoid.

"Oh, bollocks."

Graeme's gaze rose from the paper, and his eyes narrowed. "What?"

"I think they've heard about the cold case. The media, that is. Bastards will get in our way."

He turned around and looked at the TV. As he did, she could study him without him knowing. Despite her behavior the last few months, she had been intrigued by the giant Scotsman since they had been introduced. He topped six-four at least and was built like a Greek god. He'd cut his hair short, although, she wasn't sure how much she liked that. She'd had some pretty naughty fantasies about all that long blond hair. When he turned back around, she felt heat rise in her cheeks and concentrated on her food.

"How do you think they found out? Do you think your friend told them?"

She shook her head. "No way. He goes over it constantly, because I saw notes that looked to be less than a year old. While I'm not sure he believed me, I did use the story of researching for a paper."

"Okay."

"You believe me."

He frowned. "I don't know him, but I know you. You're a good judge of character."

"How do you know that?"

"You slapped me down enough. I know."

She snorted. "There is that."

They ate in companionable silence, as they both read through the reports. The noise level started to rise, and she winced as a particularly loud heavy metal song came on.

"What's wrong?"

She looked up with a frown, and wiped her mouth. "What do you mean?"

"You're wincing."

"I didn't realize I was. Loud noise...I'm afraid I'm starting to get a migraine. I have an issue with noise when they start to hit."

"How long have you been up today?"

"Since just after three. But I am going home after this." She took a sip of wine, then set it down. "Katsu wouldn't tell you where he got the gun?"

"I didn't interview him. That was Carino, because we were trying to keep it under wraps. A lot of bloody good that did. Either way, the kid has been through the system a few times, so he asked for his lawyer right off, then he passed out and was rushed to the hospital."

"*Damn.*"

Before she could say anything else, Will was at their table. "So, they say your team is looking over the Jenny Kalani killing."

She nodded and opened her mouth, but McGregor shook his head.

"Looks that way," McGregor said. "But we can't talk about it."

A twitch formed above Will's eye, and for the first time ever, Elle witnessed irritation in his expression.

"Just tread carefully, McGregor. A lot of people will see this as an attack on HPD."

"Why would they think that?" Elle asked.

Will looked at her. "Because you might question their integrity."

"That's just nonsense. We have greater chances of solving the crime now because technology has moved forward. It isn't judging anyone's work from the original case."

She felt something brush over her foot, and realized it was McGregor's boot. She glanced at him, and he shook his head slightly.

"Just be careful where you tread," Will said, before leaving them alone.

"That was a bit ominous," she said.

"Aye. I have a feeling a lot of the older cops are going to be bugging us for details, so we need to be careful. We already have a leak. Second of all, while I like Will, he was a cop here in Honolulu at the time. If there was a real cock up of the investigation, he might know the cop involved."

The ramifications of what they were doing hit her. She sighed and nodded. "*Bloody hell*, this is going to get difficult. I've met a few of them here over the last few years."

"We both need to remember to be very careful about who we talk to. This could get ugly really fast."

Graeme walked her to her car. His mother had raised him to be a gentleman and it was getting dark. Add in that they were just a few streets from one of the worst parts of town, and he couldn't let the doc go off on her own.

"You really didn't have to walk me to my car."

"My mother and my four older sisters would disagree with you."

She stopped walking and stared at him. "Four? And older?"

He nodded. "And they were mean to me."

She chuckled, the sound of it dancing over the wind to him. He rarely heard her laugh, so even a chuckle enticed him.

"I doubt that. I bet you were the baby boy, the golden son."

He made a face. "They dressed me up in their clothes and used me as a mannequin."

Now a bubble of laughter floated up out of her throat, and he stood transfixed. It was so light...so teasing, that he felt something shift through him. She was an attractive woman who had always fascinated him, but a happy Elle Middleton was a bit too much to resist. Soon, her smile faded, and Graeme realized he was staring at her.

"Is there something wrong?" she asked.

He shook his head and looked down the street. His fingers itched to brush back the single curl of hair that was dancing in the wind.

"No. Just I don't hear you laugh that often."

"Yes, well, if you deal with death as much as we do, it's hard to find those light times."

He cocked his head. "But don't you think we should find those times? It makes the days easier to bear."

She said nothing for a long moment. "Yes. Yes, you are definitely right about that."

She started walking again, and he stepped quicker to keep up with her. She wasn't a small woman. Small boned, but she topped five-ten at least. Long, lean, with curves in the perfect places. He shouldn't be thinking of her that way, but it was hard not to. When she had been dismissive of him, it was easier to ignore. Sure, he still had the thoughts, but he thought there was no chance of a romance. Now, though, she was smiling at him and being nice. It made it hard not to fantasize.

The night air carried her scent to him. It wasn't a perfume, but more of a rose soap against soft skin kind of smell. They reached her car, and he found himself trying to figure out a way to extend their night together. It was crazy, but this had been the first time since they'd met that she'd been nice to him, and he wanted it to last.

"Well, I'll go over Doc's notes some more then get them to you. You will probably be able to get more done on the profile of the person. I can help with that because I am certified in forensic psychology."

"Yes."

She looked up at him, and he couldn't seem to think of anything other than kissing her. It was insane, but just these few moments that she had been nice to him, and those walls had come tumbling down.

"McGregor, is there something wrong?"

He shook his head. "Why don't you call me by my first

name?"

She shrugged. "Everyone calls you McGregor."

"But you call others by their first names on the team. Even the boss. You call him Del."

She sighed. "I guess it was one way to keep my distance."

"So, if you finally call me Graeme, I know you don't want to keep your distance?"

She sucked in a breath, then her lower lip quivered. If he hadn't been concentrating on her so closely, he would have missed it.

"No, I just—"

"Say my name, Eleanora." He liked the way her formal name sounded on his tongue.

Her eyes softened. "Okay, Graeme—"

He bent his head then and kissed her. Just a brush of his mouth against hers. The simple touch sent a wave of fire through his body. He never took his hands out of his pockets. When he pulled back, she said nothing for a moment.

She looked as shocked as he did.

"What was that for?" she asked.

He shrugged. "I'm not really sure."

"Don't do it again."

"Why not?"

"Why not?"

"Yes. Why not?" Her voice had risen, and he fought a smile. That reaction told him he wasn't alone in his feelings.

"Because we work together, and we are working this case together. Add in the age difference—"

"How old are you?"

She blinked. He knew she used that to gather her thoughts. "Excuse me?"

"How old are you? Thirty? Two years is no big deal."

"I'm almost forty."

"Really? You don't look that much older than I am."

"Either way, I am much older, so with that in mind, it just doesn't work."

"Is it because I'm a cop like your ex?"

"No. It's not that."

"You know the one thing you didn't mention in that list of things?"

"What?"

"That you aren't attracted to me."

She frowned. "If there's a heterosexual woman who says you aren't attractive, she's blind as a bloody bat."

Delighted by her answer, he rocked back on his heels. "Is that a fact?"

She sighed. "I will not let you use that as a way to trip me up. You know you're attractive."

"Just as you are."

"And I will not let you use flattery to try to gain my acceptance. This just isn't a good idea."

"It was just a kiss, Eleanora."

She straightened her shoulders. "And that is all it will be."

He slid his hands out of his pockets and held them up. "Hey, I won't pressure you. I just wanted to let you know how I feel. What we do about it is up to you."

She opened her mouth, but her mobile rang. "Yes?"

Her frown turned darker.

"I understand. I'll be there in just a few minutes. I'm still in Honolulu. Graeme is with me."

She hung up and looked up at him. "That was Del. Katsu was attacked by someone at the hospital. He's in a coma."

HOSTILE DESIRES

Melissa Schroeder

CHAPTER SIX

The moment they stepped into the TFH conference area, Elle realized their mistake. Walking into headquarters together after working hours was sure to raise a few eyebrows. Still, there had been no way around it, unless one of them had stood outside, and that seemed silly. Elle hadn't planned it that way, but they had driven in separate cars, with him right behind her, all the way. Del, Marcus, Drew, Cat, and Emma were there. They all turned to face them both.

"Out on a date?" Del joked.

"They don't date," Emma said. "Don't you remember how much they hate each other?"

Cat snorted, but said nothing. Emma had gotten better at picking up on sarcasm, but she still had issues with it. The team called her Beautiful Mind for a reason, and they all tried to protect her feelings.

"We were going over the case. I was talking to Doc Keahi about the case, and met up with Graeme at McPherson's to talk it over," Elle said.

Emma gave her a sharp look, but said nothing else.

"Other than that, you didn't say anything to anyone

else, did you?" Del asked.

She shook her head, then looked at Graeme. He was shaking his head too.

"Once a Marine, always a Marine. I follow orders," he said.

"Well, somehow they figured out the connection," Del said. "The mayor and governor knew also, so I am assuming it came from their people. They leak like a freaking sieve when it comes to secrets."

"You didn't have a choice, Del," Marcus said. "If you didn't tell them and it leaked, there would have been hell to pay for it."

"So, can we talk about this in the open now?" Cat asked.

"I think we still need to go with our *no comment*. The one person I want to bring in on this is Rome. He will have some questions, and I'm sure he's going to be pissed," Del said.

"I'm going to call the hospital and see if I can talk to the doctor about Katsu's condition," Elle said.

"Leave the report here, so we can go over it," Del said.

"Do you want to scan them?" she asked. "I thought it might be easier to get it out to everyone. I know that we have to be careful with digital copies, and I know that everyone is really busy. Still, someone might see something in it I missed."

"I highly doubt you miss anything, Elle," Adam said.

"Still, if anyone sees anything, it might help."

"You got it," Adam said.

She nodded and pulled out the files, leaving them on the table, then she hurried toward the elevators.

"Elle, wait up," Emma said, racing toward her. "Care for some company?"

"Sure. Come on."

As they walked to the elevators, she had her mind on the case and nothing else, but once the doors opened and they stepped onto the lift, she realized that Emma wanted to talk. She was quiet, and when Emma was quiet, something was on her mind. She wasn't working on this case, so Elle knew that she didn't have work on her mind.

"Is there something wrong?"

"I'm...just the wedding is driving me nutters, and Del is trying to be sweet. But he makes it worse when he starts talking about forever and his mother coming here. I can't seem to keep anything down, and I think I have anemia again. I've lost my appetite, and every now and then, the room spins when I stand up. I suffered this after the tsunami, but that was because good food was scarce, and then I was living on the street."

Elle blinked. "Wow, that's a lot of words."

The doors opened to the basement and she stepped out. Emma looked a little green around the gills.

"Are you okay?" Elle asked.

"Yeah. I've been getting motion sickness. I get these things all separately, so I'm thinking the stress of the wedding is getting to me."

Elle smiled. "That very well could be. I didn't sleep for three nights before my wedding. Could barely keep anything down, in fact."

"Oh, good, I thought it was just me. Or maybe I was dying."

"You thought you were dying, but decided to keep it to yourself?"

"No. I came to see you, and I talked to my doctor, who said not to worry. I stress myself out, and this wedding is pushing me over the edge. Which is true. That was about a month ago, and it's getting worse."

"I can give you an exam, but not tonight."

"Yes, I understand."

Emma watched Elle as she washed her hands then dried them. Elle knew the younger woman had something on her mind, but it was always best to let Emma come around on her own.

"You called him Graeme."

The statement came out of nowhere, and it took a moment for Elle to realize what Emma had said. Dammit, she hadn't realized that she had done that.

"What?" Elle asked.

"Graeme. You called him by his first name."

She turned to look at the younger woman. She seemed so young, or looked it at least. But the horrors she had seen as a young woman, after surviving the Boxing Day Tsunami, had matured her beyond her years. Still, she had a genius IQ and barely missed a thing.

"I call lots of people by their first names."

"Not Graeme. You usually call him McGregor."

She did not need to discuss this, not right now. She had too much going on. "Well, it seemed weird calling him by his last name since we are working together."

Emma didn't believe her. Elle could see it by her expression.

"Nope. Something happened," Emma said, crossing her arms beneath her breasts.

"No."

"Yes," she said, jumping up off the chair, then suddenly swaying.

"Whoa, there, Emma," Elle said, rushing forward. "You need to take it easy there."

"Oh, that is not fun. Just like when I had anemia."

"Tell you what. I'll come by the house tomorrow and check you out."

"Don't tell Del."

"You haven't told him you aren't feeling well?"

"You know how he would freak out about it. Since that incident earlier this year, Del has been overprotective. He knows I've been throwing up, but the dizziness I've been keeping to myself."

"The *incident* was a serial killer trying to kill you, and Del saw you fall over your balcony. You act like it was just breaking your nail."

Emma rolled her eyes. "If there is something wrong,

then I'll tell him. But I think it is just the anemia."

Drew burst into the lab in his usual matter.

"I don't think I can do this," Emma said, her voice faint.

Elle patted her hand. "Have Del take you out and eat a high iron meal. Eggs, red meat, or scallops. Get some spinach."

She nodded. "I guess I better let you go so you can call Tripler. Thanks, Elle." She smiled at Drew, then left them alone, rushing out.

"What's wrong with her?" Drew asked, as Elle looked through her contacts at Tripler.

"Bridal nerves. They have less than two weeks left."

"I know," Drew said, wiggling his eyebrows. "I'm going to make my move."

She smiled. "You asked Cat to attend the wedding with you?"

"Well, we *are* driving there together. Then, I'll sweep her off her feet."

Elle smiled. "I hope you do."

She brought up a contact's name, and started dialing the number. When Dr. Myers answered on the first ring, she smiled and started talking fast.

Graeme's mobile rang before they could even get to the report. He saw Carino's number and winced.

"Carino," he said to Del.

"Read him in, and if he gives you crap, hand him off to me."

Graeme nodded and clicked on his mobile as he walked into his office for a little privacy.

"Give me a reason not to kick your Scottish ass all the way back to the UK, McGregor," Rome growled over the phone.

"Hey, I was under orders. And to save a little bit of an

issue, Del had gotten approval to read you in before the info leaked. I was going to talk to you about it tomorrow."

"Still pissed."

"Well, get over it."

There was a long pause, then a sigh. "Okay, tell me what you have."

He went over what little they had gathered, then waited for Carino to respond.

"Son of a bitch. We could have asked him about that and might have found the weapon."

"First of all, he lawyered up. Second of all, before we could sort through everything, he'd passed out."

Carino sighed again, the long day and the frustration of a case that had just gone sideways easy to hear over the phone.

"We're going over the ME's report, but why don't I come over tomorrow with the report from this case, along with the cold case, then we can put it all together and maybe come up with something?"

"I'll see what I can dig up. Nine sound good?"

"Make it ten. I'm still at TFH headquarters, and I'm not sure how long before I can head back home."

"Good. And, just so you know, I say you owe me one."

Then he hung up. McGregor couldn't help but chuckle. Carino was definitely one of a kind. He walked back out into the conference room.

"Everything okay?" Del asked.

McGregor nodded. "Aye. He's coming over around ten tomorrow to go over the two cases with us."

"Good. Carino has a good eye, so he'll help."

"More than likely, he'll be happy to dump this in our laps."

Del nodded. "From what this says, she was found under some brush, her face covered," Del said, as he read over the ME report. "Odd that he made so many notes about things like that in this."

"Both Elle and I think that the murderer might have

known her, or at least it wasn't premeditated. Definitely shows remorse."

"And the ME?"

"He's practically like an uncle to Elle. She thinks he wondered about a cover up, so the extensive notes might have something to do with that. And, she noted that he started looking at it again around the time of the Goddess Killer."

Del nodded as his mouth tightened. Graeme could understand his boss's reaction. Seeing the woman he loved fall over a balcony was enough to make Del hate even the mention of the case.

"It's such a shame the girl was ignored, but hell, you see it still today," Marcus said. "And this definitely would fall through the cracks, even right now."

"Not sure about that," Cat said. "Now that we have so many traffic cams, etc., there would have been more ways to sort through the evidence. And, remember, there is no ongoing serial killer case. With a healthy social media, many Hawaiian residents would make sure she would get attention."

That was one of the things he loved about Oahu. There were close to a million people on the island, but it was like a small town. Everyone knew everyone else...or his cousin. It was probably irritating to some, but when they needed each other, there was always community support.

"Speaking of which," Marcus said looking at Graeme, "You want to make sure you get all the evidence. I'm pretty sure Charity could do something with it."

Graeme nodded. "Let's hope there's enough."

"Well, they have her clothes from what this says," Del said.

"Do you need us for anything else, boss?" Marcus asked. "Cat and I have a meeting out at Hickam tomorrow."

Del shook his head. "You go on."

When they were left alone, Del leveled him with a look.

"Got something to tell me?"

"No."

He nodded and continued to look over the report. "So, you and Elle went out to eat?" Del asked.

"Yeah. Seems that she frequents McPherson's."

Del nodded. "I could see that. It seems like you worked through your issues."

Graeme shrugged, feeling as if Del was fishing, and he was not in the mood. His mind was on the case...*and* the woman.

"Did you ask her about her past?"

"She told me some of it."

Del nodded. "I assumed that was part of the reason she had issues with you. But I'm glad you worked it out. My mother gets here the day after tomorrow, and Emma's sick. She doesn't want me to know she is sick, but she's worried herself into a state. I knew the two of you would be able to work the case together."

"I don't know that I need the doctor around after she goes over the findings."

"True, but since she has a connection to the first ME, I thought it might help out in the case. I do want her taking off tomorrow. I want you to tell her that I don't want to see her at the office unless it's an emergency."

Graeme let one eyebrow rise up. "And you think she'll listen to me?"

Del smiled. "Tell her I said so. Then threaten her with leave. Or a call to the good old Doc Keahi. The man is like a second father to her."

"I didn't know you knew about their relationship."

"I don't miss much, but I do know he recommended her for this job, and she lived with him for awhile when she first got over here. He might not be able to get her to do anything, but he'll contact her mother. Apparently, that is the way to put the scare into Elle."

"Okay."

They heard the ding of the doors, and they both turned

toward it. Emma turned the corner into the conference area and made her way to the office. By the time she stepped into Del's office, she looked like she was ready to pass out. Her face was pale, and she didn't appear to be steady on her feet.

"Hey, Emma, what's wrong?" Del asked, as he rose from his desk.

"Nothing. I just realized I need to get some good food in me. And I need some sleep."

"You got it. I take it you'll be here when Elle's done?" Del asked.

He had planned on it. "Yes. I want to see what she found out."

Del nodded.

"Night, Graeme. Make sure she gets sleep. Elle hardly ever sleeps," Emma said.

"And you know this how?"

"I recognize a fellow insomniac when I see one."

He followed them out of the office, then watched as Del led her out into the hall. His boss was right. Emma did not look all that well, but then, he had been around for one of his sister's weddings, and that had been horrible. The memory still left him with nightmares.

Alone in the office, he decided to go over the report that Elle had given him while he waited.

Elle was practically dragging her ass on the ground as she stepped out of the elevator. She had expected Graeme would stick around, but she felt better when she saw his office light on.

Graeme. Since the moment she had said it earlier, she knew she would never think of him any other way. That was the reason she had avoided using the name. She stepped closer and realized he was reading...and he was wearing a pair of glasses. He was so focused on what he was reading, he didn't realize she was looking at him then. She felt free to take her time to study him.

He always seemed like a man from another time, a warrior without a kingdom. Maybe it was the Scots in her blood, but that accent and those piercing eyes called to her. He was the first man since her divorce, and the incident that preceded it, to make her want to be touched. And seeing him like this, intent on whatever he was reading, made her hormones pop to life.

She must have caught his attention, because his gaze rose to hers. Lord, he was sexy before, but now he looked like a warrior nerd. Then, he slowly slipped the glasses off. Okay, her ovaries might have just quivered. Good lord, she was starting to sound like Charity now.

The longer she stood there, the harder it was to take that step forward. After a few moments, she found the ability to step in the direction of his office.

"I wasn't sure if you would still be here," she said. "I did not know you wore reading glasses."

"Not a secret, but I don't need them that often."

"I talked to Dr. Myers. He works at Tripler. Seems Katsu was crashing when he came in."

"Yeah?"

"According to the admitting doctor, if he had been able to buy his next fix, it could have very well been his last. He had track marks in his arms. So very many of them. But he seemed to be okay when they got him stable."

"I sense a *but* here."

Elle nodded. "Three hours ago, he plummeted. They have no reason for it, and they have no idea why he went down the way he did."

"There was a guard at the door," Graeme said.

"Yes, but there might have been a few minutes that he was distracted. I don't have all the details on that, but Myers said he would find out. Seems like there was a fight that conveniently broke out just outside of the ICU."

"Any chance of recovery?"

She sighed. "Probably not. He's pretty much brain dead at this point. They really don't expect any kind of recovery."

"Which means, we won't be able to question him or find out where he got the gun."

She nodded.

"Bugger me."

"Exactly."

Melissa Schroeder

CHAPTER SEVEN

Less than fifteen minutes later, Elle walked beside Graeme. Nights in Hawaii were always gorgeous. Even if the trades were light during the day, the nights were bearable. The humidity from the day had burned off and nothing was left but the sweetness from the tropical flowers and the salty scent of the ocean. Still, after living in Oahu for five years, she would never get used to it.

She was wired. Too much caffeine was part of the reason. She loved her Kona coffee, but she rarely had the gallon or so she had consumed today. But part of the reason was the man beside her.

She glanced at her companion. They had parked next to each other, so for most people it would make sense. Still, this was the first time for the two of them to walk out together. Their antagonistic relationship had made it easy to avoid each other, but she knew even then he would have escorted her. When she said she had to get her things, he had waited for her. Being raised in a house of sisters had taught him well.

It had been years since she had garnered so much

attention from a man. Granted, it was because of work for the most part, but it didn't mean that it wasn't for other reasons as well. Like…to steal another kiss.

Her heart fluttered. She couldn't get that thought out of her mind. More than once tonight, her mind had drifted back to the memory of his mouth brushed against hers. She had lost her train of thought while on the phone with Tripler. Bloody hell, she was thinking like a school girl. Infatuations were not for women who were within spitting distance of forty. She had given up on fairy tales a long time ago. She knew all the experts and their advice, but she lived in reality. She might have been able to build her marriage back up, but now, she wasn't sure if she could trust a man—even for a little romance.

"So, are they convinced he had help with his crash?" McGregor asked.

He didn't seem to be preoccupied by the kiss. It was probably a very normal thing for him. He probably kissed women he knew every day. Lord knew there would be enough women who would gladly line up and pay for his attention.

She nodded. "Dr. Myers was very cagey about it, but he alluded to the fact he thought something happened. Fights don't happen every day at Tripler. They have civilians there, but the majority of the people are military or retirees and their dependents. It is suspicious that it happened like that. He doesn't know if it was on purpose, but either way, he should have pulled through. Of course, things always go wrong now and then. Katsu was pretty strung out. There were reports of drug abuse as early as twelve."

"Jesus."

"With a history like that, a bad case of the flu could send him to the hospital. His heart has been abused for years."

She clicked the button to unlock her doors as they stopped by the driver's side of her car.

"He probably wouldn't have lasted long in prison,"

Graeme said, as he held the door open for her.

"You think someone would have gone after him?"

"Yes. Any number of gangs could have gone after him, but top of the list would have been the USO."

She glanced at him. "USO?"

"United Samoan Organization Family. Most powerful gang in Halawa."

Which meant they were definitely the most violent. "I'm assuming they have some connection to the police."

"Some. You know how gangs go. There are always some gang members who have familial connections to cops, or they're from the same neighborhood. I'll assume it's even harder to break free in Honolulu. Small island, no place to go. You might walk the straight and narrow, but your buddy doesn't."

"Sounds like you're speaking from experience."

He nodded. "Although I grew up in a middleclass kind of neighborhood, there were always one or two wankers who went the wrong way. Scotland is a big place, though, and easier to move and start a new life. I would assume here some people feel trapped."

"Do you think the USO could have gotten someone into Tripler?"

He glanced at her. "Why?"

"Katsu's connection to the Kalani case only just made news. I don't think someone from that crime had anything to do with what happened at the hospital. They would not have had time to make it to Tripler, right? Even setting something like that up would be hard to do in that short a time."

"But a gang would. There's always someone ready to take revenge. Bloody hell, that could be any of them too. Joe was seen as an uncle to most of the gang members."

Because of their close connections, Hawaiians often used familial names for individuals. Being called uncle or auntie by the younger generation was a sign of respect.

"So it could be any gang?" she asked.

He nodded. "I would say the USO might have put out the hit, but there's a good chance it was left open to any of the gangs. And then you have to add in just normal folks. Joe did a lot of good in the community and someone might see it as a way to pay him back."

This time of night in Honolulu was always so peaceful. Trade winds wound through the palm trees. She always enjoyed listening to the palms shift against one another. It was something that could be rarely heard during the busy days. But at night, she could sit on her lanai and listen to them.

"I talked to Del. He wants to keep this under wraps. He's already talked to the commander at Tripler. We're keeping this from everyone but Carino."

"I can't officially say that. It would be lying."

He smiled. "Good to know you're so honest, but don't worry about it. You talked to the doctor, but you did not officially reveal anything. You are in the clear. Del said to go with the *no comment* and refer them to HPD and Tripler. You know Del would never put your career in jeopardy."

She sighed and tried to fight the feelings flowing through her at the moment. Del wouldn't turn on her like her husband had. He had reassured her of that when he hired her. She had come to trust the former Special Forces commander. He had always made sure to back up anything she said, and in that, she could trust him.

"He already talked to Carino about it. The press found out about the cold case, but that doesn't mean we have to answer any questions about the current case. Del wants people to think it's just a coincidence. He also talked to the mayor and governor."

She rolled her eyes as she pulled her keys from her purse. "Sure, that will keep it under wraps. You don't think it's connected to the present case?"

"Not sure. Because so many people are genuinely pissed off about Joe Alana's death, it could be revenge, but it could be keeping someone quiet. Either way, it's going to make it difficult to work. There are people who are still not happy about TFH being an organization outside of the HPD jurisdiction."

"I would think that after eighteen months, they would get over it."

"You were married to a cop. You should know better. Although there are some people who were happy to hand over dealing with the feds to Del."

"And yet, they blame him for taking over cases."

Graeme shrugged. "Del doesn't seem to be that bothered by it."

She unlocked her car.

"I have to talk to the Kalanis tomorrow."

She stopped and looked at him. No matter who the cop was, talking to the loved ones of the victim was always painful—even thirty years later.

"I can go with you."

He shook his head. "Adam has already offered, and Del wants you to take tomorrow off."

She blinked. "What?"

"He wants you off work tomorrow."

"Why?"

"You've worked almost twenty-four hours straight. But he said if there was an emergency, then come in. He wants to make sure you don't wear yourself out. Quit looking for a punch in the gut, Eleanora."

"Elle."

"I don't know. I like Eleanora. Like a princess."

She shook her head. "I think you're the one who needs the day off. Lack of sleep might just be going to your head."

He cocked his head to look at her. "Why do you do that?"

"What?"

"You try to pretend you're just normal, just like everyone else. You're not."

"What the bloody hell do you mean by that?"

He leaned closer, and she thought he was going to kiss her again. Her pulse accelerated in anticipation, as her mouth went dry. "You are not an ordinary woman, Eleanora."

Everything seemed to stop as he continued to stare at her. All the sounds of the night faded away, and all she could hear was the sound of her own heart pounding inside her chest.

He smiled, then stepped back. "Rest well."

Elle blinked. It took a second for her brain to start working again, but when it did, she nodded. He waited for her to get into her car, then followed her out of the parking lot, and onto the H-1. She saw him behind her until they reached the exit for H-3. He blinked his lights right before he peeled off to make his way back to Laie where he lived.

With a sigh, she continued on her way. Right now she couldn't think about him or the little kiss earlier that evening. She glanced at the time on her dashboard. Actually, that was yesterday.

Graeme had definitely been right. She had been up almost twenty-four hours. She needed a day off. She just hoped she could get sleep tonight.

Graeme bolted awake, his ears ringing from an explosion. Cordite still hung heavy in the air, as he gulped in huge breaths of air. He looked around the room and realized it was the phone that had woken him out of a nightmare he would rather forget. His ears were still buzzing from the explosion. He scrubbed a hand over his face, trying to erase the memories of the dream.

Then he realized his phone was still ringing. He glanced at the clock and saw it was just after five in the morning. Before he could reach for his mobile, Dumfries jumped onto the bed and started to lick his face. The scent of his dog's breath wafted over him. Oh, fucking hell, something had crawled into his dog's mouth and died. Graeme pushed him out of his face. His mobile continued ringing, so he grabbed it. It was his mother's ring.

"Something wrong?"

"Does there have to be something wrong for me to call my baby boy?"

He'd trained and fought for his country, killed men, and now hunted down criminals. No matter what, Francie McGregor would still see him as her baby boy.

"No. It's just early."

"Oh, bother." She paused, and he knew she was calculating the time between Scotland and Hawaii.

"No worries, as they say here, Ma. What's up?"

"Nothing. Just the normal thing. Oh, Sandra is pregnant again."

He smiled. "Another niece or nephew to add to my list for Christmas this year, smashing."

"Yes, yes, it's all brilliant. Still, you should be shopping for your own children, Graeme. Are you seeing anyone?"

The one thing that could be said about his mother was that she was never subtle. Not with him or his father. She said being subtle with a McGregor man never worked out. And she wanted him married. For his mother, he was wasting away in a morass of loneliness because he wasn't serious about anyone in particular. The moment he thought that, the image he had of Elle as a child appeared in his mind. He blinked it away. Things were complicated enough without thinking about things like that.

"I'm not even thirty."

His mother sighed. "Your father had two children by the time he was thirty."

"And seeing the way Abigail and Sinead turned out, do you think that was such a good idea?"

She snorted. "Stop that. You adore your sisters."

"I'm still suffering from Stockholm Syndrome."

"You were not a hostage."

"It felt like it, being outnumbered by females in that household."

She chuckled, and he could picture her. She was probably sitting at the kitchen table, a cup of tea in front of her, and the crossword puzzle sitting next to the cup on the table.

"When am I going to see your beautiful face?" she asked.

She tried to sound nonchalant about it, but he knew better. She wanted him married, but she would rather he be living in Scotland away from danger. She just didn't understand his love of Hawaii, or his need to do the work he loved. There was no doubt about her support though. His mother was always there to lend an ear or cheer her children on. She just wished he would find his happiness closer to home.

"I'm thinking maybe sometime this summer."

"That would be smashing." He heard the smile in her voice, and it made him feel better.

"Are you keeping busy?"

"Of course I am. Working a cold case right now."

"They give you an old case? Are you not important enough for new cases?"

The righteous indignation he heard from his mother made him smile. "No. This is important. Someone killed a thirteen-year-old girl almost thirty years ago. Left her by the side of the road. We picked up a new lead."

"Oh, that is important. Poor girl."

"I have to talk to her parents this morning."

"I cannot even begin to think about the kind of pain they are going to go through again."

"Yes. They've never forgotten. They put an ad in the paper on the anniversary of her death every year."

"I would do the same for any of my babies. Of course, once I knew who it was, I would hunt down the bastard and kill him."

He chuckled. "Now I know where I get my

bloodthirsty nature from. How's Da?"

"He's fine. You know him. Always busy at the restaurant."

His father ran one of the busiest pubs in Edinburgh. Graeme owed all of his cooking talent to his father. The women in their family were not good cooks, starting with his mother and ending with the youngest of his sisters. Boiling water was a stretch for any of them.

"I can almost taste his haggis."

"He will make you some when you visit."

He smiled. "I bet he will. I'll talk to my boss about setting a date for a two-week vacation and plan a trip this summer. When I clear it with him, I'll give you dates."

"That's my good boy. Give Dumfries a special treat from his grandmother, since he's the only grandchild you have given me."

"I will."

"You be careful, Graeme."

"I'll be careful. Love you."

"Love you, Graeme."

After he hung up, he lay in bed smiling. He had spent most of his adult life out of his home country. He loved his family, loved the closeness he had with them, but he had been called to do other things. First, to serve his country, and now...he felt as if he belonged in Hawaii. From the moment he'd stepped off the plane, he had felt as if he had arrived home.

He sat up and stretched. He needed to get a run in, and then get into work. Carino was coming by TFH at ten, so he had plenty of time. Standing, he looked out the window, then grabbed a pair of boxer shorts. When he'd moved to Oahu, he had made sure that he had a view of the ocean. His cottage sat on Naupaka Street, which lead to Laie Point. He didn't live right on the beach, as there were rocks along the shoreline, but he always fell asleep to the sound of waves. The beach was just a short walk away.

Dumfries was scratching at the back door, so Graeme

let him out then went to relieve himself. He hit the coffee machine button and sat at the tiny kitchen table. He'd been up most of the night, and when he had fallen asleep, there had been weird dreams of that sweet kiss with Elle going a lot further than just being sweet.

Dumfries barked at the back door, and he opened it to let him in.

"You're going to have to be on your own again today," he said, as he pulled out the dry dog food, filling up Dumfries' bowl. "Although, Mrs. Williams might let you come over if you promise not to dig up her garden again."

Dumfries gave him a look of disgust before he applied himself to his breakfast. He'd found the wolfhound mix roaming the streets of Bagdad. He'd barked out a warning in time for Graeme and his platoon to avoid an ambush. He became their mascot, then he'd come home with Graeme. It'd cost a fortune, but he had gotten him home. All of them knew you didn't leave one of your men behind, and they did everything they could to get him back to Scotland.

Graeme poured himself a cup of coffee then leaned against the counter. Dumfries was already licking the bottom of his bowl before he had more than one sip. Dumfries ran toward him, rising to his hind legs and planting a massive paw on each of his shoulders.

"Bloody hell, Dumfries, watch it," Graeme said with a laugh. After one long lick, Dumfries pushed himself off Graeme. His coffee sloshed over the side of his mug.

"Dammit, you big lug," he said, but Dumfries was too happy prancing around the kitchen.

"Dumfries, how about a good run this morning?"

He barked in happiness. A nice run on the beach, and then he would get into work. He had more than just a little work to do today.

After dropping Dumfries with his neighbor, Graeme made it into work earlier than expected. There had been no use going back to bed after the run and shower, so he thought he might get some work done reading up on the background of the other murders. When he turned into the office, he saw Carino sitting with Del and Adam.

"Hey, I thought the meeting was at ten."

Carino turned to face him, his irritation etched in his expression. This did not bode well since the detective was usually pretty good at hiding his emotions. Graeme glanced at his boss and the second-in-command. They did not look any happier. In fact, they looked like they'd been sucking on a lemon for the last hour.

"We have an issue," Carino said.

"What's up?"

Del stood up. "The ME report is not the only report that's missing."

"What?"

Carino rubbed the back of his neck. "It seems like most of the evidence is missing, along with the detective's report."

"You mean all the information we need to work on the case, to find the owner of the gun, all that, it's missing?"

"That sums it up," Carino said.

"Well, *bloody hell*. This case gets worse by the hour."

CHAPTER EIGHT

Adam and Graeme walked up the front path to the Kalani house. From what Graeme knew about the island, this was what they called plantation style. Dark green with white shutters, the modest house boasted a gorgeous garden.

"I vaguely remember the Kalanis being interviewed," Adam said.

"You were a babe back then."

Adam shook his head. "I looked up the case. That and the Honolulu Strangler are cases I went over and over when I was younger. Both of them had little evidence, and a lot of that is lost. But her parents have a webpage where they post things. Their interviews are posted there."

Graeme nodded. He had watched them himself that morning. Before they reached the door, it opened. A tiny Asian woman stood on the stoop. Thirty years had been kind to Mrs. Kalani, but he could see the shadows beneath her eyes. With the case back out in the public, it would definitely cause some strain.

"Aloha," she said. "I'm so happy you could make the

trip out here."

"No worries," Adam said. He pulled out his badge and showed it to her. "I'm Lt. Adam Lee, and this is Graeme McGregor. He's handling your daughter's case."

She nodded. "Nice to meet both of you. Call me Ana. Frederick is on the phone right now. Come on back in, and we can sit on the lanai."

They followed her through the modest house filled with pictures of Jenny. It wasn't in a morbid way, but it felt more like a celebration of a life cut short too soon.

"We've been getting hit with lots of phone calls today."

"I'm sorry about that," Graeme said.

"No worries. I'm just happy we have this house registered in my sister-in-law's name. It was one way to avoid people hunting us up."

She showed them out to the lanai. They took their seats just as her husband joined them.

"Fred Kalani," he said, shaking both their hands. He sat down in the chair next to his wife.

"You want to talk about Jenny. So ask," Ana said.

Adam nodded, allowing Graeme to take the lead. "I'm sure you heard the reports."

"Yes, but are they correct?" Ana asked. "So many times they just throw junk out there that isn't real. No research. We've learned not to get too excited when something hits the news."

Graeme could not imagine what it was like. Having a family member die young was bad enough, but to have it played out in the press had to be even worse. Some news people were vultures, doing anything they could so they could get a reaction for a story.

"Yes, well, some of them." Graeme wasn't sure what the press was saying because he had steered clear of it. "Ballistics are a match. The bullet that killed Joe Alana came from the same gun that killed Jenny."

"But you don't have the gun," Fred said.

"No. But thanks to you registering Jenney's DNA, we

found some of it on the bullets from this morning. We're trying to follow the trail from this incident back to Jenny's murder. If we can trace who had the gun and when, we might be able to follow it back to her killer."

Fred nodded. "Can't be easy. It's not like it was back then. Not a lot of forensics."

"Is there anything you can remember from that time that you can tell us?" Adam asked. "Even the smallest bit of information."

"Hm, not much more than would have been in the reports," Ana said.

Neither of them said anything, and Ana stared. "You have the original case file, don't you?"

"We haven't been able to locate it," Graeme said.

"Dammit," Fred said.

"Watch your language," Ana said.

"It was better than the words I used when I found out," Graeme said.

Ana smiled.

"It is difficult to deal with," Fred said. "We fought so hard to get air time for Jenny, but all they wanted to talk about was the Honolulu Strangler. The press covered her murder one day. One day!"

"Now, Fred, it wasn't that bad." Ana looked at them. "They were just overrun with people, and this was long before there were so many twenty-four-hour news stations. Sergeant Alan Smith was the main detective handling our case, but almost everyone was working on the Strangler case here and there."

"Have you had any contact with him?" Graeme asked.

Fred nodded. "Every year on the anniversary of Jenny's death, we would get a phone call from him. That is, until he died three years ago. Cancer."

"I always thought he felt guilty that more wasn't done for Jenny," Ana said. "After he passed, another detective came by. Wanted to work on this on the side, said he had a lead. Do you remember his name?" she asked her husband.

"Jeffery Abbott. I did not like him. He was shifty."

"Shifty?" Graeme asked.

"He asked for all our files, and was not happy when we refused. I did make him copies though," Fred said, as he picked up the manila folder. "And I have a copy for you. I'm not sure how much it will help, but there were things we kept track of, things her friends told us that might help."

Graeme took the envelope. "Any little bit will help."

Ana set her hand on top of his and looked him in the eye. He saw the pain there, but he also saw determination. "Just do your best to find the monster who did this."

"I will do everything in my power."

It was close to noon by the time Elle made it to Del and Emma's condo in Hawaii Kai. The door flung open.

"What took you so bloody long?"

Elle laughed. "I had to drive over from Haleiwa. Plus, I got home after two in the morning. I took everyone's advice and slept late. Then I stopped by the drugstore to pick something up."

"You left me here worrying that I have cancer?"

Elle shook her head. Emma was definitely in high gear today. The melodramatic behavior wasn't like her at all.

"Emma, you have a genius IQ. You know you don't have cancer, or you would have faced it head on."

"What makes you say that?"

"You survived on your own after the tsunami, you fought off a serial killer, and you're marrying Del. If that doesn't take some guts, I don't know what does."

She smiled, then it faded. "I just want to make sure."

"Why didn't you just go to your regular doctor?" Elle asked.

Emma made a face. "I did. She said there was nothing wrong with me. Stress. And then, I made the mistake of saying something in front of Sean, who then blamed Del." She rolled her eyes. "Being surrounded by a bunch of alpha males is not fun. I did not think I would end up in this position, since I have avoided them most of my adult life. Now, I feel as if I can't look sideways without them worrying. All this stress is causing my insomnia to get worse; then, at times, I can't stay awake. And, I've missed my period for two months."

Elle smiled. "It's nice to know you're loved though."

"Doesn't mean they're any less annoying," she said. "Give it to me straight. What's wrong?"

"I haven't done anything but look at you." She cocked her head to the side and studied the younger woman. This was completely out of character for Emma. She was hyper, and she did have ADD, but there was a desperate edge to her comments today. "I really think you're worrying too much about it."

"So, you're thinking stress too?"

"It could be that. I can understand that kind of thing. But, just in case, I picked something up on my way over."

"Yeah?"

She pulled out the over-the-counter pregnancy test and handed it to Emma. "Go tinkle on the stick."

"I'm not pregnant."

"Correct me if I'm wrong, but you told me just a few minutes ago you skipped your last two periods."

"Nothing that uncommon for me though, and we use condoms."

"Which are effective ninety-eight percent of the time. And, do you use one every time?"

Emma opened her mouth, then snapped it shut.

"I didn't think so."

"How did you know?"

"You're both healthy, young, and engaged to be married. Neither of you strike me as the cheating kind; and remember, I was there once myself." She handed Emma the box. "Go pee."

Three minutes later, Elle had to catch Emma before she fainted dead out. When she recovered, she said, "I can't be pregnant."

"Love, you *are* pregnant."

"I don't have time for this."

"You'll have to make time. You can do it, Emma. Del is going to be thrilled."

"Oh, lord, I have to tell Del? He is going to freak out."

"Believe me, a man like Del will be happy."

Emma glanced at her sharply. "You think?"

She nodded as she sat down across from Emma at the table. "I was pregnant once. I didn't find out until about a month after the wedding, but, I will tell you, Gerald was thrilled."

"You lost the baby?"

She nodded. "A month after that, I lost the baby...and then things went completely to crap afterwards. But, you're healthy and at least two months pregnant. Go see your doc, and get a recommendation for a good OB/GYN. I am wondering why she didn't have you take a pregnancy test."

Emma offered her a sheepish smile. "I might have left out the whole missed my period."

"I can't believe you did that."

"I have issues with the idea of being a mother, so I like to pretend that is way off in the future."

That was one way they were similar. They both thought they could control things that were uncontrollable.

"It's not. It is probably about 7 months down the line. Promise me you will tell Del, and you will make an appointment with the OB/GYN. Prenatal care is very important."

Emma nodded. "Now, tell me about you and Graeme."

"There's nothing to tell."

"There was something there."

She didn't really want to tell her, but she couldn't seem to stop herself. "Okay, he kissed me last night."

Emma pumped her fist in the air. "Ha, I knew it. I win."

She stared at the younger woman. "Please tell me there wasn't a bet on us."

"Okay, I won't tell you that."

"*Bloody hell.* You can't claim it."

Emma frowned. "I won. I have to."

"How did you win?"

"I bet that you would let him kiss you on a date."

"Well, you didn't win, then. We were not on a date, we were working."

"Same difference for people like us."

She did not want the entire team to know about her personal life. She had to think of something to keep Emma from spilling the beans.

"You tell the team and I'll tell Del you're betting."

Emma frowned and sat back in the chair. Everyone knew that Del didn't like the betting going on in the office. In fact, he had forbidden them from wagering on anything. They all still ignored him, but he did not know that Emma was still betting. It wouldn't go over well.

"Besides, you have more important things to talk over with Del, right?"

"I might not be a good mother."

"You will be a wonderful mother, and you have a great *ohana* to help you. You know we will all help."

She didn't say anything for a long moment, but then, slowly, her mouth curved; then she was grinning.

"Yeah. I have an *ohana* who will help."

"Why don't we get something to eat, and then you can figure out how to tell Del he's going to be a daddy?"

After grabbing a couple of lunch plates and eating

outside watching the windsurfers, Elle dropped Emma at the condo and headed to the office. She wanted to stop in and see if anything was happening with the case.

Her mobile rang just as she started walking up the stairs. She pulled it out and noticed it was McGregor.

"Hey, did you need something?"

There was a pause. "I wanted to know if you heard the latest crap that just hit."

"No. I was out this morning, stopped by to have lunch with Emma. Now I'm at the office."

She had just reached the door to the office and pushed it open. Then he saw her. In that instant, she felt a heat wave roll through her body. It was a stupid reaction, but something changed in his gaze when it locked with hers. There was something to be said about the way it felt to have all of Graeme's attention. It made every bit of her body tingle.

Bloody hell.

She clicked off her mobile.

"What's going on?"

His expression turned dark. "We have no case files. None. As in nothing."

"What?"

"Carino went over to check them out, and they just weren't there. And, there was no information on who checked them out last."

"*Bloody hell.*"

"I was thinking we could go talk to McPherson. Since the information hit the press, we can now ask people about it. He was a cop here at the time, so he might remember more about the case."

"Brilliant," she said. She looked at her phone. "He opens for lunch soon, so he should be there already."

He nodded just as Del walked into the office.

"Hey, I heard you went to lunch with Emma."

She nodded. "We got a couple of shrimp plates and enjoyed the nice trades that blew in today.

He looked at Graeme. "Carino called over and said he's having a hard time finding out who had the case last. After Abbot, the trail goes cold. Without the case files, it's going to be near impossible."

"Isn't it in the computer?" Elle asked.

"You forget that they were still filling out reports with typewriters at the time," Graeme said. "We have the name of the detective. Alan Smith, but he's gone. We do have a little bit from from the Kalanis. They kept everything in the file, and we are making copies of it so all of us can use the information."

"I thought they had inputted all the cold cases?" she asked.

"Nope. Most of them have been, but this one was not."

She looked at Graeme. "I am starting to understand why Doc thought there might have been some tampering on the case. This is an unsolved case. I would think it would have been one of the first input."

"Doc Keahi?"

She nodded. "He didn't come right out and say it, but the fact that he made copies of the report, things like that. That makes me think he thought there might have been something going on."

Del sighed. "It could have been a cop trying to cover up a bad case."

"What do you mean?" Graeme asked.

"I was talking to Adam. Things like this happen from time to time, or did before everything was computerized. Now it's hard to make things disappear. Back then, though...it was much easier. And, it might be that someone was trying to make sure he had a good yearly report. If so, we should be able to find it, but it might take a few days."

"Well, then, maybe McPherson can help us," Graeme said. "He was a cop then, and he had a pretty good memory."

"Good idea. Let me know what you find."

He headed off to his office as his phone started to ring again.

She looked at McGregor. "Ready?"

He nodded. "Let me grab my gun."

He went back to his office, and she watched as he put his computer to sleep, retrieved his gun, then attached it to his waistband. It had never been something she had watched her ex do. She had always thought she wasn't a woman who was attracted to men with guns. British police didn't carry guns on a regular basis. And she had never been intrigued by a man with a gun on his belt.

But McGregor with a gun on his belt was a completely different matter. It made him appear somehow sexier...and that was something so odd to her. She didn't particularly like guns, but then, she had never thought she would start having fantasies about a man like McGregor. Right now, she could imagine him taking off that belt and a whole lot more...then joining her in bed.

"Are you okay?"

"What?"

"You look kind of stunned."

She blinked. "Sorry. I thought I caught up on my sleep, but maybe I need to make sure I get to bed early."

Okay, she should not have said that. Now, that just furthered her fantasies. She did not need to be thinking about having a man like McGregor in her bed. He would expect things that she could not deliver. She'd been down that road in the last seven years, and it had ended badly for her.

The lunch crowd was starting to thin by the time Graeme and Elle made it to McPherson's.

"I think I'll grab myself something to eat while we're here."

She nodded, but said nothing else. She had been suspiciously quiet since they had left headquarters. He didn't know what happened, but she had been very pensive.

"Hey, there, you two. Kind of early for you to be in here," Will said as he walked up to them.

"We were hoping you could help us with the cold case," Graeme said.

Will nodded. "Ah, the Kalani case."

"Yes. But first, I'd like to order another burger."

"Anything for you, love?" he asked Elle.

She shook her head. "I had lunch already."

He nodded. "I'll put in an order for that burger, then we can get down to business. Why don't you take your regular booth, Doc?"

They headed back to the round booth once more. It seemed like it had been ages instead of less than a day. She slid into the booth and he waved her on.

"What?"

"Move over."

"Why?"

Lord, the woman was stubborn. "Because I am not sitting next to Will. Plus, you're a little shorter than I am. My legs dinna fit under that table as well."

She gave him an odd look, but she slid into the middle of the booth.

"What was that look for?"

"Your accent slipped."

"It's not like I try to hide it."

Before she could respond, Will joined them.

"Burger will be right up."

"Thanks. So, you were around at the time of the Kalani murder."

He nodded. "Although it wasn't my case. I was assigned to the Honolulu Strangler task force. Most of us who had any kind of homicide experience worked on that one for a time."

"And no one thought the two cases were connected?" Elle asked.

"At first, we had any killing of a young woman, even someone as young as little Jenny, checked out for any significant links. When it came back she was shot and there was no evidence of rape, we moved on."

McGregor noticed Elle's fingers twitched. The doc did not like that at all, but he didn't want her getting into a fight with Will. He needed more info.

"Were there any leads?"

Will shook his head. "She was found on the road she had been walking on. There were no witnesses, as it was residential. Remember, this was thirty years ago. You can imagine how much different Honolulu was then, and this was a little ways up the mountain. The report said her money was gone, and the milk her mother had sent her to buy was found on the road just about thirty yards away from her body. I know that the lead detective really worked it hard."

"And what was his name?" McGregor asked.

Will's eyes narrowed. "I think it was Alan Smith. But it should be on the reports."

Elle opened her mouth, but he broke in. "We're waiting for Carino on the report. It's not on the computer database, so we should have it by the time we get back."

"Ah. So you have to do some real police work."

McGregor smiled as the waitress set his burger in front of him.

"Do you need anything else?" the waitress asked.

"Some water would be great. You too, lass?" he asked Elle, who gave him a strange look, but she nodded.

"Do you have any more questions for me?" McPherson asked.

"No. Thanks."

Will left them alone, and Elle leveled a look at him. "Now, are you going to explain all of that?"

He waited for the waitress to hand Elle her water

before he continued. "We have to be careful who we talk to and how much info we release," he said, pouring ketchup on his burger.

"But why are we hiding the fact the case file is missing?"

"For someone who was married to a cop, you don't seem to know much about them."

"What does that mean?"

"Old cops are like women."

"I think you're digging a hole you might not be able to get out of."

He leaned closer and had to fight the urge to sniff. She always smelled like roses. He could just imagine her dabbing a bit of perfume behind her ears, then between her breasts...

"McGregor?"

He blinked. "Sorry. Old cops. They gossip. We don't want them knowing we don't have the file."

"Because the one who does might have something to do with it."

"Your doctor friend might have been right. Someone at HPD might have been screwing around with the case. They don't need to know that we don't have any evidence."

"But whoever took it would know we don't have it."

He nodded. "But he doesn't know that we might have other things. Plus, there's always a chance that he didn't take it, and it just disappeared."

"And letting him know we don't have it would have us at a disadvantage."

"Beautiful and brilliant," he said with a smile.

Elle choked on her water.

"What does that mean?" she asked.

"Not everyone would make the connections."

She rolled her eyes. "I'm pretty sure anyone with mediocre intelligence could make the connections you laid out."

He didn't like the way she dismissed her intelligence, but he thought it interesting that she didn't address the beautiful comment.

"Either way, we need to keep as much as possible to ourselves. The fewer people outside of TFH who know about this, the better."

CHAPTER NINE

Graeme was more than a little irritated by the time he made it back to the office, but he couldn't figure out just why. He hadn't expected to get much from Will, but something else was bugging him.

"Hey, how'd the meeting with McPherson go?" Adam asked.

"Boss told you we went?"

Adam nodded. "He went home a little while ago. Emma was feeling under the weather."

Graeme frowned. "Elle had lunch with her, and she didn't say anything."

Adam shrugged. "Maybe it was something she ate."

And she had eaten with Elle. "Elle didn't say anything about feeling badly."

Adam gave Graeme a strange look. "I'm sure it's just Emma. Did you find anything out from McPherson?"

He shook his head. "A little background, but not much. He was assigned to the Honolulu Strangler case."

Adam smiled. "Yeah, everyone was pretty much

considered to be on the Strangler case at the time. It's not like they knew that much about serial killers, so everyone had a hand in it, to tell you the truth."

"So, were there people assigned to it specifically?"

Adam nodded. "Yeah, sure, but they weren't turning anyone away who might have wanted to help. Lots of unis and detectives were working off the clock to catch the bastard."

"Catching him would have made someone's career."

"So, there is a very good chance that someone could have ignored Jenny's murder because they might have gotten a bigger bang out of solving the Strangler case."

"Bastard."

"Yes, but be careful who you throw that name around at."

"You're no' defending the person who did this."

Adam held his hands up. "Hey, don't attack me. I don't agree with the bastard, but you're new to this kind of work. They will stick together, especially some of the older generation. You're seen as an outsider because of your land of birth, and you've not been a cop for very long."

"That's why I told Del you should take this job."

Adam shook his head. "I think it might be better to have someone from the outside. No connections makes it easier for you to work the case, look from the outside."

"Yeah, sure. It also makes it hard to get a feel for what was going on at the time."

"Listen, you can ask me, and I can line up some of my aunties. They can tell you all the tales of Honolulu of the late eighties."

Graeme smiled. "That might work."

"They'll love talking to a *haole* like you. Blonde and with an accent...you'll be a hit. Just remember to be careful with the older cops, if you talk to any more of them."

Graeme nodded. His mind went back to the conversation with the Kalanis. "I will do that as a last resort. You know how they will react if I walk in there asking questions right off. They're already out of sorts because we have this case."

"You're probably right on that front."

Drew came walking in, a pensive expression at odds with his shirt that featured the weather forecast for Alderaan.

"What's up?" Adam said.

"I had a call in the lab for the doc, but I can't seem to get hold of her. Del said the two of you were at lunch?"

Graeme nodded. "She had already had lunch. We were talking to McPherson about the case. Who called?"

Drew shrugged. "Someone with an English voice."

"Her family."

"No. I know her parents' voices. I've talked to them before. Plus, this guy said his name was Gerald."

There it was, another ping of irritation. The fact that Drew seemed to know more about Elle's family than he knew was irritating.

"He wanted to know her mobile...I mean her cell number."

"You didn't give it to him, did you?"

He shook his head. "But I tried calling her and she didn't answer."

"She was on her way home when we got back. She said she was going to do some research."

Drew's phone rang and his features eased. "That's the doc."

"Hey, Elle. Yeah, did you get my message?" He was quiet for a moment. "No, I didn't give him your number. He said he would call back tomorrow. Okay. No problem. Bye."

He hung up and looked at Graeme and Adam. He said nothing, but smiled.

Adam glanced at Graeme, then looked at Drew. "What was that about?" Adam asked.

"Apparently, the doc's ex was trying to get hold of her for some reason. No idea why."

"She knew it was the ex?" Graeme asked.

"Yes, I left his name on her voicemail. I will say, she doesn't sound very happy to have heard from him."

Adam let an eyebrow rise. "Yeah. That probably goes with the territory, since they are divorced."

"She never talks about him. Like ever. I have an aunt who got divorced twenty years ago, and they were only married a year, and she goes on and on and on about him all the time."

"Elle's break up was not easy from what I understand, but it almost ruined her career."

"Did she sound okay to you?" Graeme asked.

Drew shrugged. "She sounded irritated, but not any more than she would be normally."

"Normally?"

"When she's irritated. She gets this tone in her voice. It's when I know to stop asking questions."

Adam coughed, and Graeme was sure he did it to cover a laugh. Working with Drew on a daily basis was bad enough, but being his immediate supervisor and trainer could not be an easy task. Elle always seemed to have an infinite supply of patience with the over eager assistant.

"She said she was going over old newspaper articles having to do with the old case."

"I was going to do that."

Drew shrugged. "Unless we catch a case, she really has nothing to do. And, she does have some payback from HPD on her covering for the last couple weeks. It's been kind of insane with the stomach flu going around."

"Ah, that might be what's wrong with Emma," Adam said.

"She's sick?" Drew said.

Adam nodded. "Del went home because she was under the weather, and since I was done with my stuff for the day, I sent him home."

"Ah. So...who is everyone bringing to the wedding? Oh, and when is the bachelor party?"

Graeme and Adam shared a look, then they looked at Drew. Drew's eyes widened.

"You're his best man, Adam. It's kind of your job."

Graeme looked at Adam.

"I already asked him, and he declined, although I do think we should take him out before his mom gets here."

"And your dates?"

"We're supposed to have dates?" Graeme asked. "I always thought it was better to go stag."

Not that he actually thought that much about it. Truth was, other than the occasional hookup, he hadn't dated anyone seriously since he relocated to Hawaii.

"What do you mean?" Drew asked.

"It's always best to come stag. Of course, that is usually to take advantage of the bridesmaids...oh, and one of them is involved with two men," Adam said.

Graeme snorted. "I would not touch that woman with a ten-foot pole. I'm pretty sure Sean and Randy would make me disappear."

Emma's half brother had two lovers, Randy and Jaime. The trio were considered some of the best security experts in the Pacific Rim area, if not the world, and all of them definitely knew how to make people disappear. Jaime, the one female of the trio, had her hands full with the two men, but didn't seem to mind.

"Yeah. But there are three other bridesmaids," Graeme said.

"Only two," Drew said. "Cat's going with me."

Again, he shared a look with Adam. "You're taking her to the wedding?"

Drew rocked back on his heels. "Yep, so that leaves Elle and Charity, and I know Charity is coming stag."

"You know, how?" Adam asked.

Drew's smile widened. "She told me. Said she liked to keep her prospects open. I have some reports to file for Elle."

And then he just left, with Adam and Graeme staring

after him.

"Now, tell me why I'm feeling like a loser," Adam said.

"Because Dead Guy Drew has a date with Cat for the wedding and we're both going stag."

"Ah, and who has the bet on their first date?"

"Damn, I think Charity is keeping track of that one."

"Someone is going to win big," Adam said.

"Doesn't matter. At the end of the day, we are both still going stag, and Dead Guy Drew has a date with a hot Hawaiian woman."

Del knew there was something really wrong. Emma had been in bed since he came home, dead to the world. He stood at the doorway to their bedroom and watched her sleep. She'd been out when he got home. A call to Elle reassured him that she wasn't really sick, but he hated that the wedding was getting to her. He felt like a bastard for insisting on having a big family wedding.

"I can feel you staring at me," she said without opening her eyes.

"Can you blame me? You have me worried, babe."

She opened her eyes and stretched. Then she smiled at him, and he felt it to the soles of his feet. Just that, and his heart started to sing with happiness.

Emma sat up and stared at him. She scooted over, then patted the bed next to her. He walked over and sat on the mattress.

"I'm sorry, Emma."

"Why?"

"We should have done a simple run to the justice of the peace, nothing big. Planning this wedding is making you sick."

She shook her head and cupped his face. Without closing her eyes, she leaned forward and brushed her mouth over his.

"It isn't the wedding, love."

Terror filled him. "Give it to me straight."

"You're going to be a daddy, Del."

For a second, the world seemed to slow to a complete stop. He couldn't think, couldn't even comprehend what she had said.

"You're pregnant?"

She nodded, as tears filled her eyes. "Probably about eight weeks or so."

"That's why you've been getting dizzy and sick to your stomach?"

"And being so sleepy."

Then, the reality of what she had just said hit him. Joy filled him.

"Are you okay?" she asked.

"Okay? No, I am not okay. I am fantastic," he said, pulling her to him in a big hug. He leaned back and kissed her then, trying to pour everything he was feeling into that one gesture.

"You made me very happy," he said.

"Well, you *did* have something to do with it."

He laughed and stood up. The room spun around him. "Whoa."

"Del?"

"I'm okay. Just a little lightheaded."

He looked down at her. She was his world. From the moment they'd met, she had been surprising him. Now, she was going to make him a daddy.

He grabbed her and lifted her up off the bed. "It's the best news."

She laughed, as he carried her into the living room. It was the most beautiful sound in the world.

"It's so weird that it isn't going to be the two of us in just seven months."

"Yes. I'm putting my money on a girl."

He set her on the stool at the breakfast bar and

grabbed the phone.

"Gotta call my mom."

"Do we have to? Can we wait until after the ceremony?"

He studied Emma for a second. "She isn't going to care that you're pregnant before the ceremony."

"Are you sure?"

He leaned down and brushed his mouth over hers. "Yes. She's going to be thrilled with a grandbaby."

Slowly her mouth curved. "Yeah?"

"Yes. And after I call her, we are going to go tell your brother."

She blinked. "Is that normal?"

Sometimes he forgot how she had grown up without much social contact. Add in being orphaned and living on the streets by the age of sixteen, she really didn't understand all of the family dynamics. The fact that she hadn't known about her half brother until a year ago added to the confusion.

"He's going to want to know, as will Jaime and Randy. They will all want to celebrate. But, first, Mom."

Elle was just pouring herself some tea when there was a knock at the door. She frowned, setting down her teapot. When she reached the door, she saw Graeme standing there.

She opened the door. "What are you doing here?"

"Well, that's a fine way of welcoming me."

"I didn't invite you."

He shook his head and tsked. "Just like a Campbell."

She sighed. "How did you find my address?"

"You're in the employee recall roster, Elle. I heard you were going over some old newspaper articles, and thought you might want to split the work."

"Why didn't you call?"

"You weren't answering, which is another reason I came over."

Oh, damn. She'd turned her mobile off to avoid her ex. She didn't think he had her mobile number, but there was a chance that he would hunt that up now.

"I'm sorry. I'm avoiding..."

"Your ex. I know. Drew can't keep a secret to save his life. I just wanted to know where you had looked, and then we could coordinate the research so we aren't wasting time looking at the same things."

"Oh, that makes sense."

But she stood there looking at him, unable to move. She still could not process the fact that he was standing there on her stoop.

"Elle, love, are you going to let me in?"

She blinked and opened her mouth to apologize when she heard a bark.

"What on earth was that?"

"Dumfries."

"As in Scotland?"

"As in my mutt, who decided to dig up his babysitter's garden again."

She stepped out onto the small stoop and looked at his truck. A massive wolfhound leaned out the opened window. His tongue was hanging out of his mouth.

"He's beautiful," she said. She slid her gaze to Graeme. "He housetrained?"

He nodded.

"Then, don't leave him out there. Bring him in."

He looked past her into the foyer that led to her tiny kitchen. "Don't worry. Nothing of great value will be where he can damage it."

"Okay, but I did warn you."

She shook her head and watched as he went to his truck and opened the door. Dumfries jumped down and galloped to her.

"Dumfries," Graeme barked out. The massive dog slid to a stop in front of her on the lawn. He sat, wagging his tail, with a doggy smile curving his lips.

"Well done, Dumfries," she said, cooing to him. She held out her hand, and he sniffed at it, then stood and moved so her hand would run down his body.

"Aren't you a pretty boy?" she said. When she smiled up at Graeme, he had a stunned look on his face. "What? Did I do something wrong?"

He shook his head, but he still said nothing to her.

"Seriously, you're making me feel weird looking at me like that."

"Sorry. Not sure I ever heard that tone in your voice before."

She didn't know what to say to that, so she straightened and waved Dumfries in. She tried to do the same with Graeme, but he took hold of her screen door and held it.

"Ladies first."

She shook her head and stepped into her house as he followed her.

"I was just making some tea. Would you like some?"

"No, but some water would hit the spot."

"I have my tablet on the coffee table there," she said grabbing a bottle of water and tossing it to him. "I have my laptop on the lanai. We can work out there because there's a nice breeze."

"Do you have a fence?"

"Yes."

"Come on, Dumfries."

His dog was sitting in the middle of her tiny kitchen watching her every move.

"Oh, I see how it is. Always drops me for the lasses," Graeme said shaking his head.

He slid her screen door open. She smiled as she made her tea, then stepped out the door, waited for Dumfries to trot out, and shut the door.

"Let's get started. I'm going to look up anything

referencing the medical examiner, and you can do anything from the police."

"Do you think you'll find much?"

"There could easily be articles in medical magazines. It's a long shot, and Doc didn't say he wrote anything about them, but someone else could have. Or it could have been mentioned in passing. I can also decipher medical double talk. I love Doc, but he was very politically correct at that time. He had a huge job, especially for someone who started out like he did. He might have not wanted to rock the boat."

"I thought he was like a second father to you."

"Yes. But I am also not blind, and I understand complex relationships with the press more than a lot of people."

He nodded. "You're not feeling ill, are you?"

She frowned. "I feel fine."

"Good. Del went home because Emma was under the weather."

"Oh, that. She's fine."

His eyes narrowed. "You know something."

"Well, since she's probably letting the cat out of the bag tonight, Emma will be fine, and we are going to be welcoming the first TFH baby in about seven months or so."

He didn't say anything for a moment, then his mouth curved. "Well, that's brilliant."

His response brought a smile to her face. "It is."

"My sister is pregnant again. Babies are amazing."

He looked down at the tablet and blinked. After setting it back on the table, he said, "I'll be right back."

As he hurried out, Dumfries barely noticed. In fact, his dog was more interested in barking at the kids in the next door neighbor's yard. Graeme stepped back out on the lanai, his glasses in hand. He sat down, slipped them on, then started to work.

It took her a moment to compose herself. Bleeding

hell, he was so pretty. How was she supposed to concentrate?

An hour later, Graeme looked up from the tablet and realized the sun was starting to set. They'd both fallen silent, intent on their research. He noticed that Dumfries was now laid out in the yard, belly up.

He turned to say something to Elle, but he forgot what the moment he saw her. The sun was off to her side, the last rays of brightness dancing over her curls. He liked that she had let her hair grow out just a bit and that it had a little curl to it.

Alabaster skin—especially in Hawaii—made her stand out, but nothing entranced him more than those sea green eyes. Even if the rest of her face was stoic, her eyes definitely showed her true feelings.

She must have felt his study, because she raised her head and looked at him. He slipped off his glasses.

"What?" she asked.

"Nothing. I was thinking how pretty you are."

She sighed. "Listen, Graeme, this isn't a good idea."

"What isn't a good idea?"

"You. Me. We can't do things like you did last night."

"Oh, you mean the kissing?"

"Yes, I mean the kissing."

"I was thinking about trying it again."

She shook her head. "No. It's...I am not a good risk for a relationship."

"I didn't say I wanted a relationship."

Once the words came out of his mouth, he wanted to take them back. Until the last year, he had been deployed most of the time. Relationships had been hard to maintain. Now, though, he was looking at her, and he was wondering what it would be like to have a long-term relationship with a woman like Elle.

"Even so, I am not a good risk for sex. You know I am a sexual assault survivor."

He had guessed that a few months ago. She had been the one who had been there for Jin Phillips after they had found her near death from a vicious sexual assault.

"Yes."

"I just haven't..." She closed her eyes as if mortified. He went on instinct and reached for her hand.

She opened her eyes and looked at him.

"No pressure."

She shook her head, as she offered him a sad smile. "Don't, Graeme. We'll both feel embarrassed, and then we will lose what friendliness we have now. It will become awkward."

He shook his head, as he pulled her hand to his mouth. He brushed his lips over her knuckles.

"Is that what happened with your husband?"

She tensed, but he didn't let go.

"I don't need the particulars, love. I just want to know what not to do."

She shook her head again. "You couldn't be any more different from him if you tried."

"You had a good marriage?"

"No. From the beginning until the end, it was a disaster. The rape just highlighted our problems. It doesn't help if your wife not only gets abducted and raped, but she's the one witness that helps you nail the bastard you've been chasing for months. He called it emasculating."

His heart broke for the woman, but rage poured through him as well. He understood that a lover would be upset, but saying something like that to a woman who had been through what she had been through...it was unacceptable.

"I have to agree with you."

"I knew you would understand."

"Understand what, love?"

"That I'm not a good risk for you. Especially at my age."

Graeme shook his head. "You act like we're Harold and Maude. You're just a few years older."

"Still."

"Age has nothing to do with it. What I meant, is that I agree that I'm no' like your ex. I'd never turn away from you."

Her eyes turned so sad. "You weren't there, Graeme. It was horrible. The papers...they were relentless. And well, Gerald, he had never been that good at dealing with pressure. When I found out he had been cheating on me, I walked out."

"I will say once again, I am not like that."

Before she could respond, Graeme leaned forward and brushed his mouth over hers again. The small touch had his blood humming and his heart singing. It was barely carnal, but it touched his soul.

Before he could push too much, he pulled back. "Are you hungry?"

She lifted her free hand to her mouth, then looked at him. The dazed expression when her gaze met his pleased him. He didn't want to be the only person stunned by it.

"Eat?"

"Yeah. How about we head over to Luibueno's and get some fish tacos?"

She studied him for a second, then slowly, surely, her mouth curved. "That sounds smashing."

As she went to get ready, he sat back in the chair with a smile. He would take it slowly. He would give her time to get accustomed to having him around. Once she was ready, he would be the one she took a chance on.

CHAPTER TEN

The next three days passed in a blur of autopsies and meetings for Elle. The flu moved through the medical examiners' office, leaving them just as understaffed. Since they didn't have a need for her, Elle had offered her lab for help, especially with Drew at her side.

"Hey," Charity said from the doorway. The forensic tech might be fabulous working on the evidence, but she had a thing about dead bodies. She didn't like spending any time in Elle's lab.

"Hey, yourself."

"Are you going to be able to come tonight?"

Charity and Cat had put together a little bachelorette party for Emma over at her brother's house.

"I wouldn't miss it, but I can't drink."

"Why not?"

"I'm on call."

Charity frowned. "That sucks."

"Not really. I'll be off all next weekend for the wedding. HPD owes me big for the last couple of weeks, and I plan on taking advantage of them."

"Oh, I guess that's good."

"And I am staying at the hotel, so I can drink all I want."

"So, are you coming by yourself?"

"To the bachelorette party?"

Charity rolled her eyes. "No, the wedding."

Elle finished the email she had been composing, then turned and looked at Charity. Today's outfit was, as usual, spectacular. The red mandarin styled dress hugged all of her curves, while she had pulled her hair up, affixing it in a bun with black and red chopsticks. She was also wearing a pair of platform boots.

"What did you ask me?"

"Really, Elle, what is with you?"

"The workload has left me knackered."

"Oh, sorry. I live in the dungeon most of the time, so I forget everything that goes on."

She nodded.

"I was asking about a date for the wedding."

"I didn't know I was supposed to bring a date."

"You don't have to, but I was wondering because Drew and Cat are going together."

She smiled. "Yeah, I know."

"She isn't going to know what hit her, is she?"

Elle laughed. "Not once he gets her out on the dance floor."

Drew slipped by Charity. "What has you two

laughing?"

"Nothing," Elle said. "We're talking about our plans tonight."

"Yeah, we're going out for dinner tonight," Drew said.

"That's it? For the alpha of the group, you guys are taking him out for a meal?" Charity asked. "That's kind of lame."

"Del said he didn't want to really do anything. I heard his future brothers-in-law offered to take him to Rough 'n' Ready, and Del declined."

Rough 'n' Ready was the only BDSM club on the island, and had a hefty price tag even for one night.

"Do you think they could get us in?" Charity asked.

Elle laughed. "I am *not* going to Rough 'n' Ready. And I have a feeling that is *so* not Emma's scene."

"Well, damn. I bet I could talk them into getting me a guest pass. I've always wanted to see the inside of that place."

Elle shut down her computer and grabbed her purse. "On that note, I'm going to head out right now. I need to clean up for our night out. Eight, right?"

Charity nodded. "Yeah."

"You filed the reports, right, Drew?"

"Yes. Everything should be taken care of. I'll lock up for you."

"Thanks. I'm off."

She made her way out into the hallway and to the lift. She got on, punched the button for the first floor. She leaned against the back of the lift as it went up. Usually, she tried to walk up the stairs once a day, but today, she just didn't care. It had been a long week, and she had been on her feet for most of it. The only thing she hoped for at the moment was to be able to sleep in.

The doors opened and she stepped off. As soon as she did, she saw Graeme coming in the front door with Adam. He was wearing another of those TFH shirts the guys all seemed to like to wear. This one was blue, which deepened the tan he had. His eyes seemed more brilliant whenever he wore that particular shade of blue. But, she got no further than that. Both men wore grim expressions. They had definitely not had a good day.

"Oh, you two look like you've had a bad experience."

Adam shook his head. "Just found another storage container filled with Chinese citizens. It wasn't a pretty sight after a couple weeks at sea."

Hawaii was a stopping place for many human traffickers from the Far East, especially places like China and Thailand. Almost weekly there was a report of a container being found filled with people, mainly young women.

"That sounds horrible. Were there any alive?"

Adam nodded. "I have a feeling they would rather not have survived. They will all be sent back."

And more than likely sent to prison. She shivered.

"Where are you headed?" Graeme asked.

"I need to clean up. We're doing the bachelorette party tonight, and I feel as if I've not showered in three days."

Graeme hesitated, then said, "Don't get too rowdy tonight."

She had a feeling that was not what he had been planning on saying.

"Kind of hard to since I'm on call."

"I know the feeling," Adam said. "See ya later."

After Adam left, she waited for Graeme to say something, but he just stared at her.

"Was there something you wanted?"

It took a second before his mouth curved. "I think I made that clear the other night."

A wave of heat spread over her body. "I meant for work."

"No. Carino still hasn't found the original file, but I am piecing it together as much as I can from the news reports, and from what the Kalanis gave us."

Then irritation moved over his expression.

"What?" she asked.

"I need to call them. I try and check in every day with them right now."

And that was the way he was. He was dedicated to his job, but it was more than that. He wanted to make sure her parents knew he took the case seriously.

"What?" he asked.

She shook her head. "Nothing. I'm sorry I haven't been able to help that much."

"A lot of your job is done. You gave me the report on the death. Her parents offered to have her exhumed."

Elle sighed. "That won't help much. We have the time of death, and we have the bullet. Doc didn't leave anything out."

He nodded, then they both fell silent.

"Well, I guess I should go."

"Yeah. Hey, I was thinking if you weren't busy tomorrow, that you might want to go over what I have so far."

"I'm not sure how much I can help with it if it doesn't have to do with the autopsy findings."

"Another set of eyes would help."

She was exhausted, and had planned on spending the day in bed. But the idea of getting to spend a little time with Graeme, even if it was for work, sounded like a splendid idea. "Okay. But I insist you bring Dumfries with you."

"I canna believe that bastard dog has stolen another woman from me. Okay. Say around noon?"

She nodded and headed out the door, feeling infinitely better than she had five minutes earlier.

Several hours later, Elle sat back in her chair and sighed. Emma's brother and his lovers lived in Kailua on the windward side of the island. The mansion they owned backed up to one of the best beaches on the island—and that was saying a lot on Oahu. The pool sparkled in the moonlight, as she listened to the trade winds shift through the palm trees. They were close enough to the ocean's edge, she could hear the waves rushing to shore.

"A woman could get used to this," Charity said. She was sitting beside her at a long table on the covered lanai. Cat and Emma sat across from them.

"Indeed," Elle said. "I can see the ocean, well a bit, but I would like to own a house next to the water some day."

"It's a dream come true for me," Jaime brought out cocktails to the poolside dining table. "I don't think I could ever take another winter in England."

Another Brit, Jaime Alexander lived with Sean—Emma's half brother—and Randy. She and Elle had not talked much, but they had chatted a bit about their homeland.

"Now, I have two virgin drinks for the doc and Emma. The rest of us are slutty."

Charity laughed, as she reached for a drink. "Now, *that* I can deal with."

"Thanks, Jaime," Elle said. "And thank you for having the party here. I am not sure I would ever want to leave my house with a view like this."

"Not to mention those two men. How do you handle them?" Cat asked, as she sipped on her drink.

Jaime opened her mouth, but Emma stopped her.

"Oh, God, don't ask. Jaime will go into detail, and it will make me want to bleach my brain again," Emma said. "I don't even want to think about the times I forgot to call to say I was coming over."

"You spoil all our fun," Charity said.

"Do it when I am not around," Emma said, sipping on her virgin lava flow.

"Okay. So let's ask Elle about Graeme," Cat said.

There was a moment of silence before everyone turned

to look at Elle.

"What?" Elle asked.

"You mean that tall blond that looks like he's ready to lead his clan to victory?" Jaime asked. "He's yours?"

Elle shook her head. "He's not mine."

"He looks at her…a lot," Emma said, leaning back in her chair. "Has for awhile."

"Your hormones have gone to your head, Emma," Elle said, not liking the direction of this conversation. She counted these women as friends, but she had made it a policy not to reveal too much. Ever since the mess in England, she tried her best to keep things nice but professional. At least, her private life—not that she had one.

Emma nodded. "There was this one time, when she had to pick something off the floor. The world could have exploded around him, and he would have kept looking at her ass."

"He did not."

Emma smiled. "He did."

"Well, either way, I told him nothing would happen."

"Wait, what?" Charity said, slamming her glass down on the table. "He's told you he's interested?"

"Yes, after he kissed me. The first time."

Emma sat up. "There's been another time?"

"Yes, when he came by my house to work. Then we went out to eat that night, and he kissed me good night. So, maybe three."

"How could you not have told me?" Charity asked, her voice filled with accusation.

"I'm sorry. Nothing is going to come of it, so it doesn't matter."

"Yeah, it does."

Elle narrowed her eyes. "We were not on a date. Emma said the bet was about a date."

Another beat of silence when everyone seemed to be trying to figure out what to say.

"Are you telling me that there's another bet on it?"

Charity opened her mouth, then she slanted a look at Cat, who shook her head.

"Just the sex part. So you will tell us when that happens."

"First, that's not going to happen. And second—"

"Why not?" Jaime asked.

"For one reason, he is almost a decade younger than I am."

"Ohhhh, a younger guy. They are so much fun," Jaime said.

"I have to agree with that," Charity said.

"You're barely twenty-five."

She shrugged. "He was legal."

Elle couldn't fight the bubble of laughter. The woman really had no problem with being honest about her past relationships.

"Okay. But still. Working together and relationships are not always the best thing."

"He's not like your ex at all, Elle, and you know it," Emma said.

She knew Emma understood, and not just because her relationship with Del made her privy to information. Emma worked for them by contract, but Elle knew that, more than likely, Emma's brother Sean would have done background checks on all of them.

She conceded that with a nod. Graeme definitely wasn't like her ex.

"Either way, I already told him I wasn't ready for something like that. I explained my issues, and told him he would be better off to just forget about anything like that with me."

"And?" Cat asked.

She took a sip of her drink before she answered. "He said he would wait."

"Oh, mama, have mercy. I bet that man said it with that thick Scottish accent. I would have melted into a puddle of lust right there," Charity said.

"Anyway, I really don't think it would be a good idea."

"You've said that more than a few times," Jaime observed.

"It's because she's trying to convince herself," Emma said.

Damn, the woman was too smart for her own good.

"I think it's a great idea. Emma and Del work together, and look how that turned out," Cat said.

"Yes, but Drew and I have a date," Cat said.

Everyone switched their attention to her.

"Yeah, now tell us how that happened," Charity demanded.

"Well, he came up to me in the parking lot and said, 'I think we need to go together to the wedding.'"

"Just like that?" Elle asked.

"Yes. Not really asking. It was kind of rude, but it was kind of a turn on too. I mean, Drew is just so sweet, but he demanded we go together and, well...I had to say yes."

Charity giggled. "Yeah, when he sets his mind on something, watch out."

"I went along with him. I was on my way home before I realized I had just made a date with Drew. Although, he didn't call it a date."

"He's sneaky like that," Charity said.

"I have to agree with Charity," Elle said. "He tends to think a long time about something, then he steps in and just makes it happen."

"Which shows you how wrong we are for each other. I like to live in the moment."

"Opposites do attract," Charity said.

Cat shook her head. "I don't believe that."

"I have to disagree with you," Elle stated.

Everyone turned to look at her. "Why is that?" Emma asked.

"My parents. They are definitely opposites."

"I thought they were both professors," Emma said.

"They are, but while my father is the quintessential English professor, my mother is a bit different. A lot. My father watches everything he says, and he only speaks when he thinks it is important. He's a scientist. Mum is a literature professor and very outspoken. She's Scottish and never lets anyone forget that they are still waiting for England to apologize."

"They sound wonderful," Emma said.

"They are," she said reflectively. "They do tend to argue a bit, but in hindsight, I have a feeling it was foreplay for them."

They moved onto talking about the wedding and babies, and Elle's mind started to drift. Had she chosen Gerald because he was more like her? If she had, she had miscalculated terribly.

"Hey, Elle," Charity said.

She realized she had lost track of the conversation.

"Sorry. Long week of work. What are we talking about?"

Soft blues music played over the speakers, as Graeme was shown to the table at Dupree's.

"We have some great Mahi today," the hostess said. She had introduced herself as May, and had one of the sweetest smiles he'd seen in a while. That is, other than when he coaxed one out of Elle.

When he arrived at the table, he noticed that Del was missing.

"Thanks, May," he said.

"You're welcome. Enjoy your night, gentlemen. Please, let me know if there is anything you need."

"I think I have to call foul on this bachelor party," Drew said. "It's my first bachelor party, and I have yet to see one stripper."

The comment earned Drew a nasty look from an uptight-looking tourist sitting at the next table. Del had requested dinner at Dupree's. It was a little bit of New Orleans mixed with a lot of Hawaiian. Graeme had been there a couple of times, and found the food and staff first rate, but he would have never picked it as a place for a bachelor party.

Considering some of the bachelor parties he had attended—including his brother-in-law's—this was pretty tame. Still, you did what the groom wanted, and this was what he wanted.

"And you're not about to see one. Del said no to all of that."

Drew frowned.

"Are you telling me you got to the age of twenty-eight and never went to a bachelor party?" Adam said.

Drew shrugged. "A lot of my friends have moved to the mainland. Not a lot of PhD jobs here in their fields."

Graeme suspected that Drew had many friends, but most of them were women. Not that he saw anything wrong with that. In fact, Graeme thought it might have given Drew the edge with getting Cat to come with him to the wedding. All the women in the office really wanted Cat and Drew together. They had been conspiring with him from day one.

Del came back to the table with a smile on his face. "I just got a call from my future brothers-in-law, who have said they are going to stop by. Jaime kicked them out of the house for the night."

"Ha, I have a feeling that sweet woman would only have to smile at them and they would do anything she wanted," Adam said.

"True," Del said. "But since I have the same affliction, I can't argue with their response."

Marcus chuckled. "This is my first time here. Can anyone give me a suggestion?"

"I think Chris Dupree is in the back tonight, so any

steak he can cook you is fantastic," Adam said. "If you are in the mood for seafood, get the mac nut Mahi, or if you want to go with Cajun, the shrimp po' boy is definitely authentic. He's from New Orleans."

Del shook his head. "Don't say the words red meat to me. With her worries over her anemia, Emma has insisted on lots of red meat. I never thought I would say this, but I'm sick of steak."

"Yeah, so how are you handling the idea of becoming a father?" Graeme asked.

"I think I can answer that," Sean said from behind Graeme. They turned around to face Emma's brother and his lover, Randy. "From what Emma said, he almost passed out."

Del frowned. "I did not. And I will mention that you got a little teary eyed."

"She's my little sister. You're supposed to get that way. You know how that is, Graeme."

Graeme didn't question that Emma's brother would know his background. He had connections in the security business that would definitely make it easy to check Graeme's background.

"Yes, and I am going to be an uncle again."

The moment he made the announcement, his phone went off. When he saw Carino's name, he answered it immediately. Rising from the table, he walked a little bit away for some privacy. Plus, Sean was kind of loud at times.

"McGregor."

"Carino. We are going to have to go on without any help from Katsu. He died tonight."

The last connection they had was now gone. "Well, bloody hell."

"And it looks like he might have had help."

HOSTILE DESIRES

CHAPTER ELEVEN

As Elle slid the drawer into the wall, Graeme walked into her lab. He had been there when she had shown up, and she knew he was waiting on her.

"Well?" he asked.

She pulled off her gloves and the over dress and threw them in the hazardous material receptacle.

"I'm not sure if we could call it homicide, as he was brain dead."

"But?"

She nodded and picked up the small glass canister. "It's going to be hard to know for sure until we get the tox report back."

Graeme frowned. Dammit, he was starting to look sexy while he frowned. What was she thinking? The man could be passed out cold and he would be sexy.

"Why? It seems like a waste. And an unneeded risk. He was dead for all intents and purposes. Wouldn't just turning off the machines be easier?"

She shrugged. "It's odd. It had to be someone who knew a thing or two about drugs. I will not be surprised if it comes back with a high dosage of something in him."

"So, why risk it?"

"Administering something that takes awhile to take effect would make for a better getaway."

"Ah, yes. Turning off the machines would draw attention to the bastard." He rubbed the back of his neck. "What was the worry though?"

"I understand that he was brain dead, but they always have those stories about people who come out of comas. Maybe he was worried about that."

"They were going to turn the machines off soon?" he asked.

"I don't know what the US statue is on that. Things here are determined by the amount of money they cost when it comes to healthcare. With no family around, I am sure he wouldn't have lasted long."

"They found no family at all?"

"When I talked to the doctors, they said he had no family. He had a sister on the mainland, but they couldn't find her. Mother is deceased, and the father was never listed. So, the worry might have been that he would linger for a long time, and they hadn't revealed he was brain dead. The worry might have been that he would wake up and start revealing information, like where that bloody gun is and how he got it."

"And that means the bastard is still alive and somewhere here on the island."

"Probably."

"*Damn.*"

She went over to wash her hands. "Once Charity runs the blood samples, we'll be able to decide what to do. She's coming in tomorrow morning to do it. It's hard to tell if he did have drugs injected. He was on IV, so anyone with a knowledge of things like that would be able to administer it easily. Put on a set of scrubs, know the procedures—he would know, if he were a cop—and it would be easy to provide a lethal dose of something."

She took a step and the room revolved around her.

"Oh, damn."

"Hey," Graeme said, catching her by the forearm. "Are you okay?"

She nodded. "I didn't get anything to eat before I came in." She glanced at the clock. "Damn, it's been about twelve hours since I ate. And it's so late now, I won't find anything here but fast food."

"You can't drive home like this. I'll drive you."

"Oh, no. I can't make you go out of your way."

"I would rather take an extra twenty minutes to get you home than worry about you. Also, I can bring you back here to get your car when you need me to."

She wanted to argue, but she could barely keep her eyes open, so she nodded instead.

So five minutes later, she was walking beside him to his truck, and Dumfries was with him.

"I can't believe you brought your dog to work."

"He'd been with Mrs. Williams all day. So after I called you, I went and grabbed him from her. We've been upstairs waiting on you."

"And it is so sweet to have such a handsome fellow to escort me home," she said.

"Aw, you do know how to make a man happy, lass."

She laughed. "I was talking to Dumfries."

"Cruel."

"I never said I wasn't cruel."

He opened the back door to the cab of his pickup. "Up."

Dumfries jumped into the back seat, then Graeme helped her up and shut the door. He walked around the hood of the truck and she watched him. The man oozed sex. She knew he didn't do it on purpose, but there was a way he strode around. Now that she thought about it, all the men on Task Force Hawaii were that way. There was just something so intriguing in that. A man who knew how to take command of a room by walking into it was definitely someone special.

He sat in the driver's seat and looked at her. "What?"

She shook her head, as she pulled on her seatbelt. "Nothing. Just zoning out."

He nodded and put his seatbelt on. "Settle back and don't worry. Dumfries and I will get you home."

As he started up the vehicle and pulled out of the parking lot, she thought there was no way she would fall asleep.

Graeme parked his truck in her driveway. She had been asleep for the last thirty minutes. An angel. Then she let out a little snore. He smiled. Okay, not a perfect angel, but an angel all the same.

"Love, we're at your house."

She said nothing really, but grumbled and turned away from him. He realized she was pretty worn out from the week.

He took her purse and retrieved her keys. Hopping out of his truck, he hurried around to get her. He unlocked her front door, then returned to the truck. Dumfries was sitting in the driver's seat. Graeme shook his head as he opened the door. Elle practically fell into his arms. He handled her easily, as she barely weighed anything.

"Dumfries."

The wolfhound climbed over into the passenger seat and jumped down. Graeme kicked the door shut, walked up the path, and into her house. It wasn't that hard to find her bedroom. The house was tiny. He laid her on her bed, removing her shoes. His fingers itched to remove the rest of her clothes, but even knowing her past told him that would be a line he could not cross without her permission.

He walked out into the living room and found Dumfries had taken up residence on the couch.

"We should go home."

Dumfries laid his head down.

Yeah, he didn't want to go home either. He knew there was another room; he opened that door and found a bed. It was twin-sized, compared to her queen, but he could handle it for one night. He didn't want to leave her without the deadbolt.

With a sigh, he decided to go ahead and spend the night. She could yell at him tomorrow. He went out to his truck and grabbed the overnight bag he kept there just in case work ran long. After locking the truck, he went back in. The couch was empty. He looked in her room, and found Dumfries on the bed with Elle.

"Don't wake her up, you idiot."

Dumfries gave Graeme a look of doggy disgust, huffed, then closed his eyes.

Seeing that he had been dismissed, Graeme headed to the spare bedroom. The idea that his dog had gotten into Elle's bed before he did was a bit much to take, but he was at least in her house for the night. That, he could handle for now.

Elle was hot. Burning up. And it felt as if she was up against a wall of fur. She opened her eyes and then closed them again. The sun was sneaking through the blinds. She turned away from the sun and ran into the furry heater again. She opened her eyes and found a big doggie face looking at her. It was Dumfries.

"What are you doing here?"

He gave her a long lick on her face.

"Where is your master?"

He said nothing, but wagged his tail as he smiled at her.

She sat up and realized she was in her clothes from yesterday. She remembered that Graeme had brought her home, but she didn't recall much after that.

"Well, I should wash up and figure out what is going

on."

She slipped out of bed and went to the bathroom. After relieving her bladder, she washed her face. Peeling off her clothes, she grabbed a pair of PJ bottoms and a big shirt. As she started brushing her teeth, she heard Graeme's voice.

"I think she's still sleeping. She had a late night last night, ma'am."

Then he was quiet.

"Yes, she does a very good job." More silence. "Yes, I'm from Scotland, like your mother. I hear a little Scots in your voice."

Bloody hell. Her mother.

She ran out of her bedroom and into the living room to find Graeme in her kitchen making coffee and chatting to her mother on the phone. He was standing there in a pair of jeans and nothing else. Oh, lord. His back was to her. He had a huge Celtic cross tattoo on his back. She had heard them talk about it at work, but she had never seen it herself. He moved and she watched the ripple of muscle beneath the flesh and ink.

"Yes, she is very smart."

"Graeme," she whispered.

He turned with a smile. In that instant, she lost her train of thought. If his back was gorgeous, then the front of him was amazing. Sculpted muscle encased in golden flesh. He had an honest to god six pack. A tiny trail of dark blond hair bisected his abs and disappeared beneath the waistband of his jeans.

"Oh, there you are, love. Your mother called," he said, handing her the mobile.

She looked at the phone, then at him. She took it, drew in a deep breath, then released it before talking. "Mum, how are you doing?"

"Doing fine, although not as well as you, love."

She snorted. "I'm sure Daddy really appreciates that."

"Just because I've been married for decades doesn't

mean I can't appreciate an attractive man. Graeme sounds attractive."

"How can someone sound attractive?"

"Show me a Scotsman who doesn't sound sexy, and he would have to be dead. Either way, Graeme sounds nice."

"He is."

"How long have you been dating?"

She glanced at Graeme, who was smiling like he knew they were talking about him. With a huff, she went into her bedroom and closed the door. She sat down on the bed next to Dumfries.

"We are not dating."

"Then what is he doing at your house answering your mobile at this time in the morning."

"We worked late; he brought me home. The rest of the night is fuzzy."

"I am happy you have a sex life again, love. Don't get so huffy."

She started to pet the dog. "I am not huffy, and I don't have a sex life. I slept with Dumfries, not Graeme last night."

"You slept with a whole city? My, that's a little more of a sex life than I expected you to get."

She sighed. Her mother had a strange sense of humor. Then she heard her father's voice asking what was going on.

"She said she slept with all of Dumfries last night."

"Dumfries is a dog."

"Oh, okay. Never mind, dear. Not the whole city, and she's still single."

"Seriously, mother, I have just gotten out of bed. I can't deal with this right now."

"I apologize, dear. I was just so surprised when a Scotsman answered the phone."

"Is everything all right?"

"I called because Gerald called me."

"Oh, damn. I'm sorry."

"He's been trying to get hold of you."

"I know."

"You're avoiding him?" her mother asked.

"For good reason."

"He got your father one day. I am afraid he yelled at him."

She winced. Her father had a particular hatred for her ex. In his mind, Gerald should have stood by her. She didn't disagree with her father, but she also hadn't liked the suggestion that her mild-mannered father offered her. Never before or since had she heard her father threaten to make a person disappear. Worse, she knew he had meant it.

"And I know what he wants."

"Well, why don't you talk to him?"

"Because, the answer would be no. Always."

There was a pause, and she knew her mother was working it all out. "Ah, this has to do with work."

"Yes. I won't *ever* work there again. Those people turned on me."

"Good for you. But avoiding him is never going to work. He will keep calling and calling." She was quiet again, and Elle waited for the next bit of bad news. "So, this Scotsman. He sounds rather sexy."

"Didn't we already go over this? Anyway, how can someone sound sexy?"

"If you don't know that, then your first husband definitely failed."

She couldn't help but chuckle. "Mum, please."

"I'm not upset dear. I am actually very happy that a man answered your phone."

"We work together."

Another pause. "So, a policeman."

"Of sorts. He works on the task force, and they are a different breed. He's former military."

"I will let it go for now. I called for two reasons. One was that bothersome bastard."

That was what her mother had called her ex from the time Elle had kicked him out of the house.

"And the other?"

"Your father is going to take a term off."

Worry filled her. Her father did not take time off. Never. The only time he had, in her memory, was after she had survived the attack. He'd taken an entire semester off so both he and her mother could stay with her.

"Nothing's wrong?"

"No, nothing's wrong, but we wanted to do a tour of the States, and we wanted to come see you."

"Really?" she asked, as she felt her mouth curve.

"Yes. It's our fiftieth anniversary, and we want to spend it in Hawaii."

Happiness filled her. It had been over a year since she had seen her parents. "That would be wonderful."

"We wouldn't stay with you."

"Well, that's rude."

"We know your house is small and, hopefully by then, the sexy Scotsman might be doing more than just working with you."

"Mum," she said in warning, but it came out with a laugh. It was hard to tell her mother to behave. She was close to eighty, and didn't give a bloody damn what anyone thought—especially her daughter.

"We'll be staying with Doc. I already called him to be sure it was okay. He has that huge house and too much time on his hands. We know you have work."

"That's true."

"Plus, we don't want you to think you need to entertain us."

"Why on earth would I think to do that?"

Her mother laughed. "You sound good, Elle."

"How do I usually sound?"

"Hmm, a little sad, maybe. Not all that settled. But you sound very happy."

"I am. I love work. It's been a little busy lately, but I

love the challenge again. It's a good team."

"Good. You deserve to be happy at work, but you also deserve to be happy with a man, Elle."

"I don't need a man."

"Of course you don't. I raised you to be independent. But wanting one...that is another matter altogether. Make sure you don't let what happened with Gerald get in the way."

"I'll try."

"Good."

"Give my love to Dad."

"I will. Be bad every now and then, love. Life is too short to always be the good girl."

She turned off her mobile with a smile. Her parents had never been very conventional. They had been very good parents, but sometimes she had felt more like the parent.

Calling her father forgetful would be the understatement of the century. A legend in the field of physics, he was often in another world, one of his own making, sorting out his next idea. Her mother spoke her mind, whether it was politics or how she thought reparations should be paid to Scotland. It hadn't been easy, but it had definitely been unconventional. By the time Elle was ten, she was reminding both of her parents when they had meetings and to take their medications.

"Is everything all right?"

She looked up and realized McGregor had opened her bedroom door. Sadly, he was no longer bare-chested.

"Oh, yes. She was just checking on me. Seems when my ex could not get hold of me, he started bugging them."

"What the bloody hell does he want?"

His irritation surprised a laugh out of her.

"It's work. He wants me to come back to England to work again. Seems I am missed on some serial case he's working. I haven't talked to him, but that can be the only reason he would call."

"You're not thinking of going, are you?"

She shook her head. "Hawaii is my home now."

He nodded. "I thought we could get something to eat, since you don't have enough to feed a dead bird in your house."

"First, how does one feed a dead bird?"

He said nothing, but crossed his massive arms over his massive chest. She really wished he was still shirtless.

"Stop that."

"What?" she asked.

His mouth curved in that way that never failed to make her pulse speed up.

"Undressing me with your eyes, lass. You keep doing that, and we won't make it to breakfast."

For a second, her brain stopped working. When it kicked into gear again, images flashed of him taking off that shirt, and laying her back in the bed.

"Eleanora," he said.

"What?"

"Stop it. I can't control myself if you look at me like that."

She shook her head trying to erase the image. "Oh, sorry."

"And what was the second thing?"

"Of what?"

"You said, first, so I assume you have a second."

"Oh." Then the conversation she had started came rushing back to her. Bloody hell, the man was killing her brain cells.

"Second, how did I end up in my bed with Dumfries?"

"I drove you back here and you fell asleep. I didn't like the idea of leaving you without your deadbolt in place, so I stayed."

He looked as if he were waiting for her to admonish him.

"And you slept in the guest room?"

He nodded, looking even more defensive. How did she

miss that this man was so sweet? He was big and loud, just like most Scotsmen she knew, but he was so incredibly thoughtful. Now that she thought about it, she realized how nice he was to all the women who worked at TFH, but he had avoided her for months, thanks to her prickly behavior. Elle didn't know a lot of men who would have driven her home then stayed there because he was worried for her safety. Most would take the opportunity to advance his case for sex.

She rose from the bed, and walked to him. Cupping his face in her hands, she brushed her mouth over his. When she pulled back, he looked stunned.

"Thank you. And I insist on taking you out to breakfast. Why don't we hit Kono's for some breakfast bombers?"

He cleared his throat. "Sounds good."

"Let me get dressed. It should only take a few minutes."

He nodded. "Dumfries, come."

Dumfries jumped down from the bed and followed his master out the door. Elle closed it behind them then turned to go into the bathroom. For the first time in a long time, she was going to just go with the flow and see where it got her. With a sexy Scotsman by her side, she figured it would at least be interesting.

CHAPTER TWELVE

Thirty minutes later, they were seated at Kono's.

They'd both ordered bombers, or what they called breakfast burritos, and were now enjoying the cool breezes and the Kona coffee. Graeme leaned back in his chair and gave his dog a look of disgust.

Elle had insisted on sitting outside. She hadn't wanted to leave Dumfries in the truck. As if the dog who braved the streets of Bagdad wouldn't be able to survive a few minutes in a truck with the windows down and the temp in the low seventies.

Now, he sat beside Elle claiming all her attention. Graeme grumbled under his breath, as he took a sip of his coffee. The dog was stealing all his thunder, the wanker. Graeme rolled his shoulders. His neck was killing him, and his back felt as if someone had stabbed him. A man of his size sleeping on a twin bed was never a good idea. That is, when he got any sleep. Most of the night he had been staring at the ceiling thinking about the thin wall that separated him from Elle.

Dumfries looked over at him, his tongue hanging out in pure dog bliss, as Elle sunk her fingers into his fur. He sneered at Dumfries, knowing it made him an idiot to be jealous of the attention Elle was giving him, but he couldn't help it. He was so hung up on her, even his dog made him jealous.

"You keep doing that, he's going to expect that from me, and then he will be disappointed," he said.

Elle slanted him a look. "I have a feeling that Dumfries doesn't hurt for attention."

He grunted and looked out over the parking lot. It wasn't too busy this early in the morning. Everyone's concentration was on getting to the beach.

"Do you always do that?" she asked.

He turned back to her. She looked good this morning. Rested. She'd thrown on a pair of shorts and a T-shirt—something he had never thought he'd see her wear. He'd imagined she always dressed up when she left the house, but instead, she was wearing a pair of flip-flops, and had foregone makeup. He liked the look on her.

She had combed her hair but left it wavy. The breeze shifted through her hair, pulling her short curls to and fro.

"Graeme?"

He blinked. "Sorry. It's habit from being in the Marines."

She nodded and took a sip of her coffee. "Of course. All cops have that sort of watchful eye. I remember when I went out with Adam a few times—"

"You went out with Adam?" he asked, his voice rising a little louder than he had meant it to.

She cocked her head to the side and studied him. Even Dumfries was giving him a look of disgust. Now he knew he sounded jealous.

Graeme cleared his throat. "Sorry. I didn't know you dated."

"We didn't. When I moved here, I think he felt a little sorry for me. Doc had introduced us. I wasn't working much, just part time at a free clinic. In fact, I think Doc wanted me out of the house. He's too accustomed to living on his own. So he called up Adam. More than likely he begged Adam to take me out."

"Oh."

"So, as I was saying before you accused me of dating Adam, Adam watched things, as did my ex. But you watch an area like Del does. Sort of looking for any possible attack. Must be the military background."

He nodded. "It's a hard habit to break."

"I don't think that you should break it, especially considering the work you're doing now. I have a feeling it was one of the reasons Del hired you."

He nodded. "I didn't think I would have a chance. I had some policing in my military background, but that is a little different than investigation."

"Yes, but we don't just handle murders. We handle terrorism as well, and you're good at that." Then she cocked her head and studied him for a second. "I wonder if that is part of the reason he assigned this case to you."

"So that I can cut my teeth leading on an old case?"

She shrugged. "It takes some old fashioned detective work to get it done. It makes you look at a case in different ways. It's sort of the way I have seen him work with everyone else."

He didn't know what to say to that, but there was a good chance she was right. Graeme wasn't about to complain, though. Working the case meant more time with Elle.

Then his mind went back to her comment earlier. "And

I didn't accuse you of dating Adam."

She didn't say anything, but her eyes were dancing over her cup, as she took a very dainty sip of coffee.

"I want to thank you for being so sweet last night, Graeme."

"That's me. Sweet guy."

She swallowed her coffee. "Well, you are."

He didn't want to be in the sweet guy territory. Those were the guys who you called when you needed a friend to take you to a family wedding. He would rather be the one *at* the wedding.

Fuck. Where did that thought come from? He pushed the thought away. He wasn't one for marriage, not yet, and not to a woman who would barely talk to him less than ten days ago.

"I was wondering if you're going stag to the wedding?" she asked.

Damn. Did she already think of him that way? Before he could answer, the waitress returned with their food. He gathered his thoughts and waited until the waitress had left.

"Why do you ask?"

"What?"

"About the wedding. Why did you ask?"

She cut into her burrito with extra care. "I was wondering if you wanted to go with me?"

Dammit, he was right. He was in friend status. She had put him in that sweet guy territory, and he would never get out of it if he didn't fight it. Fighting it, though, could lead to an argument, and then she wouldn't think of him as a friend. So he ground his teeth together before he spoke.

"As a friend?" he spat out.

She looked up at him with wide eyes.

"Well, we are friends," she said carefully. "But, I was actually asking you on a date. It's just that everyone was talking about how Cat and Drew are going to the wedding. Charity doesn't want a date, because well, she's Charity. So,

I thought maybe I would ask you. If you would rather not go—"

"No. I want to go."

"I know you are going. The question is if you want to go with me. But I understand if you do not."

"Yes, I want to go with you."

She gave him a shy smile.

"Good. It's been a long time since I've been to a close friend's wedding. I have been to some colleagues' weddings, but, you know, not one where people will know more about my personal life." She shrugged. "I just wanted to go with you."

If he thought he felt good when she smiled, he almost passed out with happiness at that comment.

"That would be brilliant," he said. "Can I ask why you changed your mind?"

"About dating you?"

He nodded.

She sighed. "I'm not really sure. Maybe it was talking to my mother this morning, who told me you sounded very sexy."

"Is that a fact?"

"Don't let it go to your head, McGregor."

He chuckled. "Hard not to."

"Mum's been worried because I haven't really dated since my divorce. She keeps saying it's been over six years since the divorce was final and I need to get out. I wasn't really ready at first, then work got in the way. It's hard to explain to people why you're on call or why you like hanging out with dead bodies."

"Why *do* you like hanging out with dead bodies?"

She smiled as she chewed her food, then swallowed it. "My mother says she blames it on my father, since he's the scientist, and I think that is part of it. I love my father, but he isn't that easy to communicate with. When I showed an aptitude for science, it gave us a connection. But, then, he says my mother ruined it, because instead of researching, I

148

turned to work with the public. So, they sort of blame each other."

"But why do you like this specific work?"

"I guess I like to think I'm helping. I am good at my job, but like my father, there are times I'm not good with people."

"Bollocks."

"No, it's true. Well, I am better now, but when I went to university, I had issues dealing with people. I am not that good with the bedside manner. But I was already leaning towards being a medical examiner."

"I think you work fine with people."

"Now, and on a smaller level. Plus, I am twelve years older than when I started working. I was definitely more awkward back then. Why do you do it?"

"I left the Marines because I was burned out. Too many deployments to war zones. But, I had skills that were handy, just not as a police officer in Scotland. I wanted something I thought would challenge me. Then, also a vacation to Hawaii. As soon as I came here, I was hooked. I heard about the job through some friends and applied. I can use the skills I learned when I was in the military and be challenged."

She nodded. "Makes sense. I gather your mother is not happy you are here?"

He shook his head. "She's mad at my sister for living on the other side of Edinburgh, but she understands. She said I was always on the move."

She nodded. "So, I was thinking that maybe a timeline would help with the case."

The quick switch in topics almost caught him off guard.

"Yes?"

She started back in on her burrito. "Maybe if we can figure out what was going on in both cases, we can find the connection."

She took a bite of her burrito as he studied her. "How

do you think?"

"We don't know what links the two killings."

"Other than the gun."

She nodded. "We need to figure out just what the hell connects it from thirty years ago. Katsu had to have a connection to the case back then."

"He was too young."

She nodded. "But it doesn't mean that someone he knew in his life didn't have a connection to it."

"And working on a timeline could give us some context. Like who could have that connection, friends or family."

"Exactly."

"That is bloody brilliant," he said.

She smiled. "Thank you."

"No, really. Del should bring you in on more cases."

"He does talk to me about some of them, especially if he needs some help with the forensic psychology of a crime."

"And he doesn't want to mess with the FBI unless he has to. That makes sense."

"He does not like to share cases," she said with a chuckle.

"If we're going to work today, I think we need to stop off and get some food. You have nothing at your house."

She nodded. "I've been so busy, it's been hard to shop."

He settled in to eat his burrito, happy with the plan for the day...and the wedding date. It definitely was a nice turn of events.

After picking up the groceries, they spent the rest of the day working on a timeline. She'd pulled out an old whiteboard and markers to use. She always did better with a big visual. Since neither of them were from Hawaii, they called on Adam. After a long conversation with him, he gave up and showed up around three to help. With calls to more than one auntie, they put together a timeline of things that had been going on in Hawaii at the time.

"Okay, now we know all of this, what do we do with it?" Adam asked.

"Now, we have to fill in what little we know. Jenny was killed in eighty-six," Graeme said, marking the timeline. "Then, here, almost thirty years later, we have Sam Katsu, who uses the gun to kill Joe Alana. He was born five years after Jenny's death. So, if the person who had it at that time had some connection to him, it definitely could be a father or uncle."

"What we need to do is go through Katsu's file. He had been arrested a lot of times, so there is a chance he ran across someone that has a connection to Jenny's murder he wasn't related to," Adam said. "Like Del thought, there's no way an ICE head like him would have held onto something like that. He would have sold it for drugs the first chance he got."

"Then why did he use it to steal?" McGregor murmured.

"He might have thought he could go for a two-fer. You know, sell the gun after gaining some cash. He'd be able to buy even more drugs," Adam said.

McGregor nodded. "ICE heads don't always think clearly."

"Your help was just brilliant, Adam. Thank your aunties for us again, please" Elle said.

He smiled. "It sounds so proper when you say aunties."

She laughed. "I hope not too proper."

Adam shook his head. "I'll see myself out."

"Thanks again," Graeme said. "You definitely helped the *haoles* this time around.

Adam grabbed his helmet, and after giving them a salute, he left. She picked up Adam's coffee cup and started to walk to the kitchen when she noticed that Graeme was watching her.

"What?"

He took his time in answering her. "I was just thinking that you fit here."

She frowned. "This is my house. Of course I fit here."

He shook his head. "I mean here, in Hawaii."

"What?"

"I was thinking about it the other day too, when I found you sitting on the bench."

"The day we got the case?"

He nodded without breaking eye contact. "You're this gorgeous English rose surrounded by all the tropical beauty, and you shouldn't fit. You should clash. But you don't. Instead, you only enhance the beauty around you."

Her breath caught in her throat. No one had ever said things like this to her, and they didn't say it with Scottish sex dripping from every word.

"And I watch you with people. You're good. And you enjoy them. Don't ever doubt your skills beyond the lab, Elle."

Again, he amazed her at how perceptive he was. "How did you know?"

"That you doubted?"

She nodded.

"Just a few things you said here and there. And, I have a feeling that you did not keep your mouth shut when that stupid ex of yours was working a case. He just probably never gave you credit."

"How do you know that?"

"Because he's been calling you trying to get your help. So I assumed you helped him before."

She sighed, and she really didn't want to tell him, but something was moving her to speak.

"We had issues in our marriage from the start. We had been working together on cases for a year and had a very hot, fast love affair, then decided to get married. We really didn't know much about each other. A month after we married, I found out I was pregnant. Just a few weeks along. We were actually elated about it. I lost it just six weeks later. That's when the problems started."

"It's tough losing a baby," he said gently.

"Yes. But, it was worse for us. We didn't know how to help each other. How could we? We barely knew each other. So, we did the only thing we understood and threw ourselves into work. It was the only thing we could talk about. By the time we started on the last case, we barely spoke if it wasn't about the case. When the last case tore us apart, there was nothing left. We didn't have work anymore, so everything dissolved."

"But he wasn't there for you."

It wasn't a question, but a statement. It told her that Graeme understood easier than many other men.

"No, he wasn't. He started working odd hours and I didn't even care. I spent a month in the house without ever leaving it. I just could not bear to be outside. Even though I know they had the bastard and I was safe, I could not get out of the house. When I learned he was cheating on me, I didn't really give a damn. I was just happy he wasn't there."

"And the people you worked with turned on you."

She nodded. "They said I had taken too many risks, but I didn't. They blamed me, which is quite ironic since they told all the victims it wasn't their fault. Colleagues I cherished, and whose houses I had visited, went to the rags and talked about how I was greedy for attention. That I had caused the department embarrassment. They spread lies about my fidelity when I was the one who had been cheated on."

"I am not going to ask what happened when you were raped, but if you ever want to tell me, I will listen."

"That means a lot. I'm not sure I'm ready yet."

He nodded, understanding filling his expression. "No rush."

He moved closer to her and kissed her forehead, then leaned back and smiled. "Why don't we walk down to the beach?"

The heaviness that seemed to lie on her shoulders dissolved. "Yeah. That is actually a smashing idea."

"Let's go, Dumfries," Graeme said. Dumfries came galloping up and then trotted beside them as they walked hand in hand down the street to the beach.

A dog on one side and his sexy master on the other. Elle couldn't think of a better way to end a Saturday night.

CHAPTER THIRTEEN

Monday arrived quietly, if you could call a main line break on Dillingham quiet. It was a common occurrence on Oahu, but it didn't make it any easier to deal with. There were only so many roads to take, and when everyone had to change their path, it ended up being a right mess.

By the time Elle made it into the office, she was already thirty minutes late. The first person she ran in to was Marcus—who was also late. He jogged up the path to catch up with her.

"I take it the main line break slowed you down too?" she asked.

Marcus nodded. "One thing I never had to worry about when I lived in DC was traffic coming to a stop because of a water main break."

She laughed. "From what I remember during my visit, traffic is always at a standstill in DC."

"I didn't say it moved, I just said water main break

wasn't the reason."

She shook her head as they climbed the steps to the back door.

"You seem different," he said, opening the door and holding it open for her.

"Different?"

"Good. You just seem happier."

"Well, it is a beautiful day, and I'm no longer on call with HPD."

"That is always a good thing."

"How's your case going?" she asked, as they walked side by side down the hallway.

"Easy. I handled this kind of thing all the time when I worked in DC."

"And the company isn't too bad?"

He slanted her a look as they walked down the hall. "Where did you get that idea?"

"Emma. You know she doesn't miss anything."

He stopped in the hall, and she kept walking to the door. This time, she held it open and waited. Marcus's eyes narrowed as he pursed his lips. She knew that laser stare had made more than one person confess their crimes. She didn't budge though.

"There's a damn bet going, isn't there?" he asked.

"*A* bet?"

"Yes. A bet..*dammit*, how many bets are going on?"

"I'm not allowed to reveal the wager or wagers. I always find it somewhat amusing that all of us get so upset when we find out we are a subject of one of the bets."

"It's all fun and games until everyone is talking about you," he said.

She waited until Marcus reached her, but he insisted on holding the door open. She rolled her eyes and stepped into the office. The moment she did, Graeme appeared like he had been waiting for her to show up.

"Morning," he said, his gaze solely on her.

He drew out the word, making it sound even more

intimate. When his accent deepened like that, it felt as if fire danced over her nerve endings. She also seemed to have lost the ability to speak. Or think.

"Speaking of wagers," Marcus said, his voice laced with humor.

She shook herself out of her stupor. "Shut it," she warned.

"Good morning. Is there a reason you're meeting us at the door, McGregor?" Marcus asked.

"I didn't want to meet you. I wanted to see Elle. She's prettier." He said all of this without taking his gaze from her. Her cheeks burned, but she didn't care. It was actually kind of...cute. He was meeting her like he was courting her.

Marcus smiled. "Can't argue with that."

"Floyd, you're late," Del yelled out from the other side of the room.

They all turned toward the sound of his voice.

"*Bloody hell,*" Graeme muttered.

"Brother, you said a mouthful," Marcus said under his breath.

She had no words. Del looked as if death had warmed over and died again. Dark circles bruised the skin beneath his eyes. Of course, it could be just shadows, but it definitely wasn't shadows that was turning his skin green.

"Del, are you feeling okay?" she asked, walking toward him.

"I'm fine." His curt response was definitely not like him. He was always straight and to the point, but this was downright cranky.

She opened her mouth, but Del decided to continue.

"What I want to know is why everyone thinks it's okay to stand around and gab in the morning after showing up late is beyond me."

Then, his face went white so fast, she was sure he would pass out right there and then.

"Del," she said, rushing forward.

"I'm fine," he said, holding out his hand to stop them

all from coming to his aid. "Just feeling a little under the weather right now. I think it is something I ate. Be with you in a minute, Floyd."

When they were alone, Marcus hummed. "Do you think he's got bridal jitters?"

"Martin Delano is not someone who would have bridal jitters," Graeme said.

Drew came walking from the direction of the bathrooms. He stopped. "What?"

"Did you see the boss?" Marcus asked.

"No. I just came up from the lab."

"I say bridal jitters," Marcus said. "Who is going to take care of the bet?"

"You were just complaining about people wagering on your sex life," Elle said.

"Wait, Marcus has a sex life?" Graeme asked. "Who won that one?"

"I do not have a sex life."

"I wouldn't be so proud of that if I were you," Graeme said.

"Shit. I do, but...never mind. Just leave Tamilya out of your bets."

"Doc, you want in?" Drew asked, ignoring the byplay.

"I'll sit this one out. I have a report to write up."

She turned to leave, but Graeme stopped her by grabbing her hand. "We still on for lunch?"

She smiled. "Yes."

"Good. See ya then."

Still smiling, she walked toward the lift. She really couldn't ever remember feeling this happy in a long while. As she waited for the lift, Del came out of the bathroom. He didn't look any better. If anything, he looked worse.

"Del, are you sure you're okay?"

He nodded. "It seems that Emma isn't the only one with a sensitive stomach right now. But I can't blame mine on pregnancy."

"And you're trying to keep it from her?"

He studied her for a second. "Yeah. She is freaking out about Mom getting here this afternoon. If I tell her I'm sick, she will assume it's because of the wedding."

"Then she will think you are having second thoughts? Is that what you are worried about?"

He nodded again.

"First, Del, you pretty much were set on having her as yours from the moment you two got together. I doubt very much she's going to think that."

"You don't know how insane she has been the last few weeks. The hormones have made her lose her mind. And she's making me lose my ever-loving mind."

Elle smiled. "And, that is the reason you might be having sympathy morning sickness."

His face went blank, then he frowned. "I'm not having morning sickness."

"It's been known to happen, which also makes me think you are going to be a good daddy—as if I had any doubt."

That made him pause. "Why do you say that?"

"That I had no doubt?"

He nodded.

It amazed her that this man needed confirmation, but everyone needed to be reassured every now and then.

"You handle this ragtag family very well. We all come from such diverse backgrounds, and you roll with the punches. We all respect you, and that is not an easy thing to acquire."

"I think you are blowing smoke up my ass, Doc."

She shook her head. "How many of your bosses have you respected, or had the respect of the entire team? I bet not many. Those men and women who follow you into danger are the top of the field. But, you also make us all feel like we have support outside of work, and that is important. We *are* a family because of you. Each of us knows if we need to reach out, you're there. You are going to be a smashing father."

"Well...damn."

Elle laughed, enjoying the way Del's cheeks pinkened. "Studies have also shown that men who have sympathetic morning sickness are often more in tune with their wives and with their children." She took his hand and gave it a squeeze.

"Truth?"

She nodded. "Keep some crackers in your desk, and cut back on anything greasy, and definitely cut back on caffeine. That will help a lot."

He nodded. "Thanks, Doc."

"Anytime, Del." She turned toward the lift, but he stopped her.

"I understand that you went home with McGregor the other night."

She glanced at him. "We did not go home together. I went too long without eating, got a little dizzy. He gave me a ride home."

"Okay."

The door dinged open.

"Anything else?"

He shook his head. "Thanks for your help."

She stepped into the lift. "Like I said, anytime. Remember, we are a family, so make sure you let us support you every now and then."

Graeme had a few people to hunt up for questioning, and since Floyd was in for the day, he decided to drag him along. It wasn't that hard of an assignment, but since it could be boring, it was always better to have someone along. Plus, you never knew if things could go sideways. Always a good idea to have someone with you when you were hanging around drug addicts.

"So, you and the Doc, huh?" Floyd asked as they got

out of the truck.

He waited until they were standing in front of the truck to answer. "Yeah. What about it?"

Floyd shrugged. "Just didn't see that one coming. She didn't like you much when you first arrived here."

"There were reasons for that, which are none of your business."

"Okay, gotcha. But I do find it interesting."

"I'm sure you do, seeing that you volunteered to help with the terrorism task force. Want to tell me your reasons for that?"

Floyd frowned. "I have a background in terrorism."

"True, but Cat was already tapped for it. They don't need both of you."

"Got it."

One thing about Floyd, he didn't pry much. He was kind of quiet a lot of the time, but that was probably because his brain was working something out. The former DC cop had the ability to look at a problem from different angles. It was one of the reasons Graeme had been happy that Floyd could come with him today. He had driven though, because the driver picked the music. Floyd had a love for Willie Nelson, and always wanted to play it at full blast. It was painful.

"So, you're looking for someone who might know anything about this Sam Katsu?"

"I have a list of known associates. This is the first one, Fred Vicker." He handed Floyd the printout of Vicker's last mug shot.

"Sounds like a damned farmer."

Graeme chuckled. "Well, Farmer Fred was tagged last time Katsu was arrested. They were both selling and smoking ICE, so there is a good chance he's high right now. From what Adam said, he heard Fred hung out here in Chinatown."

"A lot of them do."

Graeme looked over the multitude of drug addicts

hanging out in the park.

"This might take a while," he murmured.

"I'll head down to the other end. We can meet in the middle," Floyd said.

Graeme nodded, as he continued to look over the group. It was hot out and even hotter in Chinatown. The close buildings cut off a lot of the air supply, so even when they had trade winds blowing, it could get oppressive.

As he walked along the street, he ignored the prostitutes hanging out in plain view. At the moment, that wasn't his job. Truly, it wasn't his job. They were tasked with only certain things, and when they stepped over the line, it always ended up with Del dealing with the mayor.

Floyd caught up with him. "Don't see him, but there's a good chance that he doesn't look like this anymore."

Graeme looked at the picture again. "If he looked any worse, he would be dead."

Vicker was twenty-four in the picture, but he looked older. He was missing teeth, his face was pock marked, and there was a sallow cast to his skin.

He was ready to give up when he spotted the kid. He was sitting on a bench. Graeme tried to be quiet, but it was hard to hide who he was, especially in this area. The moment Vicker noticed the attention, he took off.

"Aw, damn, I hate when they run," Floyd said.

Both of them took off after him, with Floyd turning down an alley to make sure the little bastard didn't double back. Thank God, Vicker was shorter and so unhealthy from his habit that he couldn't keep up the pace he had started. Graeme caught up to him after three blocks.

"Bloody hell, Vicker, I just wanted to talk to you."

When he looked up, Graeme could see that Vicker's eyes were definitely dilated. It was bad enough they had to rely on a drug addict and a thief, but if he was strung out, questioning him was probably going to be fruitless.

The alley they stood in smelled of rotten food, produce, and feces. With the humidity, the stink hung in the air around him. It took everything for Graeme to keep from losing his breakfast.

Floyd caught up to them then. He glanced around their surroundings and made a face.

"Nice morning jog."

Graeme chuckled. "I just want to talk to you about Sam."

"What about him?" Vicker asked. He looked like he'd lost a few more teeth and dropped a few pounds. His clothes were filthy, and he stunk of ICE and body odor.

"I want to know where he might have gotten that gun."

Vicker shrugged and looked down the street. The mutinous expression on his face told Graeme that Vicker was trying his best to find an escape route.

"Listen, kid, I'm not too pissed about that little run, but if you make me do it again, I'll shoot you," Marcus said, deepening his voice. Graeme knew he was only joking, but it apparently drove home the point.

"No idea where he got it. Hadn't talked to him in weeks."

"I asked around," Graeme said. "You two were tight. What happened?"

Again, the kid shrugged. "He said he found a family member who was going to help him. I didn't know what the fuck he was talking about. Sam was always a little weird, you know?"

No, Graeme didn't know, but he nodded.

"Then, he just went off. I didn't know what the hell he was talking about half the time. He kept going on and on about how he was owed stuff. I gave up trying to talk to him. It'd been at least a month since we talked."

"A family member? Here?" Floyd asked.

He nodded. "I never thought he had anyone. That's what he always said. But lately, he'd been rambling on about some person who had left him a legacy."

"A legacy? Like money?" Graeme asked.

Vicker nodded again.

Graeme shared a look with Floyd. This could be the break they had been looking for. It was the first he had heard of a legacy, or that Katsu had any kind of family.

"Let's talk some more about it," Floyd said.

"I knew you were going to bust me, *dammit.*" He turned to run, but Floyd caught him by the collar.

Graeme shook his head. "We aren't going to bust you. I was being honest with you. We're going to get you something to eat, and maybe that will help you think."

Twenty minutes later, they watched the kid walk away, a soda in his hand, and a burger in his stomach. They'd given him a number for a treatment center, but Graeme really didn't think he would call.

"So, the way Vicker talked, it was like this family member would give Katsu something."

"A legacy. It couldn't have been much because he was robbing a store when he shot Alana," Floyd said, as they turned to walk to the truck.

"True, but what if the legacy turned out to be the gun? Or some other crap and the gun? He wouldn't want to give it away."

"Would you call a gun a legacy?"

"No, but then, I have a good solid family. He didn't. Anything that would link to the family member might have been something for him to hold onto."

Floyd nodded. "No father in the picture?"

"For a boy raised mainly on the streets and by the system, the idea his father had left him something, that might be too much to ignore. That would be special."

"In his world, a gun would probably be a legacy. He wouldn't sell it. Well, some ICE heads might, but this was a kid who had no one in the world. This was the one link to his father possibly."

"Yes, he wouldn't be able to part with it."

"So, he uses it to get money, but it doesn't go as planned."

"Yeah, and Joe Alana paid for it with his life."

HOSTILE DESIRES

CHAPTER FOURTEEN

Monday arrived quietly, if you could call a main line break on Dillingham quiet. It was a common occurrence on Oahu, but it didn't make it any easier to deal with. There were only so many roads to take, and when everyone had to change their path, it ended up being a tight mess.

By the time Elle made it into the office, she was already thirty minutes late. The first person she ran in to was Marcus—who was also late. He jogged up the path to catch up with her.

"I take it the main line break slowed you down too?" she asked.

Marcus nodded. "One thing I never had to worry about when I lived in DC was traffic coming to a stop because of a water main break."

She laughed. "From what I remember during my visit, traffic is always at a standstill in DC."

"I didn't say it moved, I just said water main break wasn't the reason."

She shook her head as they climbed the steps to the back door.

"You seem different," he said, opening the door and holding it open for her.

"Different?"

"Good. You just seem happier."

"Well, it is a beautiful day, and I'm no longer on call with HPD."

"That is always a good thing."

"How's your case going?" she asked, as they walked side by side down the hallway.

"Easy. I handled this kind of thing all the time when I worked in DC."

"And the company isn't too bad?"

He slanted her a look as they walked down the hall. "Where did you get that idea?"

"Emma. You know she doesn't miss anything."

He stopped in the hall, and she kept walking to the door. This time, she held it open and waited. Marcus's eyes narrowed as he pursed his lips. She knew that laser stare had made more than one person confess their crimes. She didn't budge though.

"There's a damn bet going, isn't there?" he asked.

"*A* bet?"

"Yes. A bet..*dammit*, how many bets are going on?"

"I'm not allowed to reveal the wager or wagers. I always find it somewhat amusing that all of us get so upset when we find out we are a subject of one of the bets."

"It's all fun and games until everyone is talking about you," he said.

She waited until Marcus reached her, but he insisted on holding the door open. She rolled her eyes and stepped into the office. The moment she did, Graeme appeared like he had been waiting for her to show up.

"Morning," he said, his gaze solely on her.

He drew out the word, making it sound even more intimate. When his accent deepened like that, it felt as if fire danced over her nerve endings. She also seemed to have lost the ability to speak. Or think.

"Speaking of wagers," Marcus said, his voice laced with humor.

She shook herself out of her stupor. "Shut it," she warned.

"Good morning. Is there a reason you're meeting us at the door, McGregor?" Marcus asked.

"I didn't want to meet you. I wanted to see Elle. She's prettier." He said all of this without taking his gaze from her. Her cheeks burned, but she didn't care. It was actually kind of...cute. He was meeting her like he was courting her.

Marcus smiled. "Can't argue with that."

"Floyd, you're late," Del yelled out from the other side of the room.

They all turned toward the sound of his voice.

"*Bloody hell*," Graeme muttered.

"Brother, you said a mouthful," Marcus said under his breath.

She had no words. Del looked as if death had warmed over and died again. Dark circles bruised the skin beneath his eyes. Of course, it could be just shadows, but it definitely wasn't shadows that was turning his skin green.

"Del, are you feeling okay?" she asked, walking toward him.

"I'm fine." His curt response was definitely not like him. He was always straight and to the point, but this was downright cranky.

She opened her mouth, but Del decided to continue.

"What I want to know is why everyone thinks it's okay to stand around and gab in the morning after showing up late is beyond me."

Then, his face went white so fast, she was sure he would pass out right there and then.

"Del," she said, rushing forward.

"I'm fine," he said, holding out his hand to stop them all from coming to his aid. "Just feeling a little under the weather right now. I think it is something I ate. Be with you in a minute, Floyd."

When they were alone, Marcus hummed. "Do you think he's got bridal jitters?"

"Martin Delano is not someone who would have bridal jitters," Graeme said.

Drew came walking from the direction of the bathrooms. He stopped. "What?"

"Did you see the boss?" Marcus asked.

"No. I just came up from the lab."

"I say bridal jitters," Marcus said. "Who is going to take care of the bet?"

"You were just complaining about people wagering on your sex life," Elle said.

"Wait, Marcus has a sex life?" Graeme asked. "Who won that one?"

"I do not have a sex life."

"I wouldn't be so proud of that if I were you," Graeme said.

"Shit. I do, but...never mind. Just leave Tamilya out of your bets."

"Doc, you want in?" Drew asked, ignoring the byplay.

"I'll sit this one out. I have a report to write up."

She turned to leave, but Graeme stopped her by grabbing her hand. "We still on for lunch?"

She smiled. "Yes."

"Good. See ya then."

Still smiling, she walked toward the lift. She really couldn't ever remember feeling this happy in a long while. As she waited for the lift, Del came out of the bathroom. He didn't look any better. If anything, he looked worse.

"Del, are you sure you're okay?"

He nodded. "It seems that Emma isn't the only one with a sensitive stomach right now. But I can't blame mine on pregnancy."

"And you're trying to keep it from her?"

He studied her for a second. "Yeah. She is freaking out

about Mom getting here this afternoon. If I tell her I'm sick, she will assume it's because of the wedding."

"Then she will think you are having second thoughts? Is that what you are worried about?"

He nodded again.

"First, Del, you pretty much were set on having her as yours from the moment you two got together. I doubt very much she's going to think that."

"You don't know how insane she has been the last few weeks. The hormones have made her lose her mind. And she's making me lose my ever-loving mind."

Elle smiled. "And, that is the reason you might be having sympathy morning sickness."

His face went blank, then he frowned. "I'm not having morning sickness."

"It's been known to happen, which also makes me think you are going to be a good daddy—as if I had any doubt."

That made him pause. "Why do you say that?"

"That I had no doubt?"

He nodded.

It amazed her that this man needed confirmation, but everyone needed to be reassured every now and then.

"You handle this ragtag family very well. We all come from such diverse backgrounds, and you roll with the punches. We all respect you, and that is not an easy thing to acquire."

"I think you are blowing smoke up my ass, Doc."

She shook her head. "How many of your bosses have you respected, or had the respect of the entire team? I bet not many. Those men and women who follow you into danger are the top of the field. But, you also make us all feel like we have support outside of work, and that is important. We *are* a family because of you. Each of us knows if we need to reach out, you're there. You are going to be a smashing father."

"Well...damn."

Elle laughed, enjoying the way Del's cheeks pinkened. "Studies have also shown that men who have sympathetic morning sickness are often more in tune with their wives and with their children." She took his hand and gave it a squeeze.

"Truth?"

She nodded. "Keep some crackers in your desk, and cut back on anything greasy, and definitely cut back on caffeine. That will help a lot."

He nodded. "Thanks, Doc."

"Anytime, Del." She turned toward the lift, but he stopped her.

"I understand that you went home with McGregor the other night."

She glanced at him. "We did not go home together. I went too long without eating, got a little dizzy. He gave me a ride home."

"Okay."

The door dinged open.

"Anything else?"

He shook his head. "Thanks for your help."

She stepped into the lift. "Like I said, anytime. Remember, we are a family, so make sure you let us support you every now and then."

Graeme had a few people to hunt up for questioning, and since Floyd was in for the day, he decided to drag him along. It wasn't that hard of an assignment, but since it could be boring, it was always better to have someone along. Plus, you never knew if things could go sideways. Always a good idea to have someone with you when you were hanging around drug addicts.

"So, you and the Doc, huh?" Floyd asked as they got out of the truck.

He waited until they were standing in front of the truck to answer. "Yeah. What about it?"

Floyd shrugged. "Just didn't see that one coming. She didn't like you much when you first arrived here."

"There were reasons for that, which are none of your business."

"Okay, gotcha. But I do find it interesting."

"I'm sure you do, seeing that you volunteered to help with the terrorism task force. Want to tell me your reasons for that?"

Floyd frowned. "I have a background in terrorism."

"True, but Cat was already tapped for it. They don't need both of you."

"Got it."

One thing about Floyd, he didn't pry much. He was kind of quiet a lot of the time, but that was probably because his brain was working something out. The former DC cop had the ability to look at a problem from different angles. It was one of the reasons Graeme had been happy that Floyd could come with him today. He had driven though, because the driver picked the music. Floyd had a love for Willie Nelson, and always wanted to play it at full blast. It was painful.

"So, you're looking for someone who might know anything about this Sam Katsu?"

"I have a list of known associates. This is the first one, Fred Vicker." He handed Floyd the printout of Vicker's last mug shot.

"Sounds like a damned farmer."

Graeme chuckled. "Well, Farmer Fred was tagged last time Katsu was arrested. They were both selling and smoking ICE, so there is a good chance he's high right now. From what Adam said, he heard Fred hung out here in Chinatown."

"A lot of them do."

Graeme looked over the multitude of drug addicts hanging out in the park.

"This might take a while," he murmured.

"I'll head down to the other end. We can meet in the middle," Floyd said.

Graeme nodded, as he continued to look over the group. It was hot out and even hotter in Chinatown. The close buildings cut off a lot of the air supply, so even when they had trade winds blowing, it could get oppressive.

As he walked along the street, he ignored the prostitutes hanging out in plain view. At the moment, that wasn't his job. Truly, it wasn't his job. They were tasked with only certain things, and when they stepped over the line, it always ended up with Del dealing with the mayor.

Floyd caught up with him. "Don't see him, but there's a good chance that he doesn't look like this anymore."

Graeme looked at the picture again. "If he looked any worse, he would be dead."

Vicker was twenty-four in the picture, but he looked older. He was missing teeth, his face was pock marked, and there was a sallow cast to his skin.

He was ready to give up when he spotted the kid. He was sitting on a bench. Graeme tried to be quiet, but it was hard to hide who he was, especially in this area. The moment Vicker noticed the attention, he took off.

"Aw, damn, I hate when they run," Floyd said.

Both of them took off after him, with Floyd turning down an alley to make sure the little bastard didn't double back. Thank God, Vicker was shorter and so unhealthy from his habit that he couldn't keep up the pace he had started. Graeme caught up to him after three blocks.

"Bloody hell, Vicker, I just wanted to talk to you."

When he looked up, Graeme could see that Vicker's eyes were definitely dilated. It was bad enough they had to rely on a drug addict and a thief, but if he was strung out, questioning him was probably going to be fruitless.

The alley they stood in smelled of rotten food, produce, and feces. With the humidity, the stink hung in the air around him. It took everything for Graeme to keep from losing his breakfast.

Floyd caught up to them then. He glanced around their surroundings and made a face.

"Nice morning jog."

Graeme chuckled. "I just want to talk to you about Sam."

"What about him?" Vicker asked. He looked like he'd lost a few more teeth and dropped a few pounds. His clothes were filthy, and he stunk of ICE and body odor.

"I want to know where he might have gotten that gun."

Vicker shrugged and looked down the street. The mutinous expression on his face told Graeme that Vicker was trying his best to find an escape route.

"Listen, kid, I'm not too pissed about that little run, but if you make me do it again, I'll shoot you," Marcus said, deepening his voice. Graeme knew he was only joking, but it apparently drove home the point.

"No idea where he got it. Hadn't talked to him in weeks."

"I asked around," Graeme said. "You two were tight. What happened?"

Again, the kid shrugged. "He said he found a family member who was going to help him. I didn't know what the fuck he was talking about. Sam was always a little weird, you know?"

No, Graeme didn't know, but he nodded.

"Then, he just went off. I didn't know what the hell he was talking about half the time. He kept going on and on about how he was owed stuff. I gave up trying to talk to him. It'd been at least a month since we talked."

"A family member? Here?" Floyd asked.

He nodded. "I never thought he had anyone. That's what he always said. But lately, he'd been rambling on about some person who had left him a legacy."

"A legacy? Like money?" Graeme asked.

Vicker nodded again.

Graeme shared a look with Floyd. This could be the

break they had been looking for. It was the first he had heard of a legacy, or that Katsu had any kind of family.

"Let's talk some more about it," Floyd said.

"I knew you were going to bust me, *dammit*." He turned to run, but Floyd caught him by the collar.

Graeme shook his head. "We aren't going to bust you. I was being honest with you. We're going to get you something to eat, and maybe that will help you think."

Twenty minutes later, they watched the kid walk away, a soda in his hand, and a burger in his stomach. They'd given him a number for a treatment center, but Graeme really didn't think he would call.

"So, the way Vicker talked, it was like this family member would give Katsu something."

"A legacy. It couldn't have been much because he was robbing a store when he shot Alana," Floyd said, as they turned to walk to the truck.

"True, but what if the legacy turned out to be the gun? Or some other crap and the gun? He wouldn't want to give it away."

"Would you call a gun a legacy?"

"No, but then, I have a good solid family. He didn't. Anything that would link to the family member might have been something for him to hold onto."

Floyd nodded. "No father in the picture?"

"For a boy raised mainly on the streets and by the system, the idea his father had left him something, that might be too much to ignore. That would be special."

"In his world, a gun would probably be a legacy. He wouldn't sell it. Well, some ICE heads might, but this was a kid who had no one in the world. This was the one link to his father possibly."

"Yes, he wouldn't be able to part with it."

"So, he uses it to get money, but it doesn't go as planned."

"Yeah, and Joe Alana paid for it with his life."

CHAPTER FIFTEEN

Just after five that afternoon, Elle stood in front of her mirror and wondered if she was dressed right. She had not been on a date since before her marriage, so she didn't really know what to wear. She blinked. Okay, she was not on a date. She was going to work.

She'd stopped off at her house to freshen up and change. Now, though, she felt she might be too dressy for the evening. She'd grabbed her birthday present from Doc, a violet sundress. Four months and this was the first time she was wearing it. It accentuated her slim waist, while giving the illusion that she had hips. The earrings her parents had sent her for her last birthday dangled, catching the light. She'd even redone her makeup, applying lip gloss and eyeliner, something she didn't do that often. She reached for her perfume and then stopped before applying any.

Bloody hell, she was getting ready for a date.

Her stomach flip-flopped. Cocking her head, she laid a

hand on it. It felt as if her stomach was doing somersaults. Why had she not realized until this moment that she was doing that? And why now?

It had been the phone call. It had to be. When she'd kicked Gerald out of the house, she'd only seen him twice afterwards before she left London. The pain and anger had festered inside of her, eating away at the idea of being involved with another man. Truth was, at that time, she had no ability to cope with it. The rape had traumatized her, and she'd been walking around like a zombie, unable to deal with anything other than getting through each day.

But today, she had stood up for herself for the first time. Well, at least the first time with Gerald. It had felt brilliant. Now she was getting dressed up for a date with Graeme.

She waited for panic. It was the reason she hadn't had a date in so long. Emotionally, she hadn't been ready. It wasn't that she had voiced that, even in her head, but now, seven years later, she accepted that her emotional balance had been threatened by the thought of dating.

Until Graeme.

Was that why she had tried to avoid him by being such a bitch when he'd first arrived? Maybe she had sensed her attraction and, in self preservation, she had decided to act out. How very juvenile of her.

And now? Now she wanted to see where it went. He was too young for her, that was true, but he made her feel happy. For right now, that was enough.

Elle grabbed her purse and headed for the front door. Graeme had given her directions to his house. She was nervous, but she was excited too. Granted, it was at his house, but there was something very sexy about a man who wanted to cook for her. Other than her father, she didn't know of any man who had done so.

With her hand on the knob, she hesitated. She planned on having dinner with two gentlemen, doing a little work, then coming home. But there was a part of her who felt she should be prepared to take a chance. She turned around and headed to the bathroom. She wouldn't go all out, but Elle had never been that spontaneous. Grabbing her toothbrush, she snapped on the travel head, and slipped it into her purse.

Happy with her decision, Elle headed to the door, stopping by her kitchen to grab the guava wine she had in the fridge. Within minutes, she was on Kam Highway heading to Laie.

As she drove through Haleiwa, she took comfort from the little shops and the waves she received from some of her neighbors. She had always loved this drive, loved her little town. After living in London for so many years, she had worried living out on this side of the island would be boring. Instead, she found solace in the slower pace. It reminded her of her upbringing in Oxford. The cute little shops and the more local feel had been just the ticket for her.

She passed Sunset Beach, and smiled when she saw a boy and his father walking down with fishing poles. She wanted to take her father fishing when he came. They had often sat in a little rowboat for hours, fishing quietly. It was one of her most treasured memories from her childhood, and she wanted recreate it in Hawaii with her father.

Elle came to a stop at a light and realized she was making plans. Real plans. First, for tonight, and then with her father when her parents visited. In the last seven years, she hadn't been making personal plans. She had focused on work and healing, but now...she wanted to think about the future.

Someone beeped behind her. She smiled and hit the gas. Yes. She wanted to have future plans, and right now they included a dashing Scotsman and his adorable dog.

Graeme had the potatoes on the grill, and he had cleaned up the house before he started on the Mahi Mahi he'd picked up. He knew how to cook and how to cook well. It was a survival mechanism. While his father was a fantastic cook, his mother had burned more dinners than he wanted to remember. None of his sisters really could cook, and if they had any talent, they hated the process. Graeme loved it.

His dad was well known for being innovative in his pub, and Graeme had learned a lot. He knew how to cook just about everything Scottish, but his father's love for experimentation was alive and well in Graeme. Granted, he hadn't done a lot of it in the last year or so, but it wasn't like he had anyone to impress before now.

He pulled out some seasonings and started to sprinkle them on the fish. Yes, he was trying to impress her. Granted, he knew Elle thought he would get over it, just move on at some point, but he knew better. She had kissed him the other day. It was the first time she had initiated affection, and it had not stopped since then. More than once, he had felt the brush of her hand against his back, and she had held his hand when they went shopping for food the other day. It wasn't much, but it was something. He knew they had turned the corner, even if she did not.

Dumfries drew his attention by whining and wagging his tail.

"No way. You are not getting this. It's for Elle."

When he said her name, Dumfries whined again. His dog seemed to have the same feelings for Elle that he did. Whenever Graeme said her name, Dumfries reacted. Worse, he seemed genuinely irritated when Graeme had arrived home without her.

"She should be here soon."

That did not make Dumfries any happier, so Graeme grabbed a treat and tossed it to him. As usual, his dog caught it in his massive mouth and wandered back to the living room to enjoy it.

Graeme glanced at the clock. He hoped Elle hadn't gotten stuck anywhere. H-2 was easy enough to navigate on a Tuesday afternoon, but if there was any kind of significant accident on Kam Highway, it could shut the two-lane road down in both directions.

He heard the sound of a car, and then a door shutting. His heart did a little dance—odd that. Graeme knew he was somewhat intrigued by Elle—okay, a lot intrigued. But, he hadn't reacted toward a woman like this since he had been a bumbling fool in his teenage years.

There was a soft knock on the door, and he waited just a second, wiping off his hands. He didn't want her to think he'd been waiting by the door. Drawing in a deep breath, he opened the door and lost all thought.

She had donned a purple dress, one that brought deepened the green in her eyes. She was...stunning.

"Hi," she said, offering him a smile. She had a bottle of wine in her hand. "I hope this will work for tonight. I had it in my fridge, and you had said something about fish for dinner. Of course, if you would rather not, we can just stick it in the fridge."

He blinked. She was babbling. Elle never babbled. She was precise in every word she used, even in social settings. Then it hit him. She was nervous, maybe just as nervous as he was.

Something loosened in his chest. It was nice to know he wasn't the only one on edge tonight.

"It will be perfect," he said, as he took the bottle from her right hand before Dumfries nudged him out of the way. "Well, that was rude, you mongrel."

Dumfries paid no attention to him. Instead, he sat down in front of Elle and offered her a paw, the wanker.

"Oh, aren't you handsome," she cooed as she shook

his paw, then petted him.

"Come on, Dumfries, let our date in the door."

The dog threw him a nasty look, but Dumfries did as ordered. Elle laughed, a light, bubbly kind of laugh that made his heart sing. He said nothing as he waited for her to step into his house.

He followed her into the living room, which was just off the side of the kitchen. It was a bigger house than hers, as he was sure he would have all sorts of relatives and military friends showing up. Plus, with a dog like Dumfries, he didn't have much of a choice. A small house would be destroyed by his dog.

"Oh, this is lovely."

The admiration he heard in her voice allowed him to release a breath he didn't realize he'd been holding. It was the first time she had been to his house, and he wanted to impress her.

"Are these your sisters?" she asked, as she looked at the photo gallery that filled his walls.

He nodded. "The one on the table is of my parents."

He set the wine down and grabbed the corkscrew to open it.

"Good lord, you are a very good looking family. Your parents must have had their hands full."

He chuckled as he watched her. "They definitely did with my sisters, but I was a saint."

She gave him a speaking glance before she moved on to the pictures from his time in the Marines.

"What? I *was* a saint. There's a reason I am my mother's favorite."

She shook her head. "First, that just tells me you're what Charity calls a mama's boy."

"That's rude."

She shrugged. "Probably the truth. But, I was talking about five children. It's hard for me to think of such a large family."

He poured the wine into the glasses and joined her in

the living room. "It was always just the three of you?"

"Thank you," she said taking the glass. "And yes. My family has always been just the three of us. I was born after years of trying and a few miscarriages, so my parents counted themselves lucky when I came along."

"I can understand that feeling."

She looked at him and sighed. "Don't make more of this than it is."

"What is it?"

"I'm not really sure. I don't know where we're going."

"I don't either."

"Our ages—"

"Don't matter."

She shook her head. "Just know that I am attracted to you, but I am not sure I'm built for relationships. Not anymore."

"And know that after growing up in a house with five women, I have the patience of a saint—as I pointed out before."

She laughed. "Okay."

"Why don't you go out onto the lanai? I need to grab the fish and the asparagus."

"Oh, you're grilling the whole dinner? That sounds scrumptious."

When she turned to leave, he found himself watching the sway of her hips and listening to the way she cooed to his dog. It was almost too homey, but it felt right. This woman, this night.

He had to pull himself out of his stupor and went about his tasks. He had a lady to impress with his culinary skills.

A couple hours later, Elle's stomach was still full from the smashing dinner and enjoying the evening. Sure, they were spending it looking over all the leads both Graeme and Marcus had dug up, but it was still enjoyable. There wasn't a beach, but she enjoyed being close to the water. She could hear it lapping against the rocks.

"Earth to Dr. Middleton," he said.

She glanced at him with a smile. "I just love that sound. Water is so soothing."

He didn't say anything, but he kept staring at her. The moment stretched out, and she felt a tickle at the back of her throat.

"What?"

"Nothing, you just seem very happy."

"Why does everyone say that like they are surprised?"

He shrugged. "You would smile sometimes, and it wouldn't reach your eyes."

She thought about it. Had she been like that? After dealing with her ex this afternoon, she felt as if a heavy burden had been lifted. She had finally said what she wanted, and she felt as if that part of her life was over.

"Good to know." She glanced out at the setting sun. "How do you not sit out here and just stare all day long?"

He chuckled. "It was hard not to after I found the house. But, then I realized I had to pay rent."

She smiled. Streaks of red and orange still filled the sky, but it would not be long before it was dark. Hawaii didn't change its clocks; and as it was, it would be well after eight, and she had an early morning.

"So, you have a list of people to look through," she said.

He nodded.

"I guess I should be on my way."

The moment she said it, Dumfries was on his feet and waiting as if he were going with her. She laughed and made her way into the house.

"Elle?"

She turned around to face Graeme. The fading sun was behind him, highlighting the golden hues of his hair. Arousal darkened his eyes. Just seeing that stirred to life her own desires.

He took her hand and pulled her slowly to him. The closer she got to him, the more her heart sped up. When he finally had her in his arms, he nuzzled her neck. For a man who seemed to be very sensual, he took his time about getting to it.

"You always smell like roses, Eleanora."

His accent had thickened, as he dragged his tongue over her pulse point. Every time he did that, her knees went weak. He tugged on her earlobe, pulling it between his teeth and sliding his tongue over it. The man was deadly with that tongue. The one thought brought to mind all kinds of naughty things. Things she wanted to do, or have done to her.

He pulled back and looked at her. It was the most serious expression she had ever seen on his face. He dropped his hands.

"All you have to say is no. I'll step away."

She looked at him then, this big, brawny warrior, and she knew that he would. No question about it. It was her choice. Always.

"I want to stay."

For a second he said nothing. The moment stretched, and Elle worried that he might be having second thoughts. Suddenly, he groaned. The sound so primal it lit through her blood and sent her head spinning. He took two huge steps to her, grabbed her by the waist, and yanked her against him. He kissed her, but it was different than before. This wasn't seductive or teasing. Raw need pulsed through her as Graeme plunged his tongue deep within her mouth. She could do nothing but surrender.

With little effort, he lifted her into his arms, then walked to the back of the house to his bedroom. He dropped her on the bed from such a height that she bounced. A laugh of sheer delight rose up from her throat, and he stopped to stare at her.

"Aw, lass, you do know how to make a man melt."

She stopped laughing as she watched him pull off his shirt, then unbutton and unzip his pants. Bloody hell, he was a bloody Scottish god. Muscles rippled beneath golden brown flesh.

Her gaze moved down his body. He was still wearing a pair of knit boxers, unfortunately. His erection was hard to miss. His cock twitched as she studied him. Graeme chuckled. She looked up at him.

"It has a mind of its own when it comes to you."

She smiled and scooted to the end of the bed so she sat with her feet on the floor. Without hesitation, she reached forward and pressed her hand against him. He groaned and she smiled.

"Sure, get enjoyment out of my pain."

Feeling a little bold, she said, "I promise to help with that."

His eyebrows rose in surprise. What did he think she was, a prude?

"You're in charge, love."

For a second, she didn't understand. Then, when she saw the glint in his eyes, she did. He was letting her take control of the situation. She stood and turned around.

"Could you unzip me?"

Again, he hesitated. Now she realized he was just as nervous as she was, and it made her fall for him even more. In the next second, she felt a slowly released breath against the nape of her neck. He eased the zipper down. She let the dress fall to the floor. He bent his head and touched his lips to her shoulder. As he moved his mouth up to her neck, he trailed his fingers down her spine, then back up to her bra. As he continued to tease her, he unhooked her bra. This time, she hesitated for a second. It was the first time a man would see her naked since the attack.

And just like that, memories of that dark night years before came rushing back to her. She closed her eyes as if that would help but, of course, it didn't. The terror, the pain, everything rushed through her, dampening the arousal Graeme had inspired.

He paused and pulled back just a few inches.

"You have the control, Elle. Just say stop and I will. No matter what."

She couldn't see his face, as he was standing behind her, but she could hear the infinite pledge in those words. He would do what he said, because Graeme always did. Warmth filled her and...trust. Love might be what the poets write about, but for her, trust was much more important. And she knew with Graeme, it was there.

She let the bra drop to the ground. He turned her around slowly, then slipped a finger beneath her chin to force her gaze up.

"Know this, Elle. When I say you are in control, you are. Stop is the only word I need to know that we have gone too far for you. Doona ever hesitate to say it. I want you, more than you'll ever know, but I don't want you to give up your peace."

Tears welled in her eyes. "Graeme."

"What, love?"

Elle couldn't bring herself to say it. Truthfully, she didn't know what to say to him at that point. Instead, she cupped his face and kissed him, trying her best to pour all of her emotions into the kiss. He groaned and wrapped his arms around her waist, pressing against her. The scent of him filled her senses. He always smelled of musk...but not a cologne. It was unique to him, and it always called to her. His warmth surrounded her, as his arms urged her closer. She could feel his erection against her belly. It sent little sparks of heat dancing through her blood and along her nerve endings.

He ripped his mouth away, then gently laid her down on the bed. In one quick move, he slipped her panties off. For a moment, he stood staring down at her, mumbling something that sounded like Scottish Celt. Then, he joined her on the bed, first kissing her mouth, then working his way down her body. His tongue and hands worked magic over her body, teasing her, tempting her.

A graze of teeth over her nipple. His fingers dancing over her belly button. When he settled in between her legs, he smiled up at her.

"You even smell like roses down here, love." His voice was thick with emotion and darkened with arousal.

He set his mouth on her sex. She was already wet, so wet she even surprised herself. If she had thought he was good before, she had been wrong. He was a bloody genius with his tongue. He slipped it between her folds, then up and over her clit. Again and again, that same motion brought her closer to completion, but not close enough. When he slipped a finger inside of her, then pulled her clit between his teeth, she lost it. A rush of heat burst through her as she bowed up off the bed. She screamed his name, as she molded her hands to the back of his head pressing herself against his face.

Just as she felt herself falling down, he added another finger, and continued on.

"Come for me again, love. I want to see you."

She could do nothing but obey his plea. Before she could stop it, another orgasm slammed through her. She screamed from the force of it, as blissful gratification washed over her.

This time, he pulled away, tugged off his boxers. She opened her eyes, as she watched him stand back up. His erection curved up against his stomach, and she licked her lips.

"Oh, love, you do know how to please a man."

He joined her back on the bed then, bending down to kiss her. She could taste herself on his lips.

He slipped an arm beneath her, then rolled them over so she was on top of him. She found herself straddling him.

"As I said, love. You're in charge." He grabbed a condom out of his bedside table and handed it to her.

Even in this, it was up to her. She undid the wrapper, then scooted down so that she could roll the condom on his erection. She did so slowly, savoring the groans from Graeme.

"Bleeding hell. I have unleashed a she-devil."

She laughed with the power of it, then straddled him once more. Again, she took her time as she sank down on his cock. Inch by inch, she took him inside of her, and that connection she had…grew. It wasn't just physical, but also emotional.

God, he was huge, and he filled her to bursting. When she finally had him inside her to the hilt, she rose up and started to ride him. Amazingly, she felt her arousal start to build again.

He rose up, and she thought he would roll them over again; instead, he pulled her close, still allowing her to set the pace, as he took one of her nipples into his mouth.

"Oh, yes, love, that's it." His teeth grazed over the tip, then he pulled her deeper into his mouth. Need blazed through her once again, lighting another orgasm, but it shimmered just out of her reach. Then, as she felt him surrender to his orgasm, she gained her release. As she convulsed against him, they fell over the edge into pleasure together.

HOSTILE DESIRES

CHAPTER SIXTEEN

Graeme lay in bed, Elle on top of him. At that moment, he decided he might just be the luckiest man alive. Scratch that. He *was* the fucking luckiest man alive. She had chosen him, and that meant she trusted him. That was more than he expected at this point.

He trailed his fingers over her shoulder.

"When did you get the tattoo?" he asked.

He had seen it earlier, but did not mention it. She'd had Scottish Gaelic tattooed on her shoulder, *neach-tàrrsainn*, meaning 'one who survives'.

"It was about a year after...well, after. I spent most of that year hidden away in Oxford and in Inverness."

"With your grandmother."

"Yes. It allowed me to spend time working on myself and not dealing with the rags in London. They couldn't find me, so they left me alone. I had time heal."

He kept running his fingers over her flesh as he waited. He knew this was a lot for her to share, a part of her soul she kept hidden. If he pushed she might retreat.

"My grannie was the one who said I should get it. I came up with the idea, and she pushed for it. She found the artist to handle it, and took me when I was ready."

"I can't think your folks were too happy with that."

She chuckled, and he could feel the delightful little tug against his cock. He was still inside of her and he liked it this way.

"My father still doesn't know. Mum likes to say my father was born middle-aged, so she decided not to tell him. But Mum, she's somewhat more liberal about things like that."

"She definitely sounded nice on the phone."

"She is, as is my father, but he's just a little set in his ways. Of course, when he comes to visit, he will see it if we are at the beach."

He liked hearing her talk about them. There was a warmth in her voice he didn't hear that often. Graeme thought it boded well for their relationship. He was very close to his family, even with all the miles between them.

He stopped moving his hand when he realized what he had just thought. Granted, he knew with her history, Elle didn't jump into bed with him on a whim, but he hadn't registered his intentions until now.

She sat up and looked down at him. The light from the living room poured in through the doorway behind her. She looked like...an angel. Right then and there, he wasn't exactly sure what was going to happen to this relationship. But the one thing he did know was that he'd fallen in love with her.

"Graeme, are you okay?"

He nodded, as his world shifted around him, then settled in a new order. It wasn't the same, but it definitely felt right. She was beautiful, but she was strong and sweet, and just the kind of woman he always thought he would marry.

"You look weird."

He chuckled. "You look like a goddess."

She rolled her eyes and turned away, but he caught her hand.

"Why do you do that?" he asked.

"What?"

"You don't take my compliments seriously. You *are* beautiful."

She sighed. "I'm just not accustomed to men saying that to me."

"Please tell me that idiot of an ex-husband wasn't *that* stupid?"

She shrugged. "He wasn't good at expressing his affection." She shook her head. "I can't believe I just gave him an excuse. My ex was a wanker, who didn't understand me at all."

He smiled. "There's the Eleanora I know."

She slipped out of bed, and he hated losing the ability to touch her—but he let her go. He didn't feel at all guilty for enjoying the view of her cute little arse as she walked into the bathroom.

Graeme pulled off the condom and threw it in the wastebasket. When he looked around for Dumfries, he saw his dog had decided to finally give them some kind of privacy. She'd shut the bathroom door, and he heard the toilet flush.

When she opened the door, she smiled at him. "You don't need to worry about pretty words. I'm not a woman who expects flattery."

"It's not flattery. It's the way I see you."

Her eyes softened, and her cheeks pinkened. Graeme promised himself to say things like that every day for the rest of their lives.

When it hit him what he had just thought, he waited for the panic. It didn't come. Instead, he felt...centered. Right. She climbed up on the bed beside him.

She leaned down and kissed him on the mouth, then moved lower. With precise moves, she skimmed her mouth over his flesh, nipping here and there, and driving him downright mental. When she reached his nipple, she twirled her tongue over it, before moving further down.

She settled between his legs, circling her fingers around his cock.

Fuck.

Elle paused. "Did you say something?"

"No," he said, but it came out as a growl. Her mouth curved.

She leaned down and licked the head...once, twice...then she took him fully into her mouth. Taking her time, she teased him, her tongue wrapping around his shaft, as she slipped her hand down to his sac. He clawed at the sheet trying to keep his control, not wanting to come just yet, but Elle was unrelenting. Over and over she took him into her mouth, until he couldn't hold back any longer.

He slipped his hands to her hair with the intent of pulling her up, but he found himself moving with her, heat curling low in his stomach. When he thought he couldn't take it any more, she gave him one long last lick, then released him. He opened his eyes. She sat there, looking so damned happy that he couldn't be mad. Frustrated, yes, but he couldn't hold a grudge against her for teasing him. Power radiated off her in waves, and it was one of the sexiest things he had ever seen. She reached over, grabbed another condom. After slipping it on him, she straddled him once again and started to ride him.

As she twisted her hips, he groaned. He watched as she threw her head back and moaned. Damned, the woman was so un-fucking-believably sensual. Then, she leaned forward, placing a hand on each side of his head and looked down at him. Over and over, she rolled her hips, not breaking eye contact.

"Come for me, Graeme," she said, her voice husky with her own arousal.

She took his bottom lip between her teeth. She released it, then increased her speed. In the next moment, her inner muscles rippled over his cock as her release hit her.

"Come with me, Graeme, now," she pleaded. He could do nothing but fulfill her request. He thrust up into her and let go.

His orgasm was a rush of heat, then pure bliss washing over him. Moments later, she collapsed on him.

The next morning, Elle walked into the office and found Graeme waiting for her again. He was dressed in a dark gray TFH shirt, which he tucked into a pair of form-fitting jeans. God, she wanted to slip her hand beneath the waistband of his jeans and tease him.

She released a slow breath and ordered her hormones to calm down. She was almost forty years old, for goodness sake. He approached her, unhurried, with his hand on the holster of his gun.

Oh, my.

"Good morning, Eleanora."

"You know," she said, just loud enough for him to hear, "you'll have the entire office betting on us if you aren't careful."

"I hate to tell you, but they're already wagering on us, love," he said.

She shook her head, even though she knew he was right. More than likely, there had been a bet on them for several months.

"What are you going to do today?" she asked.

"I'm running down a few of those CIs that we came up with last night. Checking to see who's still alive, who's still in the system."

"Have fun with that. I have to go over my notes for the Sanders' case next week. I want to make sure I'm ready."

"Lunch then?"

"If you're lucky," she said with a smile, as she walked

toward the lift.

She was still smiling when she stepped onto the lift and hit the button. There was something to be said about younger men. She could not remember smiling this much as an adult.

The doors slid open and Drew was standing there waiting on her. He was wearing one of his Doctor Who Weeping Angels shirts today, along with a pair of khaki cargo pants. She knew a lot of people would object to Drew's choice in work clothes, but she couldn't. First, he was one of the best assistants she had ever had. Second, Drew might not be wearing a suit, but he was always neat. Besides, they lived in Hawaii. Wearing a suit wasn't normal. You could always pick a *haole* by what he wore.

"Good morning, Doc. How are you feeling today?" he asked.

"Pretty good. How about you?"

"Counting down the days to the wedding."

She smiled and walked over to her desk. "I didn't see that they needed us for anything up at TFH, and we're now way down on the list for the HPD, so I thought you could help me prepare for the Sanders' case."

"Great idea. Don't want to be caught off guard."

He went to the filing cabinet and started pulling out folders. He was tapping his foot to some internal song that only he heard. She had never met anyone who was always in such a good mood. Drew was usually early to work, beating her to the office more than once, and he always wanted to help her. Her one worry was that Cat would hurt him. Not on purpose, because Cat wasn't that kind of person. But she knew better than most how an affair at work could blow up in your face.

The moment the words sunk in, she realized what she had been thinking. Here she was worried about Drew, and she was the one in the affair with someone at work.

"Doc?"

She shook herself and looked at Drew.

"Are you okay? You look a little off."

She sighed. "I just realized that sometimes we make mistakes, and there is just no way to avoid them."

He nodded. "Are you talking about you and McGregor?"

She rolled her eyes. "Is it that obvious?"

Drew shrugged. "It is to me."

"Oh lord."

"Don't worry about it. You know, you have always been nice and funny. But I don't think I've seen you truly happy until these last few weeks."

She sighed. "I don't want my happiness to depend on a man."

"Why not? And why is it that he is the only reason? My mother always says that people's love isn't based on any known scientific data. Not really. You can't predict it, right?

She nodded, fascinated by his enthusiasm.

"Sure, they can talk about the chemicals your body produces, but that initial attraction is individual. Every person has a personal experience with love and attraction. Plus, Mom says that you should never measure love by how much you need someone. It isn't always about what you need, but what each relationship builds."

She blinked. "Your mother is a wise woman."

"Yeah, she is. Dad always says she's the brains of the business."

"And he's the creative one?"

He nodded. "See, again, they built something together. Just like I want to do with Cat."

Again, apprehension hit her. Drew had been infatuated by the tough officer since they had been introduced about a year ago. Everyone knew about it, and while she knew Cat was intrigued, Elle wasn't convinced Cat understood how much Drew cared about her.

"Drew, be careful with Cat."

He laid the file on her desk. "I won't hurt her. My

mother raised me better."

"I was talking about Cat hurting you."

Drew patted her on the arm, as if to reassure her, which was odd. Elle was usually the one who was doing the reassuring.

"Cat seems all tough, and she is, but there's a soft heart beneath that armor," he said. "I plan on being the one she trusts to show it to."

She stared at him a long time. Everyone thought of him as innocent, but she knew he wasn't. Well, not *an* innocent, but everyone thought he was naïve. Then, there were times like this that he would make a comment that was so bloody insightful, he stunned her.

"You really understand her."

He gave her a wink. "I told you, my mom raised me right."

"Right. Okay, let's get to work."

"You have a lunch date with McGregor?"

She rolled her eyes. "Who texted?"

"Cat and Floyd."

"This is just getting out of hand. You know, one of these days, the HPD is going to get onto this, we're all going to get arrested for illegal betting."

Drew shook his head and said nothing, but she knew that if they figured out what had happened the night before, someone won a big pot.

"You shouldn't really care," Drew said.

"Why is that?"

"McGregor is definitely smitten with you."

"I'm not the kind of woman men get smitten over, Drew."

Drew frowned. "Why would you say that?"

She shrugged. "I was a nerd in school, and much too serious. Getting straight A's was more important than getting a date."

"I don't think you realize how amazing you are."

She could feel her cheeks heating. "Drew, I think we

need to concentrate on work."

"No, Doc. You need to know. You know I think of you as my mentor?" She nodded.

"I had a lot of trouble concentrating on work when I first got hired. I think it was your accent, which is sexy enough to hear for folks on the mainland, but even more exotic here. You are quite the catch, Doc."

"That is so sweet, Drew."

He smiled. "Thank you."

She leaned closer. "And just so you know, if Cat hurts you, I will make her cry."

He was still smiling, then it faded. "You are kind of scary."

"You don't know the half of it."

Adam parked his motorcycle on the street in Aiea and sat there. He'd been making this weekly visit to Jin's for the last few months, mostly checking up on her, and partly for himself.

From the moment she had been abducted by the serial killing duo known as The Akua Killers, Adam had blamed himself. His own personal relationship with her had always been strained. He'd been infatuated with her from the start, and she had been using him to get information. So he had avoided her, and she had almost died because of it. He should have known she would go too far. She was always pushing for the best story, looking to make a name for herself. And then, she had been given the story of a lifetime: inside information on a serial killer that was terrorizing Honolulu.

Those two bastards had known just how to play her. They pulled her in, giving her access to details no one else had. Jin was a good news reporter, but she was still a little green. Because of that, she had almost paid with her life, and she had definitely lost a piece of her soul.

With a sigh, he stepped off his motorcycle, then walked up the path to her house. She'd never been a gardener, but she had kept it somewhat clean before. Now weeds littered the lawn, and it was at least three weeks overdue for a mow. Hell, there was trash lying there. The Jin he had known before her abduction would have never allowed that.

Ignoring the mess of her yard, he took the steps up to her front lanai. He didn't know why he did this, but he couldn't seem to help himself. It wasn't that she really talked to him, and since she had left the hospital, she had only allowed him in her house twice. The second time, she had said it was too much. But, he still couldn't stop trying.

He rang the doorbell and waited. The door opened slightly.

He could see her, barely, but it still wasn't good. She had lost a lot of weight, and she rarely wore anything but pajamas. She seemed to be getting worse by the day.

"What do you want, Adam?" she asked. He hated the flat tone. He wanted the bubbly vivacious woman back.

"I wanted to see if you were doing okay."

"I'm fine."

The two words from a woman he knew meant the polar opposite.

"Did you need me to bring you anything by?"

She shook her head, and started to close the door.

"Jin, do you think you could let me in?"

She stared at him without blinking, then she seemed to wake up from a trance.

"No. Not today."

The sound of her voice, the tremble told him she still could barely handle talking to him. Frustration filled him, but he kept his voice steady.

"Okay. You still have my number?"

She nodded, not making eye contact.

"Text me once every few days, just for my peace of

mind, okay?"

She hesitated, then nodded and shut the door. He heard her lock the door. Four locks. The woman now lived in a fortress away from the world.

He waited, just for a second, wondering if he should demand more interaction, but he knew that was the wrong reaction. He turned and walked away, and realized he had fisted his hands. It was a damned shame one of the bastards had fallen off the balcony, and the other was in a mental institution. Adam really wanted to make both men hurt. Her attackers deserved to suffer for what they had done to Jin. It was hard to see the woman, who had enchanted him so easily, hollowed out. Six months since the bastards had assaulted her, and Adam still couldn't get to her.

As he reached his motorcycle, Adam decided he'd have to talk to Elle about it. He knew her history, so she might be able to give him some kind of insight. He needed to do something or he might lose Jin.

Jin peeked out her curtains and watched Adam as he drove away. It was hard on her, harder than he would ever know, to have these conversations. She stayed there, hidden by most of the material, until Adam's taillights disappeared around the corner.

With a sigh, she walked away from the window. Most people wouldn't categorize the interactions she had with Adam as conversations, but these days, it was what she could handle. Other than talking with her group or Elle, she rarely interacted with anyone. It was just easier that way.

But she lived for these days. Adam had been dropping by once or twice a week for months now. Twice, she had let him in the house. It had taken all of her courage to allow him beyond the threshold. It had been too much.

Her head started to pound. These days, any kind of stress caused migraines, which led to sleepless nights, but at least then she wouldn't have nightmares.

CHAPTER SEVENTEEN

The next day, Graeme looked over the list of confidential informants, and he wanted to groan. Forty names. He had spent all of yesterday on it, and he felt as if he had made no headway. This was going to take forever.

"I see that face, but you should be happy Adam worked the list down some," Del said.

Graeme scowled, looking up from his desk. Standing in the doorway, Del smiled at him.

"Quit being so bloody pleasant."

His smile widened into a grin. "Sorry. Can't stop it. Getting married in a few days, and I have a baby coming in less than a year. Plus, my mother is making red sauce with meatballs tonight. All is right with the world."

Del's mother had arrived the day before and apparently hit the ground running. She'd been cooking Italian dishes and babying Emma.

"Damn, you know how to make a man want to punch you."

His boss chuckled, and walked into the room to take a seat in front of Graeme's desk.

"So, how many names are you at?"

He handed over the list. "I have forty to run down. The easiest part is running them through the computer. I am assuming some of them are dead."

"Don't sound so chipper about wanting people to be dead. The mayor frowns upon it."

Graeme shrugged. "Then he should deal with this bloody mess."

"Always sunshine and rainbows, McGregor. That's what I like about you. That positive outlook is a shining example of what Marines can do."

Del paused, as if weighing what he would say next. "Is everything going all right with you?" he asked.

Graeme studied his boss. It was an odd turn in their discussion. Del wasn't the typical boss, but he rarely "checked" on McGregor.

"I'm fine."

He sighed. "Okay, I tried to be subtle. Are you having any issues? Remember, I know about your time in Iraq, read the reports. You lost a lot of your squad."

He leaned back in his chair and realized that he never really talked about it with Del. Of everyone on the team, they were the only two who had seen combat in recent years. Both of them had worked Special Forces and had seen some of the worst of humanity, so Del understood. No matter how far you were from battle, you always carried the scars.

"I'm fine. I still have dreams every now and then, but that's why I took a year off in Edinburgh with my family. I took each day as it came. Plus, there's Dumfries; he's really helped out."

"Good. I just wanted to check in."

Graeme studied him again and realized they shared

something in common. "You've lost someone?"

Del nodded. "Hard ass sergeant who couldn't deal with it when he came home. Started drinking, his wife left him."

Del didn't have to finish the story. Graeme knew exactly how it ended. Unfortunately, there were too many of them who understood too well what it was like to lose someone to suicide.

"I've had some scary moments, but I never wanted to go that route. Part of it is the thought of my mother. She would follow me into the afterlife and box my ears."

Del smiled. "Yeah. I have a feeling it would be the same for me. Sounds like you like strong women."

He nodded. "In my house, there was no doubt about it. Strong women ruled."

"I'm assuming that's why you like Elle."

He shrugged, as he started tapping on the keyboard. "More like love."

There was a beat of silence. He hadn't even realized he was going to say that, and especially not to his boss. If there was anyone who should know first, it should be Elle.

"Want to repeat that?" Del asked.

Graeme looked at Del. He should hold back, wait until Elle was ready to accept it, but he couldn't. He was just too bleeding happy, he had to tell someone. "I love her. Kind of hard to hide the fact. I would never get involved with a woman at work if I wasn't serious."

"Love her? As in marry and have babies and all that kind of thing?"

It was an odd reaction from a man who was doing just that. "Not sure about all that other stuff, but yes, spend the rest of my life kind of thing."

Del shook his head. "If that don't beat all."

He shook his head. "You Americans and your weird sayings."

"Really? You're being judgy? You eat haggis."

"My father makes the best in Edinburgh. I can't wait to get back there this summer and have some myself."

Del turned gray and made a face. "Please, my stomach's still off."

He chuckled. "Leave me to work. I want to get this done, so I can hunt a few of these wankers down."

"Sure thing."

"Oh, about that trip, I want to take a couple weeks off this summer if that's okay. I want to make the trip back to Scotland, see the family."

"Just give me the dates and we can work around it," Del said before walking out of the office.

Now that he thought about it, he would have to convince Elle she needed to go with them. She could meet his family, then she could take him to Inverness so he could meet her Granny. It was too fast, he knew that, but he didn't give a bloody hell. Right now, he just wanted to enjoy the feeling and the woman who inspired it.

Late that afternoon, Elle was ready to call it a day when the office phone rang. It was a local number and, while she didn't recognize the number, she decided to take one last call before she closed up.

"Hello, am I speaking to Dr. Elle Middleton?" a female voice on the other end of the line asked.

"This is she. Who are you?"

"My name is Amanda Anderson from Hawaii Now Blog, and I wanted to ask you about a case."

She sighed. It was part of the job, she understood that, but she did not like talking about cases. It was one of the things she loved about TFH. Del had a strict no press policy. She shut down her computer before she answered.

"Dr. Middleton?"

"I'm sorry, but I cannot comment on an open investigation."

"This one is closed. In fact, you helped close it seven

years ago. I assume you are able to talk about closed cases, correct?"

Something tickled at the back of her throat, as dread slipped over her. Dammit, what the hell was going on?

"Seven years ago?"

"Yes." Elle could hear the woman clicking on keys. "You worked with a Gerald Walton, is that correct?"

Her shocks dissolved as her anger started to rise. She would kill him. Better yet, she would tell her father, and he would kill him. Knowing her father, it would involve some kind of painfully slow-acting poison.

"I don't understand why you would call me about an old case like that. The perpetrator was caught and convicted. He's still in prison for murder."

More keys tapping. Elle wondered if she was really looking for information on the case or logging into a social media site.

"I understand that you were one of his victims," she asked. "James Farrington was convicted of your rape and the deaths of five women."

Just hearing his name had her blood icing over. She never spoke his name. She had not since the trial. Some people would call it cowardly. She called it survival.

"No comment."

"Is it true you deliberately put yourself into harm's way?"

"No comment."

"My source tells me you have a habit of doing this and causing problems with cases."

"Your source? Let me guess. He's a police officer from England, and he gave you all the juicy information."

"I can't reveal my sources."

"I have no comment on any of it. If you want to talk to me about it again, I can give you the number to my attorney."

She slammed the office phone down. Damn Gerald. She would call him and yell, but it would do no good. In fact, that was exactly what he wanted. She would not give him the satisfaction. In fact, it would be better if she used the lawyer line on him from now on. They had nothing together. No children, no property, and no connection whatsoever. This was just his way of trying to goad her into calling so he could plead his case again. It was not going to work because she would not allow it. He was the most passive-aggressive person she knew. After she had met his family, she understood it. His mother was the same way.

She closed her eyes and drew in a deep breath, using the relaxation methods her therapist had taught her all those years ago. When she opened her eyes, she realized there was one person she wanted to talk to.

Graeme.

She grabbed her purse and headed out to find him. Punching the button, she tapped her foot while she waited. If someone was on the trail of her former debacle, then it was going to hit the papers. She needed to warn Del. He knew about it because he'd had her investigated before hiring her. It hadn't bothered her then. She had expected it. Now though, everyone she worked with, everyone she knew, would find out.

A couple minutes later, Elle was still agitated when she stepped off the elevator. She knew she shouldn't be so mad at the reporter, but she didn't need to be reminded of her past. She *lived* with it. She dealt with it. It had diddly to do with her career. What she didn't want to do was lose the respect and trust of those she worked with. She had a feeling this was part of Gerald's push to get her back to England to help.

Her heart sank a little when she saw that Graeme wasn't in his office. The only one in at the moment was Adam.

"Did you need something?" he asked.

"I was looking for Graeme."

"He's on his way back. He was following up a lead.

But, since you're here, I need to talk to you about something."

"Sure."

She followed him into his office and sat down. He closed the door.

He didn't say anything until he sat behind his desk.

"I wanted to talk to you about Jin."

She blinked. "Jin?"

"Yeah. I've been by to see her a few times in the last six months, and she doesn't seem to be getting any better. I just went by yesterday, and she would barely open the door."

"Any better? Than what?"

He sighed and leaned back his chair. "I thought by now she would be moving on, or at least making progress."

"So, you have a timetable?"

"It's not that. I just wanted to know what to do to help."

"And why ask me?"

"I know your past. As second in command, it's part of the job. Plus, I know you've been counseling her."

"I cannot comment on that." That much was true. Jin had specifically said she did not want Adam to know anything, but Elle didn't even want to mention that.

Frustration stamped his facial features. "I just want to help."

"You can't."

"There *has* to be something I can do. I thought by now she would be ready to move on."

The anger she had been trying suppress came boiling to the top.

"Move on?"

"Yes. I know it's a process, so I figured in six months, she would at least be able to deal with seeing me, or talking to me."

She heard the glimmer of confused male in his voice. Any other day, she would probably give him the benefit of the doubt, but today, her anger overrode any empathy she would normally have.

"So, you think there is some kind of fucking timeline that she should be on to recover from what was done to her?"

For the first moment, she saw he realized he might have made a mistake. His eyes widened, either from hearing the anger in her voice, or her use of a vulgar word. It wasn't that she was a prude, but she didn't cuss a lot.

"It's not that."

She jumped to her feet; pain stabbed at her as rage poured through her. She couldn't stay still with so many different emotions bouncing around inside of her.

"After what she went through, the degradation, the loss of any kind of control, you think that by the six-month mark, she should be ready to bop on out for mani/pedis and be a regular girl, is that it?"

He opened his mouth, but she just ignored it. She couldn't seem to stop.

"You have *no* idea what that is like. You have *no* idea how the whole entire world knows your business, knows exactly what happened to you. You have *no* idea that the one thing you need is compassion, and you can't ask for it. Not physically. It hurts somewhere deep inside, and there is not one fucking bloody thing you can do to ease it. You need a gentle touch, but even the thought of someone touching you makes you want to vomit. What's worse is that people blame *you*."

She wiped away the tears that were now pouring from her eyes.

"They say you shouldn't have dressed a certain way. You shouldn't have been in *that* part of town. Or maybe, women are just not good on the job, and that somehow this proves it. And the people you need, the ones you thought would always be there for you, turn away from you. Blame, disgust...it doesn't matter. It is *your* fault because you can't get over what was done to you. Well,

I'm sorry, Adam. There is no timetable. The rest of her life, she will remember. She will remember what it felt like to be violated in a way that will never heal. Not completely. And until you understand that, you will *never* be able to help."

With that, she turned to walk out of his office. Before she could open the door though, she realized they had an audience. There, standing at the conference table were Drew, Charity, and Cat. The door had been closed, but she knew she had been shouting, and they had heard. Worse, she was a blubbery mess. She said nothing as she opened the door and walked out of Adam's office. She walked past the team, not making eye contact. She made it all the way to her car before she completely broke down. She leaned against the steering wheel and let the tears fall. When she felt calm enough, she wiped away her tears and forced herself to drive. She needed solace and quiet.

The moment Graeme and Floyd walked into the conference room, Graeme noticed there was definitely a solemn mood. Everyone seemed to stop talking the moment they walked in.

"What happened?" he asked.

Drew shook his head and looked at Charity.

Cat finally stepped forward. "I think you need to talk to Elle."

He glanced around for the one person who was missing from the group, other than Elle. Adam.

He turned and walked into the office and shut the door. Adam was sitting in his chair staring at his computer screen, but he really wasn't looking at it. If anything, he seemed to be in a trance.

"What the bloody hell did you do to Elle?" he asked.

Adam blinked and looked at him. "I asked her for help

with Jin. Elle took exception to it."

"That's it?"

He nodded. "But, at the time, I didn't know she'd had a call from one of the bloggers here on the island. Apparently, her ex is trying to stir up trouble. He tipped them off about her last case in London."

"And?" he asked. Adam was definitely being cagey, and that made him worry even more. It was as if he was watching every word he said.

"She yelled at me, but then she started crying."

"You made her cry?" he asked, outrage pumping through his blood. "You are *not* allowed to make Eleanora cry."

The stunned silence in the office should have told him he'd been too loud. Hell, he had been so loud that the crew outside probably heard. Adam gave him a look of regret, and he knew then that Elle had been upset when she left.

"Don't bother her any more about Jin."

He turned to leave, but Adam's voice stopped him. "I just wanted help. Jin seems to be losing her grasp on who she was."

The anguish he heard in Adam's voice made him turn around. Graeme studied him. He couldn't deny that the second in command was definitely suffering.

"You need to just let her be. You have to accept that she isn't the woman you knew before. She's different, and once she learns how to deal with it, she might be able to deal with you. Otherwise, it isn't about you or anyone else. It's about her."

"I just wanted to make her feel better."

"You can't."

Adam cocked his head. "How do you know so much about this?"

"Hell, Adam, you should know this with your sisters. And that is part of where I learned it. But I had a good friend. An American soldier. She was the best bloody shot.

Bold. Would rush right in without hesitation, and saved more than a few asses on the line. One night, she was hanging out with a man she had known for five years. A man she had trained with and fought beside. He attacked her. She fought him off, but it was a close call. She was never the same. You could see it in the way she interacted with her fellow soldiers, and the way she started to hesitate when she did her job. But it was more than that. She didn't trust her fellow soldiers anymore, and it made her second guess her judgment."

"If you're going to see Elle, make sure you tell her I'm sorry."

Graeme nodded as he left.

Drew came forward first. "I think she was going home."

"Thanks," he said, going into his office to shut everything down. After shutting off the lights, he locked the door and turned to leave.

"Tell her we were thinking of her," Cat said.

He nodded, but Charity stopped him with another comment. "Please text us when you get to her. We're really worried about her."

"I will."

He hurried out the door. As he jogged down the steps, he realized he had to make a stop before he went to Elle's. There was someone who could help her more than Graeme ever could right now. He just hoped that this wouldn't drive her back into her shell.

HOSTILE DESIRES

CHAPTER EIGHTEEN

Before leaving, and while stuck at traffic lights, Graeme had called Elle, but she hadn't picked up. As he turned onto his street, he knew not to keep calling. She wasn't ready to talk over the phone about it, and he didn't blame her. It sounded like things went to complete shit while he was out working. If he could find that bastard ex of hers, Graeme would beat the hell out of him. He tightened his hands on his steering wheel and ordered himself to calm down.

He stopped by his landlady's house to pick up Dumfries, who was barking his head off. As Graeme approached the door, the barking increased in volume. Mrs. Williams opened the door before he reached it.

"Come, take this *pupule* dog of yours, Graeme," the older woman said. From the moment he had rented his house from Mrs. Williams, she had been in love with Dumfries. She didn't want to keep a dog on her own, as she had in the past, but she loved having one around. It worked out for him because Dumfries did better with someone around. While Dumfries and Mrs. Williams were sometimes at odds over her garden, Graeme knew they both had a grand time together.

Before Graeme could stop him, Dumfries came barreling out, but instead of jumping on Graeme like he usually did, he took off toward the back of Graeme's house.

"Dumfries," he said, but the dog paid him no heed. He kept on without breaking his pace.

"Don't worry," Mrs. Williams said. "He's going to see your *wahine*. She's sitting on the rocks back there."

He glanced at his own driveway a couple doors down, and saw Elle's little convertible. Graeme had been so intent on picking up Dumfries and going to Elle's that he hadn't even seen her car.

"He's been going on and on for the last hour. I almost let him out, but I didn't know if that was the one, or if she could control him."

He gave her a smile. "She is definitely the one. *Mahalo*."

He turned to leave, but she stopped him by putting her hand on his arm. When he looked at her, Mrs. Williams wasn't smiling.

"She looked sad, Graeme. If you want her to stick around, you need to make her happy."

He leaned forward and gave Mrs. Williams a kiss on her cheek. "I will try my best."

She frowned. "No try. *Do*."

He smiled as he walked to the rocks where Elle sat. The first thing he thought was that she looked so…solitary. That is until Dumfries reached her. With a happy bark, Dumfries covered her face with kisses, and he could hear her laugh. It danced over the wind to him, and it lifted some of the heaviness from his heart.

"I was heading over to your house, but stopped by here to get Dumfries."

She turned and smiled. He saw the ravages of a good

crying jag on her face, but she appeared calm at the moment. Her eyes were red, her face blotchy, and she just looked tired.

"Aw, love, you've been crying."

He knew she had been, but he'd hoped not to see it. It made him a coward, but he didn't care. Women crying was a weakness of his. It was the one thing all of his sisters knew would break him down.

Her smile faded. "So, you've heard."

Her voice sounded very small, and he could feel her retreat. He hated it. This was not the Elle he knew. The one he knew was bold and brash, a woman ready to take on anyone who questioned her. She only go like this when they talked of her past.

"Adam is very sorry."

She stiffened at the sound of Adam's name.

"I bet he is."

"He told me a little bit, but I understand some blogger found out about your work on the case in England?"

She nodded as he sat down beside her. "Seems my ex got hold of someone here and told them about the case in England."

Again, anger swiftly heated his blood. To have been a shitty husband was one thing, but to try and damage her career a second time made him a first rate bastard in Graeme's opinion.

"I might have to hunt the bastard down and hurt him."

She snorted. "Get in line, but that would mean engaging with him, and he is best left to flounder on his own. Gerald always liked to be the center of attention. If he didn't get his way, he would do things like this."

"Has he always been like this?"

She looked at him and didn't say anything for a long time, then nodded. "I'm not sure how he is with other people, but with me, yes. He was always very passive-aggressive. I guess I didn't realize it right away. His need to control everything overrode all his other actions, but he wasn't overt. I didn't realize it until I stepped away from our marriage just how screwed up our relationship was. It's why he dragged my name through the rags when we divorced. He was mad he didn't get his way, and instead of fighting *for* me, he went to the papers and blamed me for everything that went wrong."

"Then everyone else piled on?"

Again, she hesitated. "Did you read the articles?"

"No."

She glanced at him. "How did you know then?"

"First, you told me before, but it's human nature. In their minds—and in his—they felt culpable for not protecting you. These people were your friends and, in the end, they couldn't do what they had sworn they would do. Add in the fear that they might just suck at their jobs, and lashing out at you was easier than dealing with their own feelings of guilt."

"Not my fault that they suck."

He chuckled. "There's my girl. And no, it isn't your fault. Weak people blame others for their deficiencies."

She sighed and looked out over the water.

"I like it here."

"I assumed you did, since you drove here when you were upset. Did you come to see me?"

She looked at him. "I knew you weren't here."

She sounded like she was hedging the real answer. "But you came here."

With a sigh, she looked out at the water again. "It's tranquil."

She had been there just a couple of times, but she came there when she needed solace. That should be enough, but it wasn't. He waited her out. Sometimes with Elle, it was best to wait until she worked through her thoughts.

"Fine." She looked at him. "I like being here because it's like being closer to you. Happy?"

"Ecstatic," he said with a smile.

She wrapped her arms around her legs and rested her

head on her knees. Dumfries had wandered off to explore the yard.

"You're going to be difficult to deal with now, aren't you?" she asked.

"Admit it, love. I am *always* difficult. But I promise I'm worth it."

She smiled. "That you are."

He looked out at the water. "Adam is kind of lost when it comes to Jin."

Silence greeted that comment. For a long moment, he wasn't sure if she would respond.

"It shows," she said.

Good. Her voice was no longer as harsh as it was before. "I take it he really messed up today."

"A bit, but I am more concerned about what the team will think of me. I don't want them to think I'm unfit."

"They're worried about you."

Again, she said nothing. He looked at her then.

"Worried?" she asked.

"Yeah. Cat said to tell you they were thinking of you."

"That was sweet."

"And Charity said to text her when I finally hunted you down. Of course, Drew looked like he might drive out to your house to rescue you."

She smiled again. "He is such a nice man. I hope Cat doesn't trample all over him."

"Why do you think Cat will trample on him?"

She shrugged. "He's very much in love with her. You know that. Hell, the entire office seems to know but Cat."

"I have a feeling that opposites do attract. Look at us."

Again she snorted. "You definitely have a point. I don't think anyone would have put us together."

"Now, that's just rude. And untrue. The entire office has a wager going."

"They had a wager on whether or not Drew slept with the bodies. They bet on anything."

He chuckled. "Yeah, they do."

They sat in companionable silence for a few moments, as the water lapped against the rocks below. He had always thought it calming, but he didn't realize how much it helped him through some of his worst moments.

Dumfries returned and wiggled his big arse so he could sit down between the two of them. She slid her hand through his hair, as she continued to look out over the water.

"Do you want to tell me about it?" he asked.

She continued to pet Dumfries. "About what happened now or back then?"

He shrugged, although he knew she wasn't looking at him. "Any of it."

She thought about it, then said, "Not really."

"Fair enough."

She glanced at him, surprise lighting her eyes. "You're not angry?"

He shook his head. "Just know that if you ever want to, I'm here to listen."

Her shoulders relaxed, and her expression cleared a little more. "He never asked."

"Gerald?"

She nodded, then looked out at the water again. Something caught Dumfries' attention and he ran off. Graeme took advantage of the situation and scooted closer to Elle.

"I'm not him. And you will learn that the team isn't the group of wankers you worked with in London."

She glanced at him, then back out at the water.

"How did you know?"

He shrugged. "I know you. They are worried about you, so maybe in a while, you can call them, and let them know everything is okay."

"I worry what they will think of me." Her voice had shrunk again, and he hated it. Hated that she even had to worry about things like that.

"They'll love you as much as they did yesterday. These

are good people."

She released a breath and nodded. "What made you so wise at such a young age?"

He shrugged. "Easy. I love you even more today than I did yesterday, so I assume that they will too."

Everything seemed to still around her, as she turned her head toward him. The stunned look on her face made him smile. Good, because he was still stunned by the turn of events, and he wasn't sure when he would recover.

"You love me?"

He nodded. "Especially when you sound like a very prissy school teacher like you do now. Kind of turns me on."

Her mouth opened twice before she snapped it shut and swallowed. "You do not."

"Get turned on by your prissy voice?" He nodded. "Yeah, I do. It's an illness."

"Not that, even though you might need to talk to a therapist about that. You don't love me."

"I do."

She shook her head. "I'm not a good bet, Graeme."

"Let me worry about the odds."

"What are you going to do if I can't love you back? What if I crack?"

"Crack? You?" He shook his head. "Woman, you are stronger than just about any woman I know, and I am including my mother. That is high praise."

"Coming from a mama's boy like you, it is."

He chuckled. "I like a woman with a little bite. You're just going to have to accept that I love you, Eleanora."

"I don't have to."

Instead of arguing any more with her, he changed the subject.

"Do you want to go to dinner somewhere?"

She nodded. "But let's sit here for awhile. It feels good."

He nodded and leaned closer to brush his mouth over

hers.

"Sounds good, *Mo chridhe.*"

He laid back on the grass and enjoyed the cool trade winds, the salty scent of the ocean, and the woman beside him.

The next morning, Elle found Adam waiting for her outside TFH Headquarters. It was still early, and there were very few people around. She should have known he would be there. Adam wasn't a man who shied away from adversity. It just wasn't in his nature to avoid her, and that was what made him so good at his job.

"I'm sorry," he said, before she could say anything. He held out a coffee cup to her. "Peace offering."

She took it and sipped. Of course, he had the right amount of sugar and cream in it. The man knew everything about the TFH staff.

Elle knew she could hold a grudge, but she couldn't completely fault Adam. "It's okay. Any other day, I would have handled it better."

"Still, it was insensitive. I should have chosen my words better."

"True."

He chuckled. "I do want to talk to you. I want to make sure I am doing enough to help Jin."

She sighed. "Let's sit down."

They walked over to a bench and sat down. She liked the mornings in Hawaii. The air was so sweet, heavy with moisture, and it was quiet—even in Honolulu.

"So, tell me what you have been doing?"

He shrugged. "Just checking up on her. I try and stop by once a week, and I've gotten her to agree to text me."

All the anger from the day before had dissipated, but if it hadn't, the anguish she heard in his voice would have dissolved all of it. She knew now, without the haze of pain and embarrassment from yesterday, that he truly wanted to help.

"That's good. And I know she's been making it to group sessions. I don't lead them right now. I took a couple months off since I knew I would be filling in for Dennis, as he and his wife were due now. I still keep up with her, call her every few days to check on her."

"Oh. Good," he nodded and took a sip of his own coffee. He had his mirrored sunglasses on, so she couldn't see his eyes.

"Adam, there's something else bothering you."

"I...never mind."

Then it hit her. "You feel guilty."

He glanced at her, then away. He nodded, once, almost imperceptibly. In fact, if she had not been staring right at him, she would have missed it.

"It's understandable. I assume you had a relationship with her before this?"

"Way before. We went out a few times."

He didn't continue.

"More than casual?"

"For me, I guess. Then, I found out she was using me for information, and I know how Del is about that. So, I broke it off before it really got started."

She heard something in his voice that made her study him even closer. Oh, he was in love with her. Damn, she hadn't expected that. She knew about the friendship, but Elle hadn't realized just how much he cared about her. It made her adore him even more.

"First, it isn't your fault."

"*Bullshit*. I knew she was going too far with her investigations. She was putting herself in danger."

"And she was a grown woman who was very independent. She had a job to do, and she was very ambitious."

"It was *not* her fault," he almost growled from behind

clenched teeth.

What a wonderful man. She was so happy Jin had someone like this on her side. Elle had often worried about the woman who had no family and no visible emotional support. But with Adam, she had someone who cared so deeply he hurt.

"If she had been walking down Ala Moana naked, it still wouldn't be her fault."

He sighed. "I'm sorry. I know you understand. I just hate hearing that shit."

"And, because of that, I'm going to give you a bit of advice, two bits, in fact."

He looked at her and waited. His hopeful expression made her smile.

"First, let her be Jin, or at least the Jin she is meant to be. She is completely different, and she needs to find her way back to a place she can be comfortable with herself. There is no time limit."

"And the second bit?"

"Keep checking on her. Normalcy is very important. She might not say it, but she mentioned your visits to me. She cares, but right now, she can't deal with it. You're going to have to accept she is not the woman you knew."

"I just want her happy again."

"That's up to her. No one can make her happy until she deals with what she went through. But knowing she has you to call, that will mean more than you can even imagine."

He nodded.

"And I guess things are good for you now?"

She leaned back and sipped on her coffee before answering. "Yeah. They weren't for a very long time. Add in that it was sensationalized in the press and it was horrific. My marriage fell apart and I lost my job. Thanks to my family, though, I had time to recover physically and emotionally. Now, everything is smashing—most of the time. It took me a long time to actually go on a date, and I have my moments…like yesterday."

"Tell McGregor I didn't make you cry."

She blinked. "What?"

"Yesterday, he told me I wasn't allowed to make you cry. Actually, he shouted it."

"And the whole office heard it?"

He nodded, a smile curving his lips. "Eleanora."

She closed her eyes, as her face warmed. "That goat. Then, what do you expect from a McGregor? Goats, every one of them."

"He's hooked."

She opened her eyes and watched the man in question park his truck. He slipped out of it, then strode over in their direction.

"Really, tell him I didn't make you cry."

She glanced at him. "I will, because it was more about me working through something than anything else. Make sure you think before you say things from now on."

"I will," he promised. "You're going to save a dance for me at the wedding, right?"

"Of course I will."

"Everything okay?" Graeme asked.

"Yes. I was just chatting with Adam. I have work to do, boys."

With that, she stood, kissed Graeme on the cheek. "Have fun hunting for your confidential informant."

Then, she walked into the building, feeling even lighter than she had the night before, and more centered. Today was going to be a good day.

Graeme watched Elle as she walked into the building, feeling completely enchanted. The fact that she had barely brushed her mouth on his cheek wasn't important. It was that she did it without prompting.

"And another one bites the dust," Adam said, shaking his head.

He glanced over at Adam with a smile. "Happily."

"What do you think she's going to say about that?"

Graeme knew that Adam was talking about Elle.

"Told her, she said she wasn't a good bet." He shrugged. "She'll come around."

"For your sake, I hope so. She is definitely a catch. What do you have on your agenda today?"

"I have a list of people to question about the missing CI."

Adam nodded. "Want company?"

"It might help. Elle said when I get irritated, most people can't understand me."

"I understood you just fine yesterday."

Graeme chuckled. "See. Woman doesn't know what she's talking about. Let me check in and then I'll be ready to go."

Three hours later, Graeme was ready to shoot the next person who said they couldn't remember the eighties. Sadly, he was pretty sure they couldn't. The eighties had been bad for all of them, and none of them seemed to have done better in the interim. Most of them had long rap sheets littered with drug busts. When they said they didn't remember the time period, it was because they had been too stoned.

He pulled to a stop in a nice neighborhood in Aiea. He glanced around and realized that it was a middle class area, with neat yards and houses. That was a big improvement over the others they had already visited. Most of them had lived in apartments...some on the street. None of them had probably had a shower in weeks.

"What's this one's name?" he asked Adam.

"George Thompson." Adam looked at the house.

"Looks like George did better for himself."

They got out of the truck and walked up to the door. There was a ramp for a wheelchair.

"Maybe he doesn't live here anymore?" Graeme said.

Adam shrugged and knocked on the door.

"Just a sec," a man called out. When the door opened, a Hawaiian man of about sixty sat in a wheelchair. He was a little pudgy, and he'd lost all but two strands of his hair on top of his head. But his eyes were clear, and his smile genuine.

"Can I help you?"

Adam glanced at Graeme. "I'm Officer McGregor from Task Force Hawaii. We'd like to ask you a few questions about your work as a CI in the eighties."

George's eyebrows shot up. "Well, not sure if I can help you, but I'll try. Come in."

He backed up and allowed them to enter. They stepped over the threshold, and Adam closed the door behind them.

"That was a bad time in my life. I was strung out. I would do anything for a fix."

They followed him into the living room. The inside of the house matched the outside. Neat, except for a few magazine and books lying around, and definitely not the house of an addict.

"What changed you?"

"Love of a good woman," he said, motioning to the picture of a woman. "My wife. She's at work right now. Please have a seat. Would you like something to drink?"

"No, thanks," Adam said, as they both sat down.

"What we want to ask you about is the Jenny Kalani killing," Graeme said.

"Yes. I saw that on the TV a couple days ago. I vaguely remember it."

"Do you remember anyone getting a gun around then? Anyone who said anything that might lead you to believe they had something to do with it?"

He sighed. "Let me think. There was Frankie, but I think he ended up overdosing in the early nineties, or maybe he died of AIDS. A lot of my old friends did."

"Anyone else?"

"There was another fellow. He was really tight with one of the cops in homicide, which was odd."

"Why?"

"Yeah, the homicide cops used us, but most of us were tight with Vice cops, you know.

"God, what was that idiot's name? He was always bragging that he had some kind of cop in his pocket. Chester, that was it, but I don't know if that was a first or last name."

"Are you sure?" Graeme asked.

"Yes. He was a weasely little fellow. Such a bragger too. Thought he was smart, strutting around bragging about his link to a cop."

Adam had been busily reading over the names. "Chester Fung?" he asked.

"If that was his name, then it was probably him. I just knew him by Chester. Had a big grin and an even bigger mouth. Heard he died in prison a few years later."

"But not before having a son, apparently," McGregor mumbled. He shared a look with Adam. They both knew they needed more to go on, but Graeme had a feeling they had found the man they had been searching for.

HOSTILE DESIRES

CHAPTER NINETEEN

Adam and Graeme had grabbed a bite to eat and headed back to the office to eat it. They both had a lot of work to clear up before the weekend. All of them knew they would be busy with the wedding, so both he and Adam had agreed it would better to eat at work. Graeme really wanted to talk over some of the stuff with Elle, but he knew she was busy today. She had a meeting with the DA that morning about the upcoming testimony she had to give. Just as he stepped into the conference area, his mobile rang her melody.

"Hey, there," he said.

"Hey there, yourself. How'd it go this morning? Any joy?"

"Looks like we have a lead."

"Brilliant. I'm going to be back in about an hour. I have another meeting here with the ADA about another upcoming case. His first murder trial, so I'm going to miss the afternoon meeting."

"Bollocks, I forgot about that."

She chuckled. "Don't tell me you hate meetings?"

"Any sane person hates them."

"True. I was calling to see if you wanted to share my room with me at the hotel."

"Your room?"

Adam's eyebrows rose up, but he didn't say anything. Everything had gotten quiet in the conference room. Graeme turned around and realized everyone had gathered for the meeting, including Carino.

"Bloody hell," he muttered, as he walked into his office and closed the door.

"What's wrong? You don't have to stay with me if you don't want to."

"No, I wasn't talking about that. Just office rubbish."

"Ah, okay."

"So, this room?" he said, setting his food container on his desk. Then, he closed the blinds to his office.

"Yes," she said. "I rented a suite at the hotel for Del's wedding, and I thought you would like to stay with me. They don't take dogs though."

"No worries," he said with a smile. "I had arranged for Dumfries to stay at Mrs. Williams' that night. I knew I would be gone too long for him to be alone."

"Oh, well, then, I guess that works. So, do you want to?"

She sounded so unsure of herself. It hurt to hear the self-doubt. "Yes, Eleanora, I would love to stay with you."

"Great," she said, relief easy to hear in her voice. "Oh, there's the ADA. I'll call you later. Cheers."

He clicked off his mobile, as Elle had already hung up. Graeme thought it was a good sign that Elle had invited him to stay with her. He was pretty sure he could have talked himself into her room, but it meant more that she had invited him to share her room. He grabbed his food and stepped into the conference area.

"Adam was filling us in. Sounds like a good lead," Del

said.

"Yeah, it does. Adam is calling up his uncle."

Del chuckled, and there were a few smiles.

"What?" he asked.

Adam explained. "There are uncles and aunties, and none of them are related by blood, but yeah, I'm calling a friend of my father's. He came up in the academy with Dad."

"Good. Hopefully, he can help us find out who was using this Chester Fung as a CI."

"I'll ask around, but not sure if I will get anywhere," Carino said. "A lot of the old guard has moved on to retirement, but I'll talk to Captain Pham."

"Great. Someone call the mayor and let him know that HPD and TFH can work together," Del said with a smile. He pushed away from the table and stood. "And that's it. I'm shutting down my computer and going to head out. Adam's in charge for the next week, but I'll have my phone if need be."

Adam smiled at Graeme. "We timed that right."

"I heard you," Del called out from his office, as he turned his computer off, then turned out the lights. "I am too freaking happy to care. See everyone tomorrow. You'll be there, right, Rome?"

The detective nodded. "Our first real date since the baby, so I am not missing it."

Del gave them a salute and headed out the door.

"So, if the guy is dead, does that mean you have Jenny's killer?" Drew asked.

Adam nodded. "Maybe. He had the gun, but did he own it? Did he use it, or did he use it against someone else?"

Graeme caught on to what Adam was saying. "So, we have two scenarios. He either did the killing himself, then the cop helped him cover it up, or the cop was the killer. Somehow, he got hold of that gun."

"And either way, there might be a cop involved,"

Carino said. Graeme realized he did forget something important. "Even if it is an accessory after the fact situation, it's still murder. There is no statute of limitations."

"Which means we need to match up this Chester Fung with Sam Katsu, or more importantly, his mother...what was her name?" Adam asked.

"Iris. Iris Katsu," Graeme said. "If we go back to arrest warrants, maybe we can put them at the same residence. Sam was born in nineteen ninety, so if Fung was living with Iris then, there is a good chance he's the father."

"I'll try to catch Pham before the end of the day. I'll let you know if I hear anything. See everyone tomorrow."

The moment it registered that the wedding was tomorrow, it hit Graeme he hadn't bought a present for the couple.

"Damn, I need to head out too. Got my mobile on, and I should be back in an hour." He looked at Adam. "You hear anything, call me."

Adam nodded. "Just remember, it's Aloha Friday, bruddah. Ain't no one around today."

He shook his head as he left. The truth was, he liked the idea of Aloha Friday, even though they rarely got to take advantage of it themselves. This was a good time to take the time though. They might have a case on their hands still, but they had good things to celebrate.

The next afternoon, Elle stared at herself in the bathroom mirror and tried to calm her nerves. She seemed to be repeating the pattern of standing in front of a mirror while she tried to shore up her courage.

Why had she suggested this? Because she had to be out of her bloody mind, that's why. And why was she so bloody nervous? They had slept together. But this was something different. It was somehow more intimate. While she had mostly stayed at his house, now their things were intermingled, their names linked. It was also signaling to the team that they were definitely involved.

"Are you going to spend all day in there, lass? We're going to be late."

She sighed. Grabbing her gloss and compact, she took one last glance in the mirror. She couldn't hold off any longer. Drawing in a deep breath, she opened the door. She had expected Graeme to be right there, but he wasn't. He was standing by the sliding glass door that led out to the lanai.

The sun was still shining brightly outside. It danced over his flesh and his hair, adding an otherworldly quality to him. Then, she noticed what he was wearing. He had donned a Hawaiian shirt and matched it with a kilt that she was sure were the McGregor colors. She couldn't stop the bubble of laughter that escaped.

He turned around with an amused smile. "Why are you laughing?"

"You." And dammit, as odd as it was, he'd pulled it off. Of course, he did. He was a giant Highlander dressed in a kilt. All that was missing was a claymore in his hands.

"What?" he looked down at what he was wearing, then looked up at her. "It doesn't match?"

She shook her head, unable to stop laughing.

"I brought my white shirt, so I can change. I wore this because Adam said he had to wear a Hawaiian shirt to the wedding."

Her laughter faded as she watched him. Worry moved over his expression. He cared. It was one thing she had learned about him these last few weeks. It wasn't about fitting in. It was about showing his respect for traditions. It was one of the things she loved the most about him.

Oh. *Dammit*. She loved him.

No. She didn't. She didn't want to be in love again. It hurt too much, and she definitely didn't want to fall for a cop. It was all wrong. She knew better than to make that mistake again.

"Are you okay, love?"

She blinked and looked up at him. His gray eyes were filled with concern, and he was frowning. *Dammit*, she did love him. They had only been involved for barely two weeks, but he had touched her soul profoundly. From the way he adopted a dog from a war zone, to the love she heard in his voice when he talked about his family, to the way he worked at his job. He would always take care of those he loved.

"Elle?"

She drew in a deep breath and smiled. She couldn't worry about it right now. She shook her head and blinked back the tears burning the backs of her eyes.

"You definitely pull it off."

"Yeah?" he asked, his mouth curving up.

She nodded.

Then, slowly, his smile faded as his gaze moved down her body then back up. By the time their gazes connected, his eyes had darkened. Heat flared low in her belly. God, the man always made her melt, even before he touched her.

"I don't think anyone will be looking at me. All eyes will be on you."

His brogue had deepened, drawing out the words. Her throat tightened. She loved the simple sea green dresses Emma had picked for her bridesmaids. Each of them had a style that fit her figure, and they were casual enough that they could wear them again.

"Ah..."

His mouth curved. "I have left you speechless for the second time in less than a week. I call that a win," he said approaching her.

"Don't," she said taking a step back. She knew he would touch her, and she would lose the ability to say no to him.

"But I want to."

"You'll mess up my makeup and hair. I have to look perfect for the wedding."

"Do you have anything on your neck?"

She shook her head.

He took her hand and pulled her closer. Then he bent his head and nuzzled her neck. She shivered as his tongue moved over her pulse point. God, he was killing her. The scent of his aftershave, mixed with his own personal masculine scent, filled her senses. At that moment, he could have talked her out of her dress and into bed. It should scare her. No man, not even her ex, had ever had that kind of power over her. She couldn't seem to get enough of him, or the way he made her feel when he made love to her.

He pulled back before she was ready. Leaning down, he kissed the tip of her nose. The simple gesture brought a lump to her throat.

"See, didn't mess your hair or makeup."

Then he went about gathering up his mobile and wallet, and she stood there. She couldn't move. He might have left her unmussed, but he'd captured her heart.

HOSTILE DESIRES

CHAPTER TWENTY

The sun was setting over the Pacific as the music for the first dance started. Elle sipped her champagne as she watched the bride and groom walk out onto the dance floor to take their first dance as a married couple. It had been a beautiful ceremony, including having both Emma's brother Sean and Randy walk her down the aisle, both men visibly moved by their part in the ceremony. The garden setting, the smell of the salt air and plumeria, and the soft breeze had made it that much more magical.

Emma glowed with happiness, and Elle could not blame her. Del was practically strutting. As Del took his bride into his arms, Elle's heart sighed.

"They make such a sweet couple," Cat said, stepping up next to her.

Elle glanced at her. "They do, as do you and Drew."

Cat said nothing, but kept watching the first dance of the newly wedded couple. Elle didn't miss the way the younger woman's mouth curved. Oh, this could be trouble. Granted, she had ignored her own policy about getting involved with someone at work, but this was Drew.

He was a good man, one who deserved the best.

"Just be careful, Cat."

Cat tore her gaze away from the activity on the dance floor. She studied Elle with a narrowed gaze. "What do you mean by that?"

She counted Cat as a good friend, but she loved Drew like a little brother. "He adores you. You're a decent person, just remember that when you are dealing with him."

She sighed. "I thought I would never think of him that way. I knew he had a crush on me, but I thought he was in the *friend* category. He's geeky, and has this romance streak in him that just makes me want to gag at times."

"I'm sensing a *but* here."

Cat sipped her champagne. "He kissed me."

Elle smiled. "Is that a fact?"

"I thought, no big deal. I've been kissed before. Not that I kiss every man I meet, but it's not like I haven't had more than a few dates. So, I was prepared to let him kiss me. You know, get it over with. He leaned in and I figured it would be simple."

"It wasn't?"

Cat shook her head. "No. Lord, he made my knees weak."

Elle laughed, not in humor, but for the joy of it. "Drew has a habit of surprising people."

Before Cat could say anything else, the music changed and people started moving toward the dance floor, and Drew was approaching.

"Care to dance?" he asked Cat.

"Sure, slick," Cat said, her voice as steady as usual. Elle didn't miss the way her hand shook when Cat placed it on Drew's arm. Knowing Drew, he had noticed it also.

She watched as Drew expertly drew Cat out onto the dance floor and started to dance. God, they were sweet too. She felt tears burn the backs of her eyes. She was getting sentimental. She wasn't a woman who cried when she saw card commercials, but these were people she cared about. She just wanted everyone to be happy forever.

Okay, that was a little too much. Maybe she should lay off the champagne.

A few seconds went by before a rather large hand slipped around her waist.

"That's an interesting development," Graeme said, his breath warm against her ear. She shivered.

"Yes. Seems Cat got more than she bargained for."

"Hmm," he said, as he nibbled on her ear. "I know the feeling."

She chuckled. "What have you been up to?"

"I was talking to Adam."

She glanced at him over her shoulder. "Working at a wedding?"

"First, it's not mine. Second, he just got a call from an uncle. Now that we have a name, he has his uncle checking to see how might have been using Chester Fung as a CI back then."

"Ah. Anything?"

He shook his head. "Still waiting. How do you feel about a dance?"

Giddy happiness filled her. It was silly, really, but she felt like a teenager at a dance.

"I think I would like that," she said.

He took her almost empty glass from her hand, set it on a passing waiter's tray. He brought her hand to his mouth, kissed her knuckles, then drew her out to the floor. She smiled, pushing all her worries aside, and decided to enjoy it. She was under the stars in Hawaii, dancing with a sexy Highlander wearing a kilt.

Graeme watched Elle dance with Drew. It was a swing number, and she was laughing. He couldn't really hear her over the music and the people, but just watching her made him happy. A laughing Elle made everything in the world seem complete.

"So, I understand there's a room you're sharing," Del said, as he stopped beside Graeme.

He nodded, but didn't take his gaze from Elle dancing.

"Earth to Graeme."

He blinked and looked at Del. "What?"

Del chuckled. "Nothing. Was just trying to make small talk."

"Where's Emma?"

"She's out on the dance floor," Del said, waving his hand toward the area. And sure enough, Emma was dancing with Sean.

"Oh, I didn't see her."

"I hate to do this at my own wedding, but I was just talking to Carino. He told me on one of the warrants for his arrest, Fung was at Iris Katsu's house less than five months before Sam's birth."

"Damn. So, we have the connection. If we could find the gun, or figure out how Sam got the gun, it would make it so much easier."

"Yeah, but then, this case has been stupid FUBAR since the beginning."

The music started to die down, but Emma started off running in the opposite direction.

"I think that was a little much for her stomach. Duty calls."

Then Del cut across the dance floor, nodding as he passed his new brother-in-law. But Graeme's attention was brought back to Elle and Drew. He was walking her back to Graeme.

"Have you seen Cat?" Drew asked.

"Over at the TFH table."

Drew smiled. "Thanks for the dance, Doc."

Then he sauntered over to the table the team had procured as their own, but Graeme paid him no attention.

"They had their cake and all that nonsense."

"I'm sure Emma appreciates that you called it nonsense. And I will point out that you had two pieces of cake."

"Can we go now?" he asked. He wanted to be alone with her.

She smiled. "They are going to throw the bouquet."

"Do you want to be here for that?"

"Not especially," she said.

"Good."

He grabbed her hand, then started off to the lift.

"Wait. I need my purse."

After backtracking to the table, she grabbed her purse. He saw the look in Adam's eyes, and knew he was going to give Graeme crap. He tugged at Elle before Adam could ask her to dance. He ignored everyone as he made his way out of the garden setting and into the hotel. The elevator doors opened, and they had to wait for an older couple to step off. Once they were gone, he stepped into the lift, then tugged her inside.

Graeme pulled her into his arms and kissed her. She laughed against his mouth and he pulled back.

"I kiss the woman I love and she laughs."

"We need to hit the button or we won't move."

She leaned back and hit their floor number, and he tried to kiss her again.

"Behave, Graeme. I don't want to be caught snogging."

He frowned, but did as she asked. Within minutes, he was opening the door and urging her inside their room. He backed her against the door, then cupped her face and kissed her. Slanting his mouth over hers, he stole inside, enjoying the taste of champagne as it danced over her tongue to his.

He pulled back and realized he had been a little more aggressive than he had been before with her.

"Sorry, love. I've been wanting a taste of you for hours now."

She smiled. "No worries, Graeme," she said, sliding her hand to the back of his neck. She urged him closer. "I had the same feelings about you."

She took control of the kiss now, slipping her tongue into his mouth. Heat that had been at a low boil all day, roared to life in his blood.

Graeme tore his mouth away from hers and knelt down in front of her. Taking a fist full of her dress into his hand, he hiked it up to her waist. Oh, fuck, she was wearing lace panties. Not just panties with a little lace on them. These seemed to be made of lace and bows, leaving little to his imagination—and Graeme had a very good imagination.

Without removing them, he slipped his finger beneath the leg band. She was already wet, dripping with arousal. He eased the delicate fabric aside and leaned closer. The scent of her desire washed over him, and he had to have a taste. He licked her slit then, just a simple lick, and she moaned. Bloody hell, that sound would forever be imprinted on his soul.

He slipped a finger inside of her, along with his tongue. She shivered against him and speared her fingers in his hair. Over and over, he moved within her, enjoying the way her moans grew louder with every second that ticked by.

As he felt her approaching an orgasm, he pulled back. He was a greedy bastard, and he wanted to be inside of her when she came. She growled, and he smiled as he eased her panties down her legs. He tossed them behind him, not caring where they landed.

Then, he peeled her out of that stunning dress, making sure he didn't rip it. He wanted to see her in it again. Her gaze traveled down his body. His cock was hard, easy to see beneath his kilt, since he had gone commando, as he always did with his kilt. He undressed in a matter of seconds, then grabbed a condom from his wallet and slipped it on.

He took one step towards her and lifted her into his

arms. Elle wrapped her legs around his waist, pressing her wet sex against his shaft.

"Bloody hell," he said, almost stumbling. His brain was blank of everything but that sensation.

"What was that?" she asked too sweetly.

He growled and she laughed.

He walked them into the bedroom, but instead of going to the bed, he turned to the wall, steadied Elle against it, then entered her in one hard thrust.

"Oh, damn," she said.

He immediately felt guilty. "I'm sorry, love."

"I hope not. It felt good," she said with a laugh. Then she cupped his face and kissed him.

That was enough to spur him on. Over and over he thrust into her, her moans growing louder each time he drove into her. Before he was ready, he felt his orgasm simmering, but he wanted to wait. He wanted Elle with him.

"Oh, yes, Graeme," she moaned, just as she bowed off the wall. Her orgasm caused her inner muscles to tighten against his cock, pulling him deeper into her hot, wet core. He could hold back no longer. Shouting her name, Graeme gave himself over to pleasure. As he felt himself fall, she cupped his face and kissed him. That one act connected them on a level that he had not known existed, had never experienced before.

Several moments later, he stumbled to the bed, and they fell on top of it together. She sighed, the sound filled with contentment.

"Mo chridhe," he said, kissing her temple. "I love you, Elle."

She didn't stiffen this time. Instead, she wrapped her arms around him and held on tighter. It wasn't the end goal, but it was definitely a step in the right direction.

Pleased, he let her snuggle closer as they both drifted off to sleep.

HOSTILE DESIRES

CHAPTER TWENTY-ONE

"What are you doing today?" Graeme asked her, as he held a strawberry up for her to eat.

She leaned forward and licked the tip of it.

"Bleeding hell, woman," he said.

She smiled, keeping her gaze locked with his, as she took the entire strawberry into her mouth. There was something so wonderfully decadent about being fed strawberries and cream by Graeme. It helped that they were both still naked.

She chewed it and swallowed, then grabbed the champagne. "What did you ask me?"

"I asked what you were doing today."

"I'm not sure," she said, but before she could continue, her mobile went off.

Graeme frowned, but she just shook her head. They both understood the job and what it took from them. She wasn't supposed to be working today, but she knew Graeme understood.

"Dr. Middleton."

"Elle, it's Will."

She smiled. "Oh, good morning, Will. Did you need something?"

"Yes, I need to have my blood sugar checked again. I hate to bother you, but I thought maybe I could stop by tomorrow."

"What does he want?" Graeme whispered.

She covered the mouthpiece. "Will has to have his blood sugar checked. He has a thing about needles, so I do it for him every six months."

"Elle?" Will said over the phone.

"Sorry. Tomorrow won't work because I have court."

"Damn." He paused, and she knew he was working it through in his head. "I might have to go to a regular doctor."

She heard the worry in his voice, and it registered, but just barely. She knew Will didn't want to go to the doctor because last time he passed out. With her, he seemed not to have that issue. But she was having a very hard time concentrating. Graeme had lifted the sheet and was now pulling her legs apart.

"Um, why the rush?" she asked, and almost moaned when she felt Graeme's tongue tease her slit. Bloody hell.

"I want to be sure before I go in for the insurance exam. If it is high, then I need to really watch it. I have about a week."

"Uh, a week isn't going to fix everything."

"I know that. I just want to be prepared before I go."

Graeme pressed her thighs further apart, then slipped his tongue inside of her. She barely kept in the next moan that vibrated in her throat.

"Uh, how about this morning?"

He paused. "Yeah, I can come by, but I don't want to make you come all the way back to Honolulu."

"No worries. Del and Emma had their wedding last night, and I stayed overnight."

"That would be brilliant if you could do that."

"About an hour?" Graeme added a finger and started to tease her clitoris. "Um, make that two."

"Good. I'll meet you at the lab like last time."

"Okay." She didn't wait for a goodbye. She shut her phone off and let it fall to the floor.

Graeme moved up her body. "Now, what are you going to be doing for the next two hours?"

She smiled and slipped her hands up his arms to his shoulders. "You."

He laughed and tumbled them over the bed.

Graeme's mobile rang just as he took the ramp to H-1. He needed to hit the grocery store, and then pick up Dumfries. He had special plans with Elle tonight, and he wanted to make a nice dinner to soften her up.

"Hey, Adam, what's up?" Graeme asked.

"Do you know where Elle is?"

"No. Is there a reason you need to talk to her?"

"No, but I thought both of you would like to hear the news. I found the cop who was using Chester as a CI. It took a little bit, but Captain Pham actually is the one who remembered."

"Well, spit it out." Graeme demanded.

The moment he heard the name, his blood ran cold.

"Where are you?" he asked.

Adam paused. "I'm on my way back to Honolulu on the H-3," Adam responded.

"Bloody hell." Graeme spat out.

"What the hell is the matter?"

"Elle is meeting with the man who is doing everything in his power to cover this up," Graeme responded. "Get back to TFH headquarters as fast as you can."

He clicked off his phone, then turned on his siren. Slamming on the gas, he sped around cars and took the exit to Valkenburgh Street so he could turn around. He just prayed he got there soon enough.

Elle stepped into the exam room and realized the lights had been left on. She frowned. She knew for a fact they had been turned off on Friday.

"Hello? Will?"

There was no answer, but she couldn't shake the feeling of not being alone. She hadn't had these kinds of feelings since her first year on the job. She had always wanted to be an ME, but the truth was, she had to get over the feeling of being watched by dead bodies.

She smiled as she grabbed up a needle to draw blood.

"What are you doing here?" Drew asked.

He startled her so badly, she almost dropped everything she had been gathering up.

"Andrew Franklin, you should know better."

He smiled. "Sorry. I stopped by because Cat said she left a file she wanted to read over. Why do they always want the hard copies?"

Elle shrugged. "Depends on what I'm looking for, but I know a lot of the team is kind of old school. They say they can read it better on a piece of paper."

"And what are you doing? I thought you and McGregor would be staying in today too."

"That's presuming a lot," she said.

Drew winked. "Just know that you two left before the bouquet being thrown."

She felt her face heat, but she just shook her head. "Graeme has a dog he had to leave with a neighbor, and Will called."

"Oh, another blood sugar test?"

She nodded.

"He just needs to give up drinking."

She set everything on the counter, making sure she had everything she needed. "Kind of hard when you own a bar."

"True. Well, I'm going to grab that file up and then head out. We're going to have dinner tonight," he said smiling and wiggling his eyebrows.

Then he slipped out. She heard him jog up the stairs, and she couldn't stop smiling. It wasn't going to be easy, but Drew had amazing patience. The brick wall Cat had up would have to be demolished, and Drew would do that, piece by piece.

She had everything ready when she heard Will coming down the hall.

"Hey, Will, come on in. I have everything set up."

Will stepped into the room, his face pale, his mouth a straight line.

"What's wrong? Are you feeling okay?" she asked, concern filling her. There was a chance there was more wrong with him than just the high blood sugar.

It was then she saw the gun.

"What the bloody hell are you doing?" she asked.

"I need those files, Elle, and you're going to give them to me. I need to destroy everything."

Her blood went cold. "I-I left them at home."

"Lies."

Well, yes, partially. Will should know that all the paperwork had been filed. Sure, if there was no proof, it would be easy to get it thrown out of court, but not with an eyewitness. That meant he was planning on using that gun. "No. I was in town for the wedding. It was last night. I left everything at my house."

He studied her for a second. She kept her chin raised and her gaze steady.

"Fuck. Okay, let's go. If you try anything, I'll shoot

you."

She didn't even point out that if he shot her, he would never get those reports he thought she had. When he motioned with his gun, she did as he ordered.

"You'll be seen on the CCTV."

He snorted. "You don't think I have someone who can help me with that, do you?"

Her heart sank. They went out the back way, and it was then she noticed Drew's car. He was still there, but she didn't want him getting involved. Hopefully, he would see them and call for backup.

"Seems your boyfriend isn't around."

"He's meeting me here later."

He dug the gun further into her ribs.

"Don't lie. I've been tailing you. He's on his way home, more than likely to check on that damned mutt."

She glanced around the parking lot. This was the employee parking area, and only TFH really parked there. HPD folks parked in their own lot down the street.

"Why are you doing this?" she asked.

He snorted. "You know why."

"So, your informant killed Jenny. You are an accessory after the fact, but the public will barely notice."

It wasn't true, but she was grasping for any kind of a lifeline. He laughed, but it wasn't a pleasant sound. "You really aren't that smart, are you, Dr. Elle? *I* killed Jenny."

"What?" she asked, as she slowed her steps, hoping that either Drew might be getting help, or he was staying out of the way. He was the only other person in the building at the moment.

"I killed her. She saw us doing a buy. She knew my face."

Cold seeped deeper into her soul, as she tried her best to come up with some kind of way to slow him down. If Drew was getting help, the more time she could give him, the better.

"So you killed her. Just like that?"

She couldn't even keep the horror out of her voice. Killing an innocent for money was the lowest of the lowest.

"I needed the money."

"Oh, so that makes everything okay then. I mean, what does one little girl mean in the world compared to your need for money?"

He pushed her against her car. She hit it hard, but did her best not to let him see that it hurt her.

"The high and mighty doctor passes judgment. Do you know what it's like to have nothing? To come from nothing? Of course you don't. You had everything handed to you. I was about to be forced out, with nothing. They were ready to clean house, and I was one of the ones who was going to be kicked to the curb. I had just enough years to force retirement, but it wouldn't be enough to live on. I would have had to get a job as a fucking rent-a-cop. How the fuck do you think I opened the bar? Not on a bleeding cop salary, I can tell you that."

The sound of a foot against gravel caught her attention. It had to be Drew. Fear sliced through her blood. Oh, damn, she hoped that he would have just called someone. Again, the same sound, and this time, Will heard it too. He turned in the direction of where it had come from, still holding onto her. He fired his gun, and she took the opportunity to push him away. She heard him shooting the gun again and again. Glass shattered, and Will screamed in frustration. She ran to the other side of her car, then kept running to take cover behind a bigger SUV that sat a few spaces from hers. Will kept shooting his gun and screaming. What the bloody hell was he doing? The shooting would bring attention to him. She covered her ears as she crouched down, hoping that Will would not come looking for her.

At that moment, tires squealed against the pavement as she watched Graeme come racing into the parking lot. He headed full barrel toward Will, who turned and started firing at the truck.

The bastard had lost his damned mind, Graeme thought. He had bulletproof glass, but the wanker just kept shooting at his truck. He didn't stop but he did slow down. Still, he ran right into Will, and watched as the gun fell from his hand. Will fell back onto the pavement. He parked the truck and jumped out, his handcuffs in his hand.

"Where do you think you're going?"

He turned Will over on his stomach and cuffed his hands. He pulled him off the pavement and slammed him against his truck.

"Elle, are you okay?"

"Yes, I am," she said, running toward him. The knot in his stomach loosened and the ice in his blood melted. The smile on her face was the most beautiful sight in the world.

"Why didn't you just kill me?" Will asked.

"Because you need to be held accountable and face up to what you've done."

"Where's Drew?" he asked Elle when she reached him.

"He's over near the building." She looked at Will. "I hope it hurts."

Graeme smiled as he watched her walk away. The woman definitely had a mean temper.

"Drew?" she called out.

He paid little attention as the ambulances, along with Adam, pulled into the parking lot. The noise almost deafened him, since both had their sirens going. The moment the sirens cut off, he heard Elle scream.

He shoved Will at Adam, then ran toward the sound of Elle's scream. He found her by the door, pressing on Drew's neck. Blood seeped between her fingers. Drew was gurgling as a thin line of blood dribbled out of his mouth.

"No. No. No."

She kept repeating the word over and over.

"Elle?"

She didn't look at him.

"Get an ambulance," she yelled. The medics were already rushing toward her.

"I think the bastard hit an artery."

The EMTs looked at one another.

She glared at them while she kept her hand on Drew's chest. "I'm a doctor, you idiots."

He knew she wasn't thinking straight. Both of the EMTs knew her, had worked with her more than once.

"Dr. Middleton," one of the EMT's said. "Let us take care of him."

She still refused to move, and he knew Drew needed to get to the hospital as fast as possible. He went to her. "Let them take care of him, love."

She shook her head. "I know how to fix it."

Anguish dripped from every word, and he knew she wasn't thinking clearly. "They can get him the help he needs faster. Come here."

She blinked, and he took her hand. He motioned with his head to the EMT. The man was smart enough to catch on. He pressed his gloved hand against Drew's neck. Graeme pulled Elle to her feet.

"Pulse is thready," the older EMT said. "Drew. Drew, can you hear me? We are going to get you to the hospital."

They had him up and on the gurney in record time. They were running to the ambulance as Elle tried to pull away.

"No, you need to stay with me," Graeme said. "Where are you headed?" he asked the EMT.

"We're headed to Tripler. There was a pile up on the Pali, and they were sent to Queen's."

"Thanks."

One EMT climbed into the back of the ambulance, while the other one slammed the doors and rushed to the driver's side. The sirens blared once more as the ambulance sped off.

"We have to go to the hospital."

He studied her and recognized the signs. Her eyes were glassy, and she was breathing too fast. She definitely could be going into shock.

"I think you should see a doctor."

There was no doubt about it, she was in shock, and he didn't know how much trauma this might cause her.

She was shaking her head, but he ignored her. "Let's go. Adam, can you process that bastard?"

He nodded. "We're taking him to the hospital too." He threw Graeme some keys. "I'm glad I brought my truck with me today. Take it. I'll get a ride with Floyd."

"Come, love, let's get to Tripler."

As Graeme helped her into Adam's truck, Elle's teeth started to chatter. Definitely shock. He grabbed a thermal blanket they all carried in the backseats of their work vehicles and covered her with it.

She frowned. "What are you doing?"

"Just humor me, love."

She apparently decided to not fight him on it. He shut her door, then rounded the hood of the truck. As he started the truck, he prayed that Drew made it.

CHAPTER TWENTY-TWO

Over an hour later, Elle paced the hallway outside of the surgery wing; the smell of antiseptic filled the air. She'd used her credentials and McGregor's size to bully their way into the restricted area. She didn't regret it. Now though, she was trying to keep calm, even though her pulse was still elevated.

What she did regret were her actions. Why had she not called out to Drew? Why didn't she just tell him to run when she'd heard the footsteps behind them? If she had, there was a good chance he would not have been hurt.

"Love, maybe we can get you some scrubs."

Elle shook her head and kept pacing. She wanted to be there, wanted to know right away.

A nurse came out, and she heard a doctor yell, "He's crashing."

She rushed to the door, but McGregor held her back. "Love, stay here. You will only get in the way."

She knew he was right, but she didn't like that he was right. She gave him a nasty look and pushed away from him.

"You need to change and clean up, Elle."

She ignored him. He didn't know. He didn't understand. Drew was her employee. She should have made sure he was safe. His actions had had actually kept her safe. The truth was, if he hadn't been there, she was sure her bluff to McPherson would have ended with her being hurt.

"Eleanora Middleton, you are going to clean up and put scrubs on right now."

She stopped in the middle of the hallway and stared at him. Anger swiftly took hold of her emotions. Straightening her spine, she glared at him.

"Who do you think you are?"

He stood up and towered over her. "I'm Graeme McGregor, the man who loves you. You are skating on the edge of shock, and you have Drew's blood all over the front of you. His parents will be here soon, as will Cat. They do not need to see that."

She looked down at her clothes and saw it then. Blood had been spattered all over her. Even though she had washed her hands, she could see red under her fingernails. Drew's blood.

Bloody hell.

Shards of ice sliced through her, leaving her chilled. She shivered, as her vision wavered. She realized she was crying again. Elle looked up at McGregor, whose frown dissolved.

"Oh, love," he said as he pulled her into his arms. His warmth surrounded her, comforted her, and allowed her to let go. She curled her hands into the front of his shirt and sobbed. Graeme kissed her on the temple, as he muttered nonsensical words of comfort and he rocked her back and forth. "Everything is going to be okay."

She wanted to believe that. Always. But her life didn't always turn out brilliantly.

"You don't know that."

He leaned back, and she looked up at him. "I do. You have to believe in the good things, Eleanora."

She nodded and stepped back, as she wiped her tears away.

"Now, let's get you changed. I have some scrubs here. It will only take a sec, and then we will be back to watch for news."

She let him lead her into the bathroom. He helped her out of her clothes, which she noticed he put into an evidence bag. Her heart ached thinking that they could be evidence in a murder trial. Drew's murder.

She pushed that thought aside. Graeme was right. She needed to keep her head on straight and think positive. He easily helped her put on a pair of green scrubs. He'd even brought a pair of nonskid socks.

"Come, let's wash your hands better."

She did as he instructed, allowing him to lather up her hands and arms. Then, he helped her wash her hands and arms, drying them with paper towels. When they stepped back into the hallway, Marcus and Adam were there, both of them wearing grim expressions. Her heart sank.

"What's up?" Graeme asked.

"McPherson is in with the doctor," Adam said, just as the door opened again to reveal Del and Emma. The new bride and groom rushed in.

"Any word?" Del asked.

"No. He's still in surgery. The bullet shattered on impact, causing it to splinter." Elle had heard the explanation, but now that she said it herself, she realized how horrible it was.

She shivered. Graeme trailed his fingers down her spine, then slipped his hand around her waist. She leaned into him, accepting his comfort. His body heat surrounded her—steadied her.

"Has anyone gotten hold of Cat?" Del asked.

Adam nodded. "She's on her way with Drew's parents."

Just then, the doors to the operating surgical wing opened up, and the doctor came walking out.

"Well, you seemed to have acquired more people who believe in abusing their power."

She ignored that. "Please, doctor."

He smiled. "It was touch and go there for a few minutes, but we pulled him back. That young man is a fighter, that's for sure. It's going to be a long road to recovery, but I think he's up for it. And if not, he apparently has enough people to help him. We'll have to watch him. There is always a chance of blood clots."

Happiness and relief filtered through Elle. Her vision wavered again.

"Thank you," she said.

The surgeon nodded. "He'll be in recovery for awhile, then up to ICU."

"Is there news?"

They all turned to find Cat standing with Drew's parents. His mother had asked the question.

Elle stepped away from the comfort of Graeme and nodded.

"He is on his way to recovery right now. They will come to get you when he is in ICU."

"So, he's okay?" Cat asked.

Elle nodded. "He's going to need some therapy, and recovery isn't going to be easy, but he should pull through."

Cat nodded and walked away. Elle blinked.

"What?" she asked and looked at Graeme.

He patted her on the shoulder. "I'll talk to her."

She watched as he followed Cat out.

"Can you tell us what happened exactly?" Drew's father asked.

She nodded, led them to some chairs, and started the long story of just how their son had probably saved her life.

Cat was already at the lift by the time he caught up with her.

"Where are you going?" he asked her.

She glanced at him, then back at the door as if willing it to open. "I have things to do."

He crossed his arms over his chest. "Like what?"

"Just leave it, McGregor."

"No, I will not leave it. Drew is one of our team, and you need to be there."

"He has all of you, and we aren't going to be allowed in ICU. You know that. Elle might be able to weasel her way in there, but not us."

"Cat—"

"It's my fault."

"What?"

"He went by to pick up a file for me before our dinner tonight. He got shot because I asked him to be there. My fault."

He should have seen it. She would think it was her fault, just as he knew that Elle thought it was hers. But he knew what Cat was doing. She was trying to get away, to avoid the pain. It was scary almost losing someone you truly cared about. Being soft would not work on Cat though.

"The only person at fault is McPherson, and there's a good chance if Drew hadn't distracted the bastard, Elle would be dead. Drew saved Elle. Blaming yourself diminishes his sacrifice."

"Yeah, I know. I'm a bitch." Her flippant tone was at odds with her expression and her actions.

"That's no' the word I was thinking of."

She glanced at him. "Is that right?"

"Coward is the word I would use."

She said nothing, but the quick intake of breath told him he had hit his mark. He felt like a bastard for doing it to her, but he wanted to save her the regret of this mistake. It would haunt her forever, eat away at her gut, and leave her a shell of who she was now.

He thought she was ready to crack. Something shifted in her expression, but in the next instant, the doors to the lift opened. Charity came barreling out of the elevator.

"Sorry," Charity said.

Before Graeme could stop her, Cat jumped on the elevator. As the doors closed, he saw her expression. She might have acted a little cowardly, but she was in pain. She looked up just as the doors closed, and there were tears in her eyes.

"I got a text from Emma. All good?"

He nodded. "Come on."

He walked Charity to where everyone was waiting. The first person he saw, the one that he would always see first, was Elle. She was holding Mrs. Franklin's hand, as she talked to her softly.

That moment when he thought he might lose her, when Will was shooting wildly throughout the parking lot, he had realized he didn't want to go on living if she'd died.

She glanced at him, offering him a tired smile. That one little gesture told him that she was going to be okay. And that was all he needed for his world to be right again.

Graeme woke just before sunrise and reached for Elle. He found an empty bed. Sitting up, he looked around, and realized his dog had abandoned him also.

Grabbing a pair of jeans, he stepped into them, zipping but not buttoning them. He looked out his bedroom window and saw his dog and his woman sitting on a rock. He stood there for a few moments watching the two of them. In just a couple of short weeks, this woman had become all that was important to Graeme. Nothing else mattered in the world if things with Elle were not right. He needed her to be okay, to be happy.

After a quick trip to the bathroom, he went into the kitchen. The coffee had brewed, so he poured them both a cup—doctoring hers how she liked it—then headed out to her. He approached her, and realized she was wearing one of his T-shirts. She was sitting next to his dog, wearing his shirt, and enjoying his view. It felt good. It felt right. This woman, this place, with him.

"Did you have problems sleeping?" he asked.

The moment Dumfries heard Graeme's voice, he rose and trotted over to say good morning. It was as if his dog understood the duty of protecting Elle, and he was handing off the job to Graeme. After a sniff at the coffee, Dumfries ran off to explore.

She smiled back over her shoulder. "Not really. Just a bad dream, and I couldn't go back to sleep. I could hear the water and decided to come out here."

He handed her a cup.

"Thank you," she said. When she took a sip, her eyes widened and then she smiled. "You got it just right."

He sat down beside her. "Of course I did."

She snorted. "Ever the McGregor."

They sat side by side, sipping their coffee.

"What are you thinking about?" he asked.

"Nothing really. I just wanted to hear the water lapping against the rocks. It smells so good out here. Then I started thinking about yesterday."

He understood the confusion he heard in her voice. It still hurt that Will had been the killer all along. Of course, he was refusing to comment, and had decided to hire one of the toughest criminal defense attorneys in the state.

"Do you think they'll ever find the gun?" she asked.

He shrugged. "Not sure. I have a feeling he ditched it somewhere. I'm still surprised we didn't find it in his house."

She nodded, apparently agreeing with him, but she said nothing else. The sun was just starting to peek over the horizon, and the morning buzz of birds was starting.

"I was thinking."

"That is always a dangerous thing," she said, humor lacing her voice. She glanced at him with a smile on her face, but it faded. Probably because he was trying hard to stay serious. This was a serious discussion. "Is there something wrong?"

He shook his head. "No. Just, you seem to like it here more than at your house."

"I can hear the water. I like that."

"Aye." Bloody hell, he was starting to sound like an extra from Braveheart. "And there is a little more room in my house."

She looked at him. "What are you getting at?"

"What would you think of moving in here?"

She didn't say anything right away, and he panicked. "I know that you might not want to live here with us without anything permanent."

"Us?"

"Dumfries and me."

She smiled as she took a sip of her coffee. "Of course."

"I want to marry you."

Coffee sloshed over the top of her mug. "Oh, bloody hell, that was hot."

"Marriage scares you that much?" he asked.

She sighed. "I'm not sure I want to be married. Not this fast. I'm not sure I'm ready to move in with you either. We've only been involved for a couple of weeks, Graeme."

"I'm good enough to sleep with, but not marry?"

She blinked. "I married Gerald after knowing him for less than a year. We were in such a rush, and it wasn't until later that I realized what was wrong."

"What?"

"I thought I loved him, but there was always a part of me that must have known I did not. I didn't truly trust him, and that was one of the biggest failings in our marriage. Looking back on it, I can tell that neither of us trusted the other, or we would have been honest with our feelings."

Irritation sparked. He knew it wasn't fair, but it angered him...and it hurt.

"Well, great. You didn't love him, but you married him."

"Yes, and look what happened. First problem was the loss of the baby. Then, we used work to communicate, to make it feel like a marriage. When that went wrong, everything fell apart."

He looked out over the water. He hadn't planned on proposing to her, and he shouldn't have done it. It wasn't the right moment, not with everything that had gone on the day before. He wanted her to be his. He didn't need a bloody ring on her finger, but he wanted some kind of commitment. It wasn't exactly logical after their short time together, but he didn't want to waste another minute.

"Graeme, please look at me."

He hesitated, not wanting to face her...to face the fact that she had married another man she didn't trust or love.

"Graeme." This time her tone was more insistent.

He turned to look at her. The trades had picked up and were tossing her short curls around. Graeme barely noticed because she was smiling at him.

"I know I love you, Graeme, so I want to make sure we get it right. I don't want just for right now. I want forever. I think we both deserve it."

His heart sang, but he had to be sure. "It's not because of what happened? You're not saying you love me because of what happened with Drew?"

She shook her head. "You know when I realized I loved you? Saturday."

He thought back to the wedding, to the way everything

had progressed that day. He had known there was something different, felt it.

"When we were dancing?"

She shook her head. "No. Before the wedding. You were asking about the kilt and the Hawaiian shirt, and I just couldn't help it. You were so worried about making sure you honored Del and Emma with the way you dressed. You care so much for the people around you. It touched my heart and opened my eyes. I love you, Graeme Arthur McGregor."

"How did you know my middle name?"

"Looked it up in your file," she said with a laugh.

"I love you, Eleanora Catherine Middleton." He leaned closer. "You're not the only one who can look things up in files."

She laughed and brushed her mouth over his. She pulled back before he was ready.

"I like the idea of moving in here, but I have a couple months left on my lease."

For a moment, he wasn't sure he heard her right. His breath seemed to tangle in his chest, as his brain tried to compute the words. A second or two later, he could breathe again. She wanted to move in with him. She wanted to be his.

Graeme cleared his throat. "We can work that out. It will give us time to rearrange my house for your things."

"Smashing," she said. "And, you have to agree that if either of us feels pressured, we tell each other. I don't want secrets like that between us."

He nodded, content with the plan, then wiggled his eyebrows. "How about we go christen the deal?"

"That sounds brilliant, but first, I want to sit here and watch the sunrise with you."

Graeme couldn't argue with that request. He slipped his arm around her, and she settled her head against his shoulder. Together, with the the birds singing their morning songs, and the scent of plumeria in the air, they watched the sun rise over the water.

ABOUT THE MELISSA SCHROEDER

From an early age, USA Today Bestselling author Melissa Schroeder loved to read. First, it was the books her mother read to her including her two favorites, *Winnie the Pooh* and the *Beatrix Potter* books. She cut her preteen teeth on *Trixie Belden* and read and reviewed *To Kill a Mockingbird* in middle school. It wasn't until she was in college that she tried to write her first stories, which were full of angst and pain, and really not that fun to read or write. After trying several different genres, she found romance in a Linda Howard book.

Since the publication of her first book in 2004, Melissa has had close to fifty romances published. She writes in genres from historical suspense to modern day erotic romance to futuristics and paranormals. Included in those releases is the bestselling Harmless series. In 2011, Melissa branched out into self-publishing with A Little Harmless Submission and the popular military spinoff, Infatuation: A Little Harmless Military Romance. Along the way she has garnered an epic nomination, a multitude of reviewer's recommended reads, over five Capa nods from TRS, three nominations for AAD Bookies and regularly tops the bestseller lists on *Amazon* and *Barnes & Noble*. She made the USA Today Bestseller list for the first time with her anthology The Santinis.

Since she was a military brat, she vowed never to marry military. Alas, fate always has her way with mortals. Her husband just retired from the AF after 20 years, and together they have their own military brats, two girls, and two adopted dog daughters, and is happy she picks where they live now.

Keep up with Mel online:
Facebook.com/melissashcroederfanpage
Twitter.com/melschroeder
Pinterest.com/melissaschro
Facebook.com/groups/harmlesslovers – Mel's private fan group!

Don't miss the first exciting book in the Task Force
Hawaii Series. **Seductive Reasoning**!

*He's got a killer to catch and no time for love. Fate
has other plans.*

Former Army Special Forces Officer Martin "Del"
Delano has enough on his hands chasing a serial
killer and heading up TASK FORCE HAWAII. He
definitely doesn't need the distraction of Emma
Mitchell. From the moment they meet, she knocks
him off his feet, literally. Unfortunately, she's the
best person to have on the team to make the
connections to help them catch their killer.

For Emma, it's hard to ignore the lure of a man like
him. Tats, muscles and his Harley cause her to have
more than a few fantasies about Del. He'd never be
interested in a geek like her, but she can't resist
toying with him. When she pushes the teasing too
far, she ends up in his bed. She convinces herself
she can handle it until the moment he steals her
heart.

Del can't help falling for the quirky genius. She's
smart, funny and there's a sweet vulnerable side to
her that only he can see. As Emma gets more
involved with the investigation, she becomes the
target of the psychopath. When the danger
escalates, Del promises to do anything to save the
woman who not only captured his heart but also his
soul.

HARMLESS

A Little Harmless Sex
A Little Harmless Pleasure
A Little Harmless Obsession
A Little Harmless Lie
A Little Harmless Addiction
A Little Harmless Submission
A Little Harmless Fascination
A Little Harmless Fantasy
A Little Harmless Ride
A Little Harmless Secret
A Little Harmless Rumor

THE HARMLESS PRELUDES

Prelude to a Fantasy
Prelude to a Secret
Prelude to a Rumor, Part One
Prelude to a Rumor, Part Two

THE HARMLESS SHORTS

Max and Anna

A LITTLE HARMLESS MILITARY ROMANCE

Infatuation
Possession
Surrender

THE SANTINIS

Leonardo
Marco
Gianni
Vicente
A Santini Christmas
A Santini in Love
Falling for a Santini
One Night with a Santini
A Santini Takes the Fall

SEMPER FI MARINES

Tease Me
Tempt Me
Touch Me

TASK FORCE HAWAII

Seductive Reasoning
Hostile Desires

ONCE UPON AN ACCIDENT

An Accidental Countess
Lessons in Seduction
The Spy Who Loved Her

THE CURSED CLAN

Callum
Angus

Logan

BY BLOOD

Desire by Blood
Seduction by Blood

BOUNTY HUNTER'S, INC

For Love or Honor
Sinner's Delight

THE SWEET SHOPPE

Cowboy Up
Tempting Prudence

LONESTAR WOLF PACK
The Alpha's Saving Grace returning 1/26/16

CONNECTED BOOKS

The Hired Hand
Hands on Training

A Calculated Seduction
Going for Eight

SINGLE TITLES

Grace Under Pressure
Telepathic Cravings

Her Mother's Killer
The Last Detail
Operation Love
Chasing Luck
The Seduction of Widow McEwan

COMING SOON
Constant Craving
A Santini's Heart

CPSIA information can be obtained at www.ICGtesting.com
Printed in the USA
LVOW11s1723250116

472164LV00009B/1006/P